About the Author

The author is an ordained spiritual leader, offering counseling and spiritual companionship at Wisdom Ways of Being. Active in land-based and indigenous rights, she tends half a million honeybees and blogs at Thinklikeabee.org. Residing in New Mexico with her spouse and two cats, her first book, *Soul Tending: Journey into the Heart of Sabbath*, was published in 2018. You can find more information at afamstutz.com

The Bee Priestess

A. Fisher

The Bee Priestess

Olympia Publishers
London

www.olympiapublishers.com
OLYMPIA PAPERBACK EDITION

Copyright © A. Fisher 2023

The right of A. Fisher to be identified as author of
this work has been asserted in accordance with sections 77 and 78 of
the Copyright, Designs and Patents Act 1988.

All Rights Reserved

No reproduction, copy or transmission of this publication
may be made without written permission.
No paragraph of this publication may be reproduced,
copied or transmitted save with the written permission of the publisher,
or in accordance with the provisions
of the Copyright Act 1956 (as amended).

Any person who commits any unauthorized act in relation to
this publication may be liable to criminal
prosecution and civil claims for damage.

A CIP catalogue record for this title is
available from the British Library.

ISBN: 978-1-80074-914-6

This is a work of fiction.
Names, characters, places and incidents originate from the writer's
imagination. Any resemblance to actual persons, living or dead, is
purely coincidental.

First Published in 2023

Olympia Publishers
Tallis House
2 Tallis Street
London
EC4Y 0AB

Printed in Great Britain

Dedication

I gratefully dedicate this book to girls and women everywhere who have faced sexual violence, trauma, and marginalization. May you find your authentic voice, and a place of solace in the sisterhood and on Mother Earth as you heal your body, mind and heart. May we become societies that honor all women and live in reciprocity with all living beings.

Acknowledgments

As a sisterless young girl, I thank all women who have become spiritual sisters in this struggle for women's rights, trauma healing, and the courage to 'become'. You teach me how to live courageously and with heart in these times. Thank you to Singeli Agnew for lending her amazing casita in the northern New Mexico mountains to midwife this book. Most of all to my supportive partner in life and the circle of friends and family who see and know me best.

CHAPTER ONE

The Waxing Fullness of Her Moon

My love reached in for the latch
And my heart
Beat wild.
I rose to open to my love,
My fingers wet with myrrh,
Sweet flowing myrrh
On the doorbell.
I opened to my love
But he slipped away.
(Song of Songs 5:2–6, 3rd c. BCE)

There was a column of joy, an invisible source of gladness that arose and animated Althaia that day. She began to dance slowly on the marble floor, with the sounds of birdsong swirling around. She twirled amidst the colonnades of the open portico. She felt one with the sun's rays warming her skin. She bent and swayed like a sapling in the wind, her arms radiating outward, her slender hands making graceful shapes above her head.

She couldn't put her finger on it, what was happening to her body. It felt like the potion that Daphne, her servant, offered when her headaches came upon her like the fierce grip of a hawk's talons on her scalp. As the herbs took effect, the grip loosened, and her body soared among the clouds, floating across the sky.

The medicine flung her out of the pain and limitation of her fleshly boundaries for a time. The addictive quality of the herbs kept her body always wanting. It was an escape from the severe constriction of her life at home.

"Child!" the shrill voice of her mother came from inside the darkness of the cavernous room. "What keeps you? It is time to fit you for your costume."

Althaia came crashing back to earth. "I'm here, Mother."

She could feel her ire rising. Mother controlled every aspect of her life. There was no room for what she wanted. Oh yes, she was grateful for the opportunities that Father's wealth as an exotic textile importer afforded them. Lessons in reading, writing, mathematics, literature, and music. Through her tutor, Althaia, her sisters, and her brother had the opportunities to develop intellectually.

But this was where the equality ended.

Her brother would go on to study at some of the best philosophical schools in Athens. Althaia would be pawned off on an older mentor, a man who would make her wise in the worldly ways of culture and in being a good female citizen of Greek society. It would include tutoring in the intimate ways of her budding sexuality. Althaia dreaded the day.

She had a secret that no one knew but her best friend, Helena. Today, she savored the delicious memory.

The marketplace was thick with people, the day she met him there among the throngs. Songs of the lute player and drummer plied the crowds for a coin or two. The smell of coffee and baked bread rose along with the heady scent of herbs and spices. Mounds of rosemary, mint, sage, freshly ground cloves, cinnamon, nutmeg, and turmeric wafted in the air, their colors seducing the eye. Densely assembled stalls with wares lined the city square. Tables were heavy with brocade and silks the color of earth, stone, and flower. Semi-precious gems were carefully fingered by men with fine tunics, their heads bent toward the seller as they haggled. Women pulled children along, their arms laden with heaping baskets of ripe fruits and colorful vegetables. The atmosphere was eager and joyful. Althaia was with her little brother, Egan. Daphne accompanied them. Mother had sent them to procure some figs, pomegranates, bread, and cheeses for Father's meeting with his employees.

In the stall next to them, Althaia was magnetized by the Roman soldier. His eyes were a cerulean blue, as deep as the Mediterranean Sea on a placid day. His short, curly brown hair was tousled, and his cheeks were ruddy from the windy ride through town. He had an unusually wide, chiseled chin and an aquiline nose. Althaia found herself transfixed by his presence, his clever humor, his silly, boyish laughter as he haggled with the vendors of leather goods in Greek vernacular. She observed his small, even, white teeth with a gap between the front ones when he laughed. The easy, languid movement as he walked among the stalls.

He held his galea, or soldiers' helmet, cradled in his arm. His tunic covered his lithe body, a bright red cape dangling off his shoulder, a belt cinching at his slim waist. His golden legs were smooth and muscular, carried along by sturdy leather sandals. He had a satchel casually slung over his left shoulder.

The Romans had been in Greece for so long now that only the old ones remembered the stories of conquest, and felt the bitterness in their mouth of the oppression of their country. Soldiers walked the streets now as part of everyday life. The Great Pax Romana had absorbed this small country and its economy completely. People went about their daily business, usually ignorant of the occupation and the cost of the wars.

Egan tugged at his sister's hand.

"Sister! I want one of those!"

The small boy pointed at the stall next to the leather stand. The owner smiled and nodded as their gaze landed on crates and crates of small animals: birds, hares, roosters, mice.

"I want one for my game tonight! Sister! Sister!"

"Yes, yes, little brother. Don't pull my hand so hard," Althaia scolded him.

Noticing the Roman boy at the leather stall next door, she exchanged an affirmative nod with Daphne and allowed Egan to pull her over to the stand. The stall owner eagerly squatted down to Egan's height and began to animatedly ask him which animals he wanted to hold.

"I want that! We will fight him tonight with my rooster, Aeneas!"

It was a pastime that Althaia hated, a game that was cruel, but popular, amongst the boys.

Egan pointed at the crate with the rooster, its tail feathers a rainbow of colors and with a comb of brilliant fire red. As the door to the crate slid open and eager hands slipped in to grasp the bird, it began to squawk fiercely, pecking and flapping, its claws unleashed upon the fingers invading its space. The rooster evaded with all its might. As the bird popped out of the cage, Egan screamed in fright and excitement. The rooster was loose. The crowds at the market parted and shouts went up as the owner raced after in hot pursuit.

The Roman turned to Althaia; his eyes almost green in the sun. The merriment in his eyes lit up his whole face. Althaia rolled her eyes and threw her head back and a deep belly laugh erupted, even as she pulled her little brother away from the chaos.

"Sister! I wanted that rooster!" he cried with a mournful note.

"No matter," she said. "Daphne is almost done shopping, and we must go find her at the cheese stall."

"Where might you live, young lady?" the Roman asked. Althaia looked into the pools of his sea-colored eyes and took a deep breath, knowing that her parents would disapprove of her speaking with a Roman soldier.

"We live outside of Athens, near the Aegean Sea," she said.

"I am Adrian, my post is here in the city. I've never seen you before! Might I accompany you home with your servant and brother to make sure you are safe?"

"Oh, no, no," Althaia said hastily. "My father has an office here in the city where he imports fabric. We will meet him there after shopping, and he will accompany us home."

A momentary cloud passed across the Roman's face. A slight unhappiness at the rebuff. Althaia felt her brother tugging at her hand as Daphne approached with her woven baskets weighing down her forearms.

"It is time to go," Daphne said in her no-nonsense, clipped tone, unaware of the unfolding drama of boy and girl.

"Come," she snapped, as she noticed Althaia hesitating.

Without turning her head, Daphne's eyes rolled sideways to glance at the Roman soldier. His presence seemed to pin a frown on her face; contempt snarled her lips.

"Come," she growled. "We have no time to waste. Your father is waiting."

Before Daphne could proceed any further, Adrian touched her arm and asked, with chivalrous kindness, "Please. Let me take your bags. They are heavy."

Confused for a wicked moment by this soldier's gap-toothed, boyish smile and easy fluid Greek, Daphne relented as he pulled the heavy weight from her arms.

"You are a Roman soldier. Father says you are worthless," the tiny boy spouted.

"Shhhh," Althaia said, her smile freezing on her face.

"Father says the occupation is destroying us Greeks," he mimicked the language of the adults around him.

Althaia put her hand on her brother's shoulder and stooped down to his level.

"We must be hospitable to others, no matter who they are," she said.

"No fear, he's only a child. I'm not offended," Adrian offered as he began to walk, easily bearing the burden of Daphne's groceries.

"Where to?" he questioned.

Bewildered, Daphne pointed him down the main thoroughfare as she followed behind, grabbing Egan's other hand as he whispered loudly, asking why the soldier was coming with them.

The awkward procession made their way through the thronging market, down toward the docks where the ships waited for their treasures to carry to the Orient and back.

Althaia released Egan's hand to Daphne and fell in stride with this boy-man who carried their load. He magnetized her. His kind and laughing face, his beautiful body. Though almost a child herself, only fourteen years old, she felt a throbbing at the base of her tailbone, an aching to know more of this Roman named Adrian.

"May I be so forward as to inquire of your name?" Adrian spoke as they walked along.

"Yes, Althaia Adamos. I am my father's eldest daughter."

"And what does he import?" Adrian asked.

"Fine silks and textiles from the Far East," Althaia countered.

"And what is it you love to do, Miss Thaia?" Adrian's eyes smiled at her as he toyed with a nickname.

"Well, I love all my studies, but music is my favorite. I play the flute. Quite well, I might add!"

"I have no doubt. I would be delighted to hear you play!"

There was a mischievous quality now, a flirting that caused Althaia's pounding heart to beat faster.

"Well, you may come to Athena's Ceremony, down at the center of town, on the next full moon. I will be there," she said boldly.

Adrian's eyebrows raised ever so slightly, and a smile curled at the edge of his lips, a dimple playing in his cheek.

"I will be there, Althaia."

As he spoke her name, a fire was unexpectedly lit at the core of Althaia's being. The cord between this man and her heart was illumined. Fate was sealed. Something untouchable for a young woman had been touched, leaving her hungry.

"Here, here. Leave those baskets here, young man!" yelled Daphne. "We will take them ourselves the rest of the way to Mr. Adamos' office."

She looked around furtively, hoping no one known to the Adamos family would see a Roman soldier carrying their bags.

Adrian bowed as he set the woven bags next to Daphne.

"Thank you for allowing me to accompany you," he said, his lips parted to show the small, straight teeth with a slight gap between the front ones.

Althaia nodded her head slightly in gratitude, feeling as though her breath was squeezing her throat and the words would not form. She raised her right hand in a gesture of farewell, picking up Egan's hand, and hurrying after Daphne, who rolled her eyes and picked up the load again, marching toward her goal.

On this day, Althaia slowed her dance on the portico, her face tipped upwards, drenched by the morning sun, as she savored and tasted again the sweet, seductive danger of this first meeting. It temporarily sedated her anger as, once again, her mother's voice, like a sharp knife, cut through the air, and she came to the arched door to the portico, her hands on her hips.

"Althaia, I have been looking for you all morning. Where have you been? You *know* that you have a place as the head flautist with the girls' quartet for your father's event next weekend. Come. We must take your measurements for the tailor. Soon he will be here to show us the scrolls of imported silk that your father has secured from afar."

The events were an endless parade of young virgin girls showing off the wares of their musical prowess for older men. All this in service of eventually marrying off their daughters to older men, who would care for all their needs, even as they became a prisoner to the daily household requirements and to rearing the children.

Althaia felt her resentment below the surface. She imagined a love marriage between equals. Beyond culture and time, the unimagined tenderness of such a connection made her giddy. She fantasized about the Roman soldier.

As promised, Adrian came to Athena's ceremony when the moon grew full. Without his Roman soldier uniform, he looked smaller, softer, ordinary. His body was still lithe and tall, but without the regal uniform that set him apart from the others gathered at the ceremony. He hung out in the shadows, away from the shouting and laughing Greek men with tall glasses of plum-colored wine and platters of olive oil and fruits and bread.

And then the moment came when the torches were lit, and the girls filed onto the stage in their simple, colorful peplos, pleated and draping around their young, ripe bodies.

The audience of women, men, and children playing around their feet were silenced by the sound of flutes shimmering and hovering above the heads of the crowd, lilting and mesmerizing those gathered.

At intermission, Althaia and Helena chattered and shrieked with laughter, making fun of the boys ogling them and their awkward attempts at engaging them in conversation. Hand in hand, they moved toward the edge of the light as the servants rotated, offering them drink and food.

Suddenly, out of the shadows emerged the face that Althaia remembered so vividly.

"Althaia! What beauty! The music is like a siren! I am at your service, whatever you want, madam!" Adrian laughed.

Althaia's heart missed a beat. Helena glanced closely at her best friend and then at the man.

"Who are you?" Helena asked innocently, knowing full well this was the man Althaia had told her about.

The Roman soldier for whom she longed.

Adrian bowed in an exaggerated manner. "I am Adrian, Roman citizen, at your service."

Helena's wide eyes crinkled in laughter, and she dissolved into giggles.

"Well, sir, can you manifest a Roman soldier for me?" she volleyed.

"Why of course, I know many of them!" he countered.

"I will await his courtship at our next full moon ceremony

then." She smiled coyly.

Looking at her friend slyly, Helena said, 'I'm going to find some pomegranate juice. I'll see you back on stage!"

Alone at last in the noisy crowd pulsating around them, Adrian took Althaia's hand in his, and an electric current flowed between them.

"I hope to see you again. I pray this will not be the last time!" He earnestly looked deep into her eyes.

Hearing the musicians assembling, Althaia quickly withdrew her hand as though she had touched a hot stove.

"Yes. Yes. I want that. But we must not let my family know. I am to marry my father's chosen one, which I hate. I… I must go."

Althaia flushed, turning from Adrian, but not before she said, "Come down to the seaside, Asteria at Glyfada and we will share some bread and poetry as the moon wanes on the fourth day, at high noon. I shall think of some excuse to get out of the house."

And she was gone.

Days dragged by after Athena's ceremony. On the appointed day, Althaia reported to her mother that Daphne must take her and Helena to the beach, the Athenian Riviera, Asteria at Glyphada. Mother was distracted that particular day. Father had sprung yet another dinner with fellow importers on her.

"Go, go! But be home by supper. And make sure you have your math lessons done," Mother snapped.

Daphne was clearly unhappy about the mandate to spend time at the beach with two adolescent girls. She grumbled, annoyed at being taken away from her tasks.

Helena, delighted at an outing, was pulled back by Althaia as they walked with Daphne.

Conspiratorially, she filled her friend in about the

preordained meeting with Adrian.

"Please, you must keep Daphne occupied so I can meet him," she pleaded.

With an exaggerated sigh, Helena widened her eyes.

"Is he bringing me a nice young Roman soldier boy? Otherwise, I cannot keep your secret." She pouted, with a smile tugging at her lips.

"Helenaaa!" Althaia wailed.

"Okay, I'll keep your secret, but you will owe me. Remember that, Thaia!" Helena laughed.

At the edge of the white sands was an outcropping of stones—the place of meeting. Althaia led her friend and Daphne down the beach from this meeting place to a cove where Daphne set down the blanket and spread out the picnic. As the girls ate and giggled, Daphne curled against the edge of the sand, falling into a deep sleep. A rare thing for servants in the middle of the day.

Helena brought out her rolls of papyrus and began to read, her head sinking deeper into the manuscript as Althaia whispered, "It is almost high noon, I must go!"

Helena waved her off.

As she ran along the simmering blue-green waves of the Aegean Sea, waving ebony hair flowing down her back, Althaia could see a form in the distance walking toward her. It was Adrian. They met and began to run together from the outcropping of rocks far beyond to a small grove of trees inland from the water, mossy, soft grass around their feet.

The electricity of youth became like a fire as their hands touched. Adrian was a seasoned young man, much older than Althaia's fourteen years.

Plopped among the cypress trees, Althaia coyly withdrew

her hand from his as she fell back on the sand, catching her breath, her breast heaving from the short sprint. They were alone. She had never been left alone with a boy, much less a man. Who was this man, Adrian?

"Where do you come from?" Althaia rolled to her side, raised herself up, and propping her face in her hand as she gazed at this beautiful man. She smiled sweetly at him.

"I come from a small town in Northern Italy. My father was a vineyard owner," Adrian began.

"I miss the countryside and the animals we kept," he said wistfully. "I always thought I would go back and take over the land and the business. But then I was conscripted into the Roman army and have been roaming about the Roman Empire for a decade now. They send me hither and yon, wherever they have need of more manpower. I have seen the greater Mediterranean region in my travels. My younger brothers stepped in to help my father when they were only children, ten and twelve."

"Oh," Althaia said softly. "How many siblings do you have?"

"I have two brothers and one sister, who is already married off to a good Roman citizen."

He looked pensive for a moment. Suddenly, his brilliant eyes were downcast. Althaia thought she saw a glimmer of tears.

"My mother is a widow. Father died early on after I left home. I was on duty and unable to return for his funeral. What is there for me to return to?" Adrian's voice was suddenly rough and strained.

He looked out at the placid horizon, over the blue green Mediterranean, his eyes suddenly steely.

"It is my brothers' home now. There is no room for me. They will marry and raise their families there. They will take care of my mother's every need. She adores them." He drew in a heavy breath, exhaling slowly.

"Ah, but Thaia, I did not come here to talk about me!" He pulled her hand, toppling her from where she was propped up in front of him.

She felt herself guided toward him. Here was a man, not a boy. It passed through her mind briefly that he was a worldly man who had seen much in his travels. Fleetingly, she wondered how many women he had known. How had he assuaged his suffering from his boyhood longings and loss of his dreams?

As the sweet, musky air of the sea surged around them, Althaia felt as though his lust was consuming her body. There was a hunger there that she recognized in herself. A longing to be loved. To be seen. A budding girl-woman wanting to be known beyond the restrictive and unhappy bounds of her mother and father's household. Instinctively, she pressed against him. There were no words as their lips met. She felt his manhood harden, a bewildering and excited feeling as her body mounted up to meet him. In the soft grass, they fell, her small breasts rising to his touch, his mouth. He pulled open her dress, and she reached her hand under his tunic, opening him up to her. As Adrian's ocean filled her, she cried out with pain and ecstasy. No one had ever told her it would be like this: pleasure unparalleled alongside a searing ripping of her tissue down there.

Adrian's breath was heavy, mingling with hers, his body shaking. Suddenly, he subsided, and they began to laugh together. The pungency of his breath on her face, their skin against skin, the hardness of their bodies softening and curling into one another. He rolled with her over and over on the grass as they laughed, their passion finally spent.

Althaia looked into this boy-man's eyes adoringly. So tender. So strong. He was hers. She savored the after-moments.

Only then did she hear the sound of Helena's voice, calling and calling her name.

Eyes widening, Althaia quickly pulled her peplos up around her shoulders, gave Adrian a final kiss, resisting as he tried to pull her back down, his gap-toothed smile disarming her.

"I must see you again, Thaia."

There was an urgency to his voice, his long-boned, slender brown fingers reaching for her as she stood up.

"Yes! yes. I am at Heracleous St. on the outskirts of Athens. It is at the end of the road, near the park of cedar trees. There is a large marble arch at the gate. Leave a message under the lion's statue at the gate, under the loose brick, telling me where we may meet in the public square," Althaia said breathlessly, as she pulled away to meet her friend.

Althaia's reverie and the delicious memory was suddenly smashed into a million pieces.

"Althaia! Come at once, please stop daydreaming." Mother stood before Althaia, reached out, and gripped her arm, bruising her as she pulled her along. "I have no time for your stubbornness. You are an evil girl and forget your place in this household. I am in charge and you must come now. The tailor is here."

Nothing could destroy the warm glow, the powerful surge of life force that permeated Althaia. Not even her mother's mood.

A moon was mysteriously growing in her body, and it was like the delicious waves of the Aegean Sea, the blue-green eyes of the soldier man, the sweetness of the flute song soaring through her.

CHAPTER TWO

Athena's Daughter

At night on my bed I longed for
   My only love.
I sought him, but did not find him.
I must rise and go about the city,
The narrow streets and squares, till I find
   My only love.
I sought him everywhere
And could not find him.
   (Song of Songs 3:1–5, 3rd c.BCE)[1]

Every day, she checked beneath the loose brick under the lion statue that guarded her home of marbled porticos, arched ceilings, fountains, and many rooms. Despite the fountain of gladness that had originally animated Althaia to dance on the portico after that day at the beach, something uneasy began to grow also.

There was something pathetic, more stooped about Althaia, as each day she came away with nothing in her hands. Bereft, she wept bitterly in her room or in secret places in the garden full of birdsong and water fountains. How could he forget her? Did he

---

[1] ("Song of Songs: The Shulamite", excerpt from <u>Women in Praise of the Sacred</u>, Ed. Jane Hirshfield(New York: HarperCollins, 1994)24

throw their moment of union and bliss into a trash heap, like all the other forgettable experiences of his life? He was a man of the world and unknown to her. How could she have been so stupid?

Althaia felt the sickness of longing, as well as the indelible print that her surprise encounter with Adrian had left upon her heart. Her mind was in motion constantly with memories of their fleeting time together. She examined every glance, every touch, every dimpled smile, every laugh. The short space between their meeting and the consummation had been as brief as a falling star. But its meteoric impression was infinite.

Along with other lessons, the flute quartet resumed its practice on her family's portico. Concentration was practically impossible for Althaia.

"Althaia! Are you watching me? Do not play when we are all taking a breath. Where is your mind, young lady?" The flute master, whose wand was frozen midair, looked down his nose at her, glaring.

Helena rolled her eyes sideways at Althaia, stifling a giggle. Althaia could feel the heat rising in her cheeks as all her musical friends stared at her.

"Yes, Master Andino. My deep apologies."

"Let's take a moment and return shortly to complete this piece, ladies," the stern master barked. "Clearly, one of you is living in an altered universe. And, of course, it makes all of us pay for such inattention to details. I expect full concentration when you all return."

"Yes, Master Andino," the girls spoke in a chorus of voices.

Althaia stood up so quickly that her seat toppled over and crashed to the ground. Helena hurried over.

"What is *wrong* with you, Thaia!" she whispered loudly, grabbing Althaia's hand as they raced out into the garden.

Althaia pulled her friend down hard onto a marble bench.

"Ow!" Helena cried.

Althaia sighed deeply and began to tell her childhood friend, haltingly at first, then in a gush, about that day on the beach with Adrian.

Helena's eyes widened, her black eyes signaling disbelief.

"Althaia," she hissed. "How could you be so promiscuous? Will you ever see him again? What will happen when your mother finds out?"

"Or," she emphasized, "your *Father*? They will be so, so angry. What will become of you? This is not what we are allowed to do. You know our future is ensured by our family name and their wishes. What will happen to you?" Helena wailed.

Althaia began to sob. "I... I don't know. It felt so natural. I couldn't stop myself. I told him to leave me a note in the wall beneath the loose brick, under the lion that guards our wall. He has not come. I cannot stop thinking of him. My mind has a sickness I cannot shake off. I must see him again. I must speak to him!"

"Girls! Girls, come quickly," the flute master shouted.

Althaia and Helena traded a final, tragic look, their eyes frightened and filled with grief, their hands molded together in solidarity. Althaia wiped her eyes on the wrap that overlaid her long tunic. Helena tugged at her hand and they were off, back to join the other two girls in the quartet and their very stern master teacher.

Althaia took a deep breath and exhaled slowly. She could feel some of the weight of her suffering lifted, now borne by Helena, her dearest and best friend. She would not be destroyed by a sorrow shared.

Weeks passed. No word from the Roman. Althaia sank further into a depression. One evening at dinner, mother was in a cheerful mood, an unusual event. Father had received a large bonus on one of his textile imports, which would allow them to take a small holiday this year. Althaia's younger twin sisters, Calista and Calliope, chattered eagerly.

"Mama! May we go to Constantinople, along the sea?" Calista's eyes were shining. "Or Egypt, the Nile? I have been learning about it in my lessons!"

Calliope jumped up on the chair and took a pose, with her hands shaping a pyramid.

"Now, now, girls! Your father and I will tell you where we will go. Meanwhile, you must continue your lessons."

Althaia was silent.

Egan shouted, "Thaia! Where do you want to go?"

Althaia sighed. Her mind was occupied.

"I will be satisfied wherever Mama and Father decide. May I please be excused?"

"Althaia?" Father looked closely at her. "Are you ill? You look pale?"

"I'd like to go to my room now and rest, please."

"Yes, my dear. Is it another headache coming upon you?" Father pursued.

"No, no. Just a slight stomach upset." Althaia arose.

"I'll send Daphne with some medicine, dear," Mother injected.

But Althaia was already off and running as fast as her feet could carry her to the bowl where she would throw up until her stomach had nothing left in it.

What was wrong with her? Was she so sick from longing that her stomach was now retching with grief?

"Althaia, I have a tonic for you. Your mother requested it," came Daphne's voice from outside the curtain.

Althaia smoothed her hair and splashed water on her face. Taking a shallow breath, she pulled the curtain aside and took the proffered jar. Bringing it to her lips began an unhappy sequence of events. Her nose flared as her stomach began to roil. She could feel her bile begin to rise, burning in her throat as she gasped and yanked the tonic away from her.

"No, thank you, Daphne. I think I am feeling better and the medicine only tortures my stomach further."

Daphne rolled her eyes. "Child, what is troubling your stomach? Why are you so unhappy these days?"

Daphne was a simple woman who had raised a daughter of her own while also caring for children of wealthy patrons, whom she loved as her own. As a woman with the generational wisdom of herbs, she knew that there were some things that made the heart sick. These could not be cured by any herb.

"Althaia, look at me and tell me what is making thy heart so ill?" Daphne implored her eyes by cupping her face with both hands until she could look nowhere but into her servant's kind eyes.

Althaia began to sob, "I want to see Adrian, the Roman we met in the market. I am sick with longing. I have seen him once and await his word for another meeting. But he has left me destitute in my heart."

She was inconsolable.

Daphne pursed her lips, dropping her hands from Althaia's face. She sighed knowingly. This did not bode well.

Another day of flute practice. This time it was at Jacinta's home in the more modest quarters of the city. Her father had a small shop where he sold juices and fruits and nuts, and his family lived above the shop.

After quartet practice that morning, Jacinta's mother offered the girls fresh pomegranate juice.

"Girls, you are ready for the next festival of the goddesses! So lovely! Maybe we will see if someone on the lyre can join you!"

But Althaia was not in that circle of happy girls. She sat in the bath quarters after practice, doubled over with a morning sickness that overtook her almost every day now. The joyful, dancing energy rising up the column of her spine had receded into misery.

She heard the staccato steps on the tiled floor coming toward the bath.

"Althaia," came the loud whisper of Helena. 'I've come to walk you home. Are you okay?"

"No, I am not," came the clear response as Althaia poked her head around the door. "But the waves of sickness have subsided and I will go with you."

Helena looked knowingly at her friend, taking her hand as they bade farewell and headed down the cobbled street.

"I know what is wrong with you, Thaia," she said matter-of-factly. "When Mother was pregnant with Sebastian, she threw up all the time. It was disgusting. She was very miserable. She looked pale as white marble, like you."

Althaia froze inside. She was two years old when her twin sisters were born. She did not remember her mother being so sick when she carried them. Egan was nine years younger. Still, Althaia did not remember seeing her mother sick during that pregnancy either.

Could it be?

"Lena. If this is true, I will be banished. I am promised soon to a male mentor who will teach me the female ways of being with a man. Father has already begun to hunt for the right man with a proper dowry."

Terror contorted her pale face.

Helena held her hand tightly as they walked along the Aqueduct. She was silent.

Althaia abruptly stopped and her hand tore from Helena's.

"I am ruined!" she wailed.

She fell into her friend's arms, wracking sobs shaking her slim shoulders. Helena stroked her hair.

"Will you tell your parents soon? They are worried for your health."

Althaia lifted her tear-stained face, red and blotchy, sucking air into her lungs with staccato intensity as she faced Helena.

"I don't know. I don't know. I. Don't. Know." Her heaving, breathless weeping continued.

She was all alone in the world. Not even the Roman could come to her aid at this time.

Helena and Althaia walked the long way home as Althaia tried to pull herself together, Helena at her side.

Finally, they came to the gate. Althaia was spent, utterly exhausted in her body and soul.

"Thaia, where is this loose brick you told the Roman about?" Helena asked, to distract her.

They stood gazing together, side by side, at the noble carved lion.

Althaia walked toward the wall and dislodged the loose brick to show her friend.

To her surprise, there was a fragment of papyrus that fell to the ground. Both girls seized upon it, eyes wide with excitement.

Helena grabbed it and playfully began to run until Althaia, giving chase, stepped upon the heel of her sandal, causing her to fall. Her hair splayed out on the ground, her head tilted back in regaling laughter, Helena rolled on the ground, protecting the papyrus as Althaia grasped for the paper, relieved by this moment of gaiety.

Finally, Helena released the paper and Althaia, gasping in laughter, carefully unfolded the creased note.

She read it out loud. It said simply:

"*I must see you.*

My apologies for being gone for so long.

I was sent to the occupied territory of Palestine for a time. But now I am back.

Your beauty lives in my mind. Come see me at the market stand of the leather maker tomorrow at full noon."

"So, your soldier has not deserted you!" Helena smiled.

Althaia's shoulders relaxed. Her head dropped back as her breath released long and slow.

The laughter began in her belly and came out in a shriek as she jumped to her feet and began to twirl with the paper cradled against her bosom. As Helena jumped to her feet, the two girls reached for each other's hands and began to twirl together.

The lightness of their being reached the heavens as they lifted their voices in the clear bell-tone of the Orphic hymn to Athena.

Pallas, you only-begotten One, born of mighty Zeus, awesome you are, and divine:

Goddess so blessed, lifting high the turmoil of the fray,

Mighty One unspeakable yet so well spoken of!

Great-named One at home in a vault of stone,

Caught up in haughty hills and wandering the shaded

mountain's ridge,
You who put a dance in the heart and glory in embattlements…
Hear my prayer, and grant us an abundant peace, fulfillment, good health.
Make prosperous the hour, gray-eyed One, inventor of Art, The object of the people's ceaseless prayers–
My Queen!

The moon was full that night. It streamed through the thin curtains and fell in dizzying patterns on the tiled floor. Althaia slept fitfully. Tomorrow, she would see Adrian! Anxiety drenched her brow with sweat. Excitement was like a spoon, whipping up her stomach juices into a frenzy.

Between bouts of nausea, she had begun to feel the presence of another energy within her after two months. It was a quiet sensibility. A peaceful joy. A stable, cheerful breath beneath the turmoil of life and her emotional storms.

What would she tell Adrian? How would she let him know that his seed was planted in her womb? What would he say?

In the deep hour of the night, Althaia stirred herself to life, and her feet pushed into her embroidered slippers. She crept along the shining path of the moon, down the wide, marbled stairs into the garden where her familiar, Athena the owl, sat watchfully in the wide, spreading cypress tree. Althaia remembered Adrian also mentioning his childhood connection with the animals of his birthplace.

Athena had come as a tiny owlet from Althaia's father. Her mother had been killed by a raptor in the forest down near Father's office. The tiny owlet would cling to the edge of the branch near the nest and shriek daily. Because of their culture's deep cultural regard of owls as a symbol of higher wisdom, the feminine, and the goddess Athena, the little owlet would soon find itself ensconced in the elaborate gardens of the Adamos family.

Egan was delighted, and like any little boy, he was soon eager to catch any rodent to feed to the tiny, budding owlet.

But Athena the owl would come to be Althaia's familiar, perching on her shoulder during the day, sometimes sleeping as Althaia attended to her daily lessons. A large cage in Althaia's room housed Athena. Soon, her wingspan grew, and Athena practiced flying and hunting lessons in the nearby forest outside the garden.

But she always came back to perch in the garden when she heard Althaia's voice calling her, "Whoo-whoo, whoo-whoo."

Back would come the response, "Hoo, hoo, hoo."

And the great winged being would silently arrive on the ancient Cypress tree, the strong talons curling around the bark, her head turning full circle, her yellow eyes blazing as she looked for Althaia.

This night, Althaia had donned her leather wristlets that reached up her forearms so Athena could perch on her arm.

"Athena, whoo-whoo, whoo-whoo. Come swiftly, my beautiful, winged companion," Althaia whispered loudly beneath the tree. "Please help me! My womb has the fruit of my beloved, Adrian. The time is upon me. I must go tell him the news. Tomorrow, I see him at noon."

The owl did not come immediately.

"Athena, my spirit companion, please intercede on behalf of the Great Goddess, and bring kindness and wisdom to me.

"You have never known what it is to birth tiny ones, but I know you will tell me what I need to speak when the time comes.

"First I must tell Adrian. After him, it will be Mother and Father. I tremble inside, imagining what they will say. Come to my aid, send your spirit with me to visit my beloved tomorrow!"

As Althaia confided, the owl watched her with its great yellow-globed eyes in the moonlight. Soon, she unfolded her wings and came to perch on Althaia's forearm. Feeling the power and presence of such a large and magnificent being so close to her heart never failed to take away Althaia's breath. Standing in the moonlight, with Athena staring trance-like into her eyes, Althaia began to gently, almost imperceptibly sway, singing,

You who put a dance in the heart and glory in embattlements...

Hear my prayer, and grant me an abundant peace, fulfillment, good health.

Athena the owl was like a fortification for her soul. Althaia sensed that tomorrow would bring a difficult reckoning when she met Adrian. Her heart began to thud; her breath became shallow. This night of her soul was only the first test in her young life as a budding woman.

The weight of the owl reminded her of how far Athena had come from her first tiny owlet days. She remembered that the death of Athena's mother brought her familiar here to her. Perhaps hardship and tragedy could bring unexpected twists and turns, good things, in life.

Quietly, she began to speak to Athena. Reminding her of how special her powers and prowess were. How shining and glorious her feathers. How precious her companionship, her guardianship from the creaturely world. Athena's head swiveled around, her gaze coming to rest on Althaia.

They stood in the moonlight together—marvelous giant owl and the diminutive fourteen-year-old girl with ebony hair flowing down her back, the small bump forming in her belly, silhouetted by the white glow.

The next day dawned as usual, brilliant and arid. The summer heat was not yet oppressive. Althaia took extra care to dress herself. Her favorite peplos was a shimmery lavender with gold braids around the neck, waist, and hem. As she descended the marble stairs, she could see her siblings eating out in the garden at the end of the long colonnade. Only Daphne was present; Mother and Father were noticeably absent.

"Thaia's got a boyfriend! Thaia's got a boyfriend!" shouted Egan as he saw Althaia approach.

"Stop it! Stop it, Egan! You are being stupid." Althaia could feel her stomach roil at his teasing, which was undergirded by an uncanny sense of the truth.

"I saw her talking to a Roman soldier! I saw him. I saw him," Egan said in a sing song voice.

"Thaia's eyes were all googly," the boy said, watching his sister closely for a rise.

Calliope joined in the chorus, "Well, look at that dress, it must be true. You never put on your shimmery silk unless it is a special occasion!"

Calista held her counsel, her face revealing a map of emotion as she turned her head from Egan to her twin sister with wide eyes.

"Egan, now that's enough!" Daphne interjected sternly. "All of you, stop it. Your sister has not been feeling well. Perhaps she needed to raise her spirits by dressing fancy today."

Barely glancing at Althaia, she said, "Come now, sit down, and have your morning juice, missy. Do you want cherry or apricot?"

She indicated the thick syrupy juices in their urns.

Althaia pointed to the cherry and sat on the edge of her chair to drink her morning cup, ready to flee.

"That's all I can take, Daphne, lest my stomach becomes upset again. I need to go meet Helena this morning. We are studying our lessons at her house." The lie came easily. "Where are Mother and Father?"

"Your father needed to go to the office early. Your mother's sister sent a messenger before dawn asking her to come for an emergency with your cousin, Phile. I will go later to take some herbs for her. She has a fever."

Without waiting for further conversation, Althaia jumped off her seat as though it had burned her and took leave.

"Okay. I'll be back this afternoon. Please give Phile my best regards."

Daphne nodded and turned back to her siblings.

It was already mid-morning when Althaia set out. She took her embroidered shoulder bag to give the semblance of carrying her lessons.

She had already vomited and felt the emptiness of her stomach. There was a buzzing in her body and a lightness in her head from the lack of food. The mid-morning heat was bracing, brightening her already golden skin to a deeper hue.

Althaia took her time walking along the aqueduct into the center of the city. Helena's home was just around the corner. That would have been an appropriate distance for a young girl alone. But a fourteen-year-old girl unaccompanied into the city was not proper. It was a thirty-minute walk and would take all she could muster without the sustenance of her morning meal.

In the distance, the Acropolis stood nobly above the city, with the white buildings teeming around it. Her feet were becoming dusty, and she could feel blisters forming. It was rare that she walked this far. Her father's servants were always ready with a chariot.

The sweet sound of birds filled the air, and the walk calmed Althaia at a deeper level. The fresh air and brisk exercise strengthened her body.

Finally arriving at the market in the center of the city, there was still some time before high noon. Althaia roamed the market stalls, picking up clay trinkets, rubbing frankincense and amber on her skin, holding to her ear lobes semi-precious lapis lazuli earrings. She found herself completely immersed in the baubles and fascinating wares of the bustling marketplace. Suddenly, she felt a hand on her shoulder.

Dropping the marble jar in her hands, which shattered into pieces, Althaia gasped. Adrian's gap-toothed, dimpled smile shone down on her. He knelt and began to pick up the wreckage. The stall owner pulled his arms into his abdomen and shook his hands at her animatedly, a scowl on his face.

"What do you think you are doing? Don't touch my wares again. You will pay for this."

Adrian quickly pulled some coins from his pocket and placed them on top of the stall.

"We're sorry. It was an accident. Can't you see? Don't be so harsh with the young lady," he said firmly.

With that, he took her arm and steered her away from the stalls of the marketplace, down a side street, and to the end, where there was a small park with public benches.

"I'm so sorry to have startled you," Adrian said, tenderly brushing from her face a stray hair that had come loose.

"I missed you, Thaia," he said quietly.

His lips brushed hers.

He took her hands and whirled her around.

"You are absolutely stunning in that dress. My heart is so glad to see you, my beautiful one."

Althaia blushed. She could feel her heart in her mouth. Her desire washed over her.

Adrian, noticing her reticence at seeing him in his Roman soldier clothing, pulled apart slightly. He was sensitive to her anxiety but could feel the heat of her desire even amidst her inner conflict.

They sat down on the bench, Adrian keeping ahold of one of her hands, hidden in the folds of her dress.

"How have you been? I deeply regret my late reply to you after… after… well, I meant to leave a note sooner. It is not for a loss of longing, Althaia. I did so want to see you after we met on the beach."

His blue-green eyes carefully attended to every facial movement and gesture as Althaia cast her eyes down under his intense gaze.

Suddenly, the heat, the midday sun, the long walk, the moment with her beloved made her feel faint. Her breath became erratic as she bent over, trying to take deep gulps of breath. Gathering herself, she sat back up and looked into his eyes.

"I missed you so. You… you cannot even imagine my longing, Adrian. It has been months." She began to cry, despite herself.

Adrian moved closer, touching her tears with his long index finger, tasting the salt of her tears.

"I am so sorry. I am a lout. I must admit that my work is very unpredictable. But here I am. I want to be with you."

"It's… complicated, Adrian." Althaia wept. "How do I tell my parents? How can we see each other in the daylight without keeping secrets or hiding? I tell you, they are poised to prepare me for the womanly duties of marriage with a Greek man."

A cloud passed across Adrian's face. "I must admit, I don't understand the complexities of your society, but I am far from my home in Italy, and I want to forge my own choices based upon love, not obligation."

"I do too!" she wailed. "But I am here in the center of my family and culture. What can I do?"

"Well, I will come and meet your father in civilian clothing." Adrian eyes lit up. "He will never know that I am Roman!"

"No, no, no! Of course he will know." Althaia rolled her eyes. "You look sooo Roman. My father can smell a Roman, especially a soldier, from afar."

"Ha!" Adrian's boyish laugh rang through the air. "I am willing to do whatever you want, Thaia."

As she imagined her parents' reaction to Adrian, suddenly a sick feeling began to well up. As though she were viewing a Greek tragedy, she could see her mother throwing her hands up in the air and falling on the ground in a heap, screaming and trembling in anger.

Her resolve hardened.

"Adrian, I have something to tell you."

His face was so close to hers, she could smell the muskiness of his breath, the amber scent of his neck.

"Since we last met, two full moons have come and gone. I am now with child."

It was as though he had been slapped. He recoiled from her, dropping her hand, turning his head away as he inhaled through his mouth. Now it was Adrian's turn to take deep breaths. She could see the straight slant of his nose and slight flare of his nostrils, his jaw tightening and working in circles.

The Greek tragedy continued. Althaia felt as though she were dissociating from her body, sitting and looking down from the cedar tree above them. Her tears had dried. She felt the vise in her head begin to clamp down.

"Althaia!" a familiar voice cut through the fog. "Althaia!"

Before she could gather her wits, Father and his associate were upon them. He sneered with contempt at the young man in a Roman tunic, dressed as a soldier.

"And who is this?" Father practically spat the words out.

"Father, please," Althaia said in a low voice. "'Please. I simply met this man in the market, and we came here for some solitude to talk about Greek culture."

The lies came readily.

"Come with me immediately. No daughter of mine will ever, ever be seen again with a Roman soldier. This is an insult to our family."

His hand was upon her shoulder, compelling Althaia to stand and follow along with him. The associate looked bewildered, standing silently as his employer dealt with an intimate family situation.

Adrian stood up, his face now slack. His shoulders slumped, his long fingers clenching and unclenching. His boyish smile was wiped away, lips parted as though to say something, his breathing shallow and fast. Adrian, who had been so utterly charming, was suddenly just a boy, responding to the fury of a father.

"Master Adamos, let me explain..." His voice trailed off, traumatized by not only the rage of this man he had never met, but doubly by the news he had just learned.

"Let us go, Althaia. I will have the chariot take you home immediately." He shook his head, and the furrow between his brow deepened. "Why were you here at the market alone in the first place, my daughter? We will have much to talk about with your mother this afternoon."

The last view Althaia had of Adrian was a side glance as her father steered her forward, the associate in hot pursuit. Adrian's eyes were torn open by hurt, the veil of suave confidence replaced with the terror of a small child facing an unknown beast.

CHAPTER THREE

I Am Virgin, I Am Whore

I am the first and the last
    I am she who is honored and she who is the scorned one
    I am the whore and the holy woman.
    I am the wife and the virgin
    I am the mother and the daughter ...
    I am knowledge and ignorance...
    I am shameless; I am ashamed. I am strength,
    And I am fear... I am foolish and I am wise... I am godless, and I am one whose God is great.[2]

The vise grip of Althaia's headache made her eyes squint. Small, white spots danced before her, searing her brain. Father's grip was stern, guiding her to the small, horse-drawn chariot that he took to work. She knew better than to speak. Father's jaw was set. She could feel his rage emanating like a cloud around him, invading her body with the violence of his emotion.

Father said goodbye to his colleague, who had become frozen from the interaction he had witnessed. Stiffly, he bowed and turned from the small side street to Father's office to take his leave down the main boulevard.

---

[2] (Thunder: Perfect Mind, NagHammadi Library, Tr. J. Robinson, HarperCollins, NY, 1977, 271–4)

Shame burned in Althaia's stomach and head. They connected her chest and heart, lungs and throat, in one ball of fire. A track was being laid down her spine, conveying a patterned response of fear, hyper-vigilance, and seething grief. How could she have brought such unmitigated disgrace, such tainted ugliness to her Father's household? Soon, they would become pitiable objects in the eyes of Father's reputable world.

The journey home was insufferable. They passed the lion-studded arch, and a servant hurried to relieve Father and escort the horse to the stable.

Lander Adamos showed little emotion as he hopped down from the chariot and came around to help his daughter step down. He struggled to gain control of his anger, withdrawing deeper into his mind as he imagined the scenario that laid before him. His wife was high-minded, to put it mildly. Unhappiness seemed to pervade her daily duties. He did not know when she had become this way. Discontented, harsh with the children, quick to judge. The children relied on him for a reasonable and balanced opinion, while Phaedra Adamos' reaction was always swift and hard.

When Lander first met Phaedra, it was at an all-male business dinner. That evening, she was one of the many female dancers performing a classical Greek dance. Her fine beauty overcame him. Curling, chestnut hair was braided in a frame around her heart-shaped face. She had high cheekbones and tiny rosebud lips, which parted to small even teeth, and a slightly upturned nose. In their brief introduction, he was struck by her high-spirited confidence and hearty laugh. To Lander, a man with large dreams for his life, who had already begun to accumulate wealth through his business acumen, such a woman would be a great asset. He began negotiations immediately with her family, which was her uncle from the Island of Thira, presenting a dowry unparalleled by any of her other suitors at that time.

Soon, Phaedra was his very own, eager to join him in planning a family and in the purchase of their very large home on the outskirts of Athens. She discontinued her cultural pursuits and dancing, pouring her boundless energy and efforts into decorating their soon-to-be marbled and colonnaded vast manse, gardens, outdoor theatre, servants' quarters, and stables.

Soon, they became well known in the public arts circuit as wealthy patrons. Phaedra's life was a dizzying whirlwind of meetings. Their young passion was unmatched and soon the children came. Althaia was the first child, the apple of her father's eye. Lander brought her special gifts from the Orient in his travels for textile imports, as well as dolls from many countries and cultures.

He could see that she mirrored and imitated her mother's high-spirited nature. They clashed as soon as the tiny daughter indicated she had a temper and a strong will. Phaedra grieved that her firstborn was a girl instead of a boy child. Boys were insurance and wealth for the future. They were a sign of blessing and a rung in the ladder of success.

It seemed that the girl child somehow could do nothing right. Her mother's wrath came down upon her often, even for unintentional childish things, such as a broken vase or a spilled cup of juice. It only made Althaia stronger in her resolve to resist, fleeing to Lander frequently for comfort and a circle of safety against her mother's heavy-handed discipline. Lander was alarmed at times and tried to mediate his wife's temper. But it only seemed to inflame her further, and she turned on him. As his work increasingly took him away for long periods of time, Althaia had no refuge from the violence of her mother.

The twins, Calliope and Calista, came two years later. Good-natured and silly, they were a balm for Phaedra's nerves. She had grown increasingly frazzled by the endless requirements of a good wife and rising socialite. The twin girls could entertain themselves—another mark in their favor. Phaedra's role as a householder, while raising three girls with her husband increasingly distant emotionally and absent in his travels to the far east, began to take their toll.

She would not be great with child again for nine years. The seed of her last child, a boy, was sown on a special holiday with Lander to the island of Crete. As they roamed the beaches and played in the waters, sipping fresh drinks in the sunshine, their passion for one another again ignited. This time, the baby growing in her womb would be strong, engaging in many athletics even in utero. She was ill many mornings, secreting herself away from the girls, asking Daphne to care for them in her absence.

When the boy child was born, they named him Egan, *'little fire.'* He would be Phaedra's heart and soul, pride and joy.

Father guided his eldest daughter through the front door. The twins were shrieking and chasing Egan in a game of tag.

"Children, children!" Lander raised his voice. "Please go out and play in the gardens. Now."

"Hello, Father!" The twins raced over and wrapped their arms around his waist, clinging on to him, refusing to let him pull their skinny, twining arms away.

Even he could not keep from smiling as their breathless laughter surrounded him, dragging them along as he tried to walk.

Egan, a mischievous smile on his five-year-old face, threw a ball at his sisters clinging onto Lander. The girls screamed again and released their father to grab their little brother and the ball, dragging him outside to continue their game.

Althaia's heart pounded, grateful for the playful reprieve by her siblings. She dreaded this meeting with her mother. Her childhood had taught her not to cross her mother, if at all possible. Beatings with a willow whip, words to shame and curb her spirit, and looks of contempt had only hardened her heart against her mother.

She could not wait to leave home. Meeting Adrian had opened up a window in her imagination—the possibility that she could have a love marriage with a peer rather than become a chattel for a wealthy older man.

Lander's fury was spent.

"Come, daughter," he beckoned.

They walked toward the sunny drawing room where Phaedra often spent time making schedules and planning her day. In the late afternoon sunshine, she would often sit with her feet up, drinking ouzo, alcohol mixed with herbs, to ease the day's exhaustion and stress.

Althaia's only hope was that Father's more measured, reasonable nature and close, affectionate relationship with her would guide the conversation.

Mother was indeed in her drawing room. She looked up from her lounging chair, smiling and offering her hand and cheek to Father to kiss. He obliged.

"Well, look who you found!" She smiled, rolling her eyes as they fixed on Althaia. "I heard you were studying with Helena today. How did it go? Surely you didn't need to dress so fancy? What were you girls up to?"

She looked closely at her daughter. "You don't look well. Do you have another headache?"

"Althaia?" Father's eyes registered hurt. "You told your mother you were at Helena's?"

Althaia looked at the floor, studying her shoes. Her head continued to throb painfully.

"Yes, Mother, I have a headache. May I go lie down please?"

"Althaia!" Lander commanded as he sucked his breath in and released it through his nose.

She could hear the anger rising again in his voice.

Her voice was small, "I'm so sorry. I didn't go to Helena's. I was in the city. I... um, I met a friend."

Her increasing distress was evident as she felt sweat on her neck, brow, and upper lip.

"A *friend*?" her father said accusingly.

Tears began to flow down her face as she closed her eyes, and her body began to shake.

"It was a Roman soldier, a man. I spied them on a bench in a public space." His eyes met Phaedra's and held them as she blinked quickly, her nut-brown eyes questioning his face, flashing as they moved from his eyes to her daughter's face.

He continued, "Why was she with this man, touching him, so close in a public space? Did she know him from before? How long? She brought dishonor to myself and our house today. The very sight of her with the enemy, the occupier, was a distortion of our family name."

Althaia began to moan, her stomach roiling, whether from her head spinning with fear or the baby, it did not matter. Her stomach was forcing waves of nausea up through her body. She leaned over, grasping her stomach as she began to heave.

Phaedra rose to stand before her daughter as her intuition came alive like a feral animal. Her voice was livid and cold as stone.

"Are you pregnant? What is this? Tell us. *Now*."

Father had walked to the door, and she heard it close, the thick cedar door sealing the sound of their conversation, her despair, and the fate of her future. She could not escape. Althaia's breath became ragged as she began to hyperventilate, falling down on the marbled floor slick with her stomach juices.

"Althaia. Tell us. You heard your mother. What is this all about?"

She heard her father repeat what Mother had said.

Then, came the sound that was familiar: Mother screaming, "Are you *pregnant*? What is this? Answer us."

Althaia pulled herself up to standing. Something in her became like the stone in her mother's voice. The love that had never been consummated between them held her steady. She was silent as she faced her mother, her dress soiled, her face streaked and blotchy. Her jaw had become like the marble floor. She stood, refusing to answer.

"Answer me." Phaedra slapped her eldest daughter's cheek hard, as Father's voice suddenly became impotent, his body sagging, the truth beginning to sink in.

"Harlot! Loose woman!" Mother's low, enraged whisper was almost more fearsome than her screams. "I should have let you die when you were born."

Althaia knew all too well about the cultural infanticide of girl children, especially if the eldest child, the first one, was not a male.

"Yes, I am pregnant," Althaia heard her dispassionate voice.

Everything stood still, as though in a dream state. Althaia wondered if there was any air left in the room as she breathed heavily, in and out, her cheek sore and stinging, her head on fire.

Mother's ire had subsided. She dropped into her chair.

"Lander, she is *your* daughter," she said accusingly. "But I will tell you what I believe we need to do with her, and I expect you to heed my advice. This cannot continue… the Roman. This unwanted pregnancy. But you must agree, *if* you do not want your reputation and our family's sullied further."

Now they were in a heated but whispered argument, Father's back to her, leaning over Mother in her chair. Althaia bent over to ease her head, then fell to her hands and knees to quell the rising dizziness. She could only catch a few words here and there. *Witch. Herbal formula. Three days.*

It did not matter; her heart was broken into a million pieces on the ground. She must find Adrian. Surely he would know where they could go to find safety.

"Daughter." Father finally came to stand over Althaia.

"Take my hand, Althaia. Stand up," he commanded. "What is the name of this *Roman* soldier?"

He contemptuously spat the words out.

"Adrian. His name is Adrian. I, I… I don't know his last name," she wailed.

"And where did you meet him?" Father continued.

"At the market a few months ago. When I was with Daphne and Egan. He carried our baskets, which were heavy. We spoke. That's all."

The untruths were stacking up, though there was no protection for her as each deceit was laid out.

"So, he is stationed here in Athens. I will go at once and speak with his superior."

"No!" Now it was Althaia's turn to scream.

Stunned, she pleaded, "No, no, no. Please, Father, please, please, no, no, no."

She began to weep, grasping for her father's hands, which

he withdrew as she fell again in a heap onto the cold floor.

Her mother's straight spine against the chair had become a wall of solidarity with her husband.

"I will find Daphne, and we will get to the bottom of this story," she said coldly.

"She will also clean up the floor here and bring you some tea. Go to your bath and wash up, Althaia," Mother said, with disgust edging her voice.

Again, Father offered his hand. When Althaia refused, he put his arm beneath her shoulder, bidding her to stand. She stood, miserable and numb.

"Go, daughter. Clean yourself. Rest. We will come to you with our decision this evening."

Althaia stepped out of the lavender silk dress, letting it slip to the floor. She poured the crystal-clear water of the pitcher into her bathing bowl, dripping in a tincture of lavender drops to calm her nerves. As she washed her face and neck, moving down along her breasts and the small, soft bump of her abdomen, she lingered for a moment with her hands caressing this growing being.

Spent by her emotions, she felt a small spark of joy as she remembered her time with Adrian by the sea. What would become of him? What would happen to the tiny fire of their love that had been kindled? A tear slipped out of the corner of her eye. She dressed in her simple white nightgown, feeling her body begin to relax, though her brain still felt foggy and inflamed.

Daphne came bustling in the door with a decanter of ginger-lemon juice and a simple platter of olives, flat bread, and olive oil. She also offered a steaming cup of tea.

"Here, child, try this. It's chamomile infused with linden and licorice herbs to settle your stomach. You *must* eat. I worry about you, Thaia. Your headaches, and now the nausea. Please eat and drink these things to soothe yourself. I slipped a bit of mead into the juice, my dear," she winked.

Clearly, Mother and Father had not spoken to her yet. She was only aware that she must minister to Althaia's suffering.

"Thank you, Daphne. I am so grateful."

Sipping the juice, she felt the slow tide overtake her—a combination of lightness of being and her brain finally slowing down. She laid down on her bed, finally feeling the ache of her body and the gnawing psychic pain recede slowly.

"You are welcome. If my daughter ever had this kind of pain you have, I would take them to a doctor. I'm sorry you must bear this burden alone."

Daphne, despite her rough edges, was kind at heart. She was truly the only mothering figure Althaia had ever known.

Althaia reached her hand toward Daphne, inviting her to approach her bedside. Her servant gently stroked her hand, and a smile that often looked like a grimace, softened her face.

"Thank you," Althaia said again, ever so softly. "I love you."

Daphne looked startled, but continued to stroke her hand, finally brushing her forehead with a kiss before taking her leave.

Althaia sighed as her mind floated. She watched the designs on the ceiling as the shadows lengthened into evening. Her young mind struggled to understand the rigid social mores and confusing messages of her class, her family, her parents, and her society. She was meant to hate the Roman soldier. She was meant to save herself and her virginity for a negotiated bargain between her father and an older man. Her body was not hers to offer freely to the first tender words and respectful touch that opened the hunger of her longing. There was no wise woman mentoring her in the ways of femaleness and the mysteries and secrets of her budding woman's body. No one to guide her into the adventure of loving another, while keeping her safe from pregnancy until she was prepared and her beloved was ready.

And now, for the first time in her young life, she had felt her passion opened up. She was no longer a girl. She had become a woman in the stroke of that moment. The key to her heart unlocked by this boy-man. Eager, impetuous, and headstrong, she joined and met him to explore the unknown interior rooms that no one had opened to her before.

It seemed that the great and holy Athena, goddess of war and protectress of Athens, had not covered her daughter, Althaia, with protection. She had betrayed this one who had played for her on the flute from childhood. She had been left abandoned, ignored, without wisdom and skill for the moment before her. And now she was disdained and shamed by her parents.

As the moon rose in the blackening sky, Althaia startled at a blood-curdling scream. It sounded like a woman in distress. Then she heard the loud whoosh of wings as Athena, the owl, took flight. Althaia let her head drop backward, her cheeks wet.

With one unexpected encounter, Althaia was no longer the virgin. She had suddenly become the whore. She fell into a fitful sleep.

CHAPTER FOUR

The Fruit of Her Womb

I am the barren one and the one with many children.
　I am she whose marriage is multiple, and I have not taken a husband.
　I am the midwife and she who does not give birth.
　I am the comforting of my labor pains.[3]

Althaia awoke often during the night, trembling at the curtains that closed the scene of last evening's drama. Her headache became a dull thud, reverberating through her whole body at times. She awaited the promised visit from her parents. They never came.

The sun rose and poured through the sheer curtains of her bedroom, encasing her in light. Althaia heard the shouts and arguments of her siblings moving from the house to the garden as Daphne's sharp voice reminded them to settle down for breakfast.

Then she heard Mother and Father's voice at the bottom of the wide, marbled stairs in hushed tones. She remained in bed, paralyzed by her anxious foreboding. Tangled up with the nausea was a knot of terror and grief.

---

[3] 1 (Thunder: Perfect Mind, NagHammadi Library, Tr. J. Robinson, HarperCollins, NY, 1977, 271–4)

None too soon, she heard a rap at her door. Before she could speak, the door opened, and Mother and Father strode in and stood over her.

"Althaia, we have come to a decision," Father spoke deliberately.

"Today, I will go into the city and speak with this man, Adrian's supervisor. I will use my influence to have him removed from Athens and restationed. You are never to lay eyes upon him again."

Althaia sucked in her breath as her chest began to shake. Her grief, like bile, rising in her throat with loud, jagged sobs. She hung her head. She could no longer meet their eyes.

Mother continued without affect, "You will stay home today from lessons. We have summoned the midwife to come this afternoon. We have also spoken with Daphne. She deeply regrets that she ever let that Roman soldier carry our things. She will go with your father this morning and identify the young man."

With that, they strode out of her room, her father taking one last glance at the heap of misery that was his eldest daughter, his face contorted with sorrow and compassion, before closing the door.

Althaia continued to hear the sounds of a wakening household. But she stayed prone and paralyzed in her bed. Soon, the door opened, and Daphne poked her head around the edge. She had a tray in her hands. Putting the breakfast down, she sat quietly on the edge of the bed, rubbing her hands together. Digging in the bosom of her dress, she pulled out a piece of linen and handed it to Althaia, indicating that she could use it to dry her tears and blow her nose.

"Oh, Daphne. I never, never, ever wanted to bring shame to my family," she wept bitterly.

"There, there," Daphne again took her hand and stroked it gently.

"I never wanted to put you in such a compromised situation. Please forgive me."

Daphne closed her eyes and nodded her head. She had raised this girl from a tiny baby and felt a maternal closeness, as though she were one of her own. Since she was not responsible for the discipline of this child, she could offer only kindness. Her heart hurt as she saw how broken Althaia's spirit was. If it were one of her own daughters, they would've found a way to care for the baby. But Daphne was well aware of the class system in Greece. A wealthy family would betray its reputation by such an act. Mercy was rare in the higher castes. Everything was commodified.

"My little love," she said, using a pet name that Daphne had not employed since Althaia was tiny. "You must eat. You must rest. Soon the midwife will be here to check you and see how you are doing and how far along you are in your womb time."

Althaia offered a small, pained smile, leaning over to hug her longtime servant. They embraced for a few moments, Daphne stroking her hair slowly. The sunlight held them in a spotlight and then began to shift, ever so minutely. Drawing away, Daphne stood and brushed off her apron, becoming all business again.

"I must go and prepare your sisters and brother for their lessons. I will come again and take the tray. I expect it to be empty," she said, nodding emphatically.

Althaia fell back in her covers. Food was the furthest thing from her mind. She had not seen Helena for days now. She longed for her friend: the comfort of her laughter, the way her eyes widened and glowed with a clever idea or joke, her arm pulling Althaia close to her as they walked and shared secrets together.

Despite her throbbing head and the low ebb of nausea, she stood up and went to her satchel with her papyrus sheaf. She would write two letters: one to Adrian and one to Helena.

Then she would ask Daphne to deliver them both to Helena, whom she would beg to pass along Adrian's letter.

She began.

Dear Helena,

Trouble has come to our household. Mother and Father have found out about Adrian. Mother also sensed that I am with child. The scene was ugly and frightening. I have no words to speak of the horror of that evening. They threaten to have Adrian stationed far away from Athens. I am not to see him ever again. I am drowning in a sea of tears. My heart is broken into a million pieces. I am not repentant for my love of the Roman soldier, nor of our sweet but brief time together. But I do feel regret for dragging the Adamos name through the dirt. Mother is enraged and on her high horse. Father has become tight-lipped. He is no match for mother. Please come to me when you can. I miss you, my friend.

Althaia

The sun's shadow lengthened and circled to the window in the south. Althaia picked at her food, managing a few bites of the egg and flatbread dipped in olive oil. Her head was beginning to clear, and the dull thud receded as she rested with the lavender silk pillow on her eyes.

At exactly mid-afternoon, she heard the staccato of her mother's step and a swishing of slippered feet attempting to stay abreast. They followed each other up the wide, banistered, marble stair steps.

The door swung open without a knock. Her mother

presented in her usual long, elegant, silk gown. This one was the color of calendula. With her was a strange, stooped older woman.

"Althaia, here is the midwife. Her name is Eileithyia," Mother said formally.

Althaia knew well what the name meant: Goddess of childbirth. The ready-comer. She nodded in acknowledgment. The woman was much older than Mother. Probably past her moon-time. A crone.

"Get. Out. Of. Bed. Eileithyia has come from across the city to see you." Mother was still infuriated, her voice was tight.

Althaia's breath became shallow. She swung her feet over the side of the bed and stood in her thin linen nightgown as the midwife looked her up and down.

"Do you know how many months you are along?" the midwife questioned.

Althaia shrugged her shoulders to her ears. "Ma... may... maybe two months?"

"Althaia, speak clearly. You *know* how long you have been with child. Tell her," Mother spoke accusingly.

Althaia's hands began to shake. "Yes, that's right, two months."

Eileithyia nodded. "Let me check you."

She was a practical woman. Not unkind, but neutral. Her experienced hands had delivered many babies. She stepped next to Althaia and began to palpate the small bump forming around her navel. She asked Althaia to lie down so she could examine her pelvis.

Althaia squirmed with discomfort as she laid flat.

"Madam Phaedra, please give us a moment," Eileithyia spoke directly to Phaedra, a voice of confidence and experience that left no room for debate.

Phaedra's lips pouted and her cheekbones became rigid.

"We are paying you a good sum of money. Please be thorough and give me a report when you are done."

At that, she stepped out of the room, clearly fuming at this woman brave enough to challenge her authority.

The midwife was quick. She washed her hands carefully and examined Althaia's pelvic width and noted her small hips and fine bone structure.

"You are correct. It is two months. Aside from the nausea, is there anything else that you experience? Pain, bleeding?"

"No," Althaia said in a tiny voice, ashamed of being seen by this strange woman in such a private way.

"Okay. Pull your underclothing up and I will speak with your mother."

The midwife was gone.

Althaia could hear their tones, up and down, her mother's high-pitched indignant sound, Eileithyia's low monotone voice.

Her ears strained to understand what they were saying. It was no use.

Soon they came back into the room.

"Eileithyia will give you some herbs," Mother said in a clipped tone. "You are to take them now, after dark, and tomorrow morning. She will remain in our household until you are complete."

Mother turned and walked out of the room, her steps receding down the stairs.

"I shall be right back," the midwife stated. "I must get some warm water and prepare my herbs."

After what seemed an eternity, Eileithyia returned. She brought a decanter and a chalice in which to pour the tonic.

"I am giving you this, child, at your mother's command. I

shall remain near if you need anything."

"What is in the potion?" Althaia questioned, her brow drawn.

"It is a mixture of tansy, rue, wormwood, yarrow, and essential oil of pennyroyal. Here, child, drink this… to the last drop."

Before Althaia could ask any other questions, the proffered cup was put into her hand and the old midwife encircled her fingers around Althaia's, encouraging her firmly to her to put it to her lips and drink.

Althaia hoped it would keep the nausea at bay. She drank and then spat it out, slamming the cup on her bedside table. The bitterness upon her tongue brought up her gagging reflect. She turned away, her face to the wall.

"I cannot!" Her voice was shrill.

"Yes, you will," the woman said firmly, not unkindly. "It is your mother's wish. You do not want to answer to her, do you?"

Althaia's affect went flat. "Will it help the nausea?"

"Yes." The midwife's emotionless eyes met hers.

Breathing deeply, Althaia picked up the cup again and, without taking a breath, gulped the entire drink down.

"There's a good girl. Now, you rest. I will be back to check on you later as the shadows of the evening deepen."

"Please, send my servant, Daphne," Althaia pleaded.

"Certainly."

And the midwife was gone.

Phaedra Adamos was a striking figure. Tall and slender as a willow, she had once been a rising classical dancer in the Mediterranean Near East. How many times she would perform at the colonnaded Parthenon temple of the Acropolis, rising above the city of Athens. She remembered well the clarity of the

Grecian air and the arid Azul sky. How the globe of the sun warmed her hair, bronze skin, and limbs as she moved gracefully before the appreciative audiences. It was as though she had transcended to Athena herself, rising above the bustling city of mortals below.

Growing up in Thira, a small island in the Aegean Sea, Phaedra could see it in her mind's eye as though it were yesterday. The whitewashed, simple homes clinging to the cliffs, rising above the bejeweled sea. There was her mother, Lydia, washing clothes in the open-aired courtyard, her countenance downcast. With five daughters, her lot in life was to not only birth them, but find them good husbands and dowries. After her husband disappeared in a strong storm while at sea in his fishing boat, she struggled to get out of bed each morning and care for them. Five young daughters could keep the household going, but none could replace a mother's love. Lydia's moods swirled like the sea. Like the darkness of the moonless island nights, her soul could no longer see her way forward. She was sinking.

Phaedra remembered how she longed to flee this island and ply her artistry in the world beyond. She wanted to go far away from the depression that lingered like a thick and diseased breath, a smell surrounding she and her sisters every day. She could not comprehend what it was like to be in her mother's body. Only that it was a fortress of sorrow against her own needs as a child.

On the day she met Lander, it was a business event in Athens. As she entertained the Bacchus crowd of young men with her dance, she could see he wanted her. Handsome and smart, he could offer her the freedom to leave the island and the weighty sorrow of her childhood. They married. As his fortunes rose from his oriental trading business, she finally felt the security that she never had in her youth. The children came. Life was busy. Her first child, a daughter, Althaia, was as headstrong and beautiful as she was once upon a time. Yet, she had pushed that life far away, and in her amnesia, Phaedra could not understand this child who wanted to push against the rules and flout the family reputation.

Her work was to preserve the good family name that she and Lander had worked so hard to achieve.

As the night wore on, Althaia noticed the residual taste of the strong bitter herbs on her tongue. She also noticed that her throbbing headache had receded.

She took up her ink and papyrus again and began a letter to Adrian. She would ask Helena to deliver this to him quickly, before he was gone.

My dearest Adrian,

Beloved of my heart. Our absence aggrieves me. I long to see you again. Can you make a way for us to meet? How can I speak of the sorrows since our last meeting? Please forgive me for the unexpected news. Surely it was a shock, and my father's appearance only further alienated you. I am so sorry.

My parents want to keep us apart and they will seek to have you sent away. I am not certain what will become of me here in their household. Mother continues to be enraged.

Please come to me. Leave a note under the lion's brick. Tell me what to do! I will do anything to see you again. Our love is the fruit of my womb. I will protect this seed with my whole life.

Yours truly,

Thaia

There was a knock at the door.

"Come in!" Althaia called, cheered by her letter to Adrian and the thought of seeing him again.

Daphne came in bearing a tray with food, Egan popping in behind her.

"Sister! Sister!" he said excitedly. "Are you sick, Thaia? May I come and sit by your bedside, and we can play a game?"

"No, little brother. I am not fully well. Come tomorrow and we can play then."

Egan's face was downcast. "The twins will not play with me today. They ignore me and play mean tricks on me."

Despite herself, Althaia laughed and welcomed him to come and sit on her bed, where she hugged him.

"Sisters are like that. Tomorrow will be fine. You'll see. Their moods are like the wind that blows."

Egan squirmed away.

"Come now," Daphne took Egan's hand and led him out the door.

"Oh, wait! Daphne, come back!" Althaia shouted.

Daphne popped her head back in the door.

"I have two letters for Helena. Can you promise to deliver them safely and that their contents remain in confidence?"

Daphne glared at her. "Of course, child. Who do you make me out to be?"

She snatched the letters, carefully sealed with wax, both addressed to Helena, and grabbing Egan's hand, she left the room in a huff.

As the hours dragged on, Althaia read her lessons, stared out the window, and rested in bed. Within three hours, she began to feel cramps. At first, they were mild.

Within a half hour, they began to come in widening waves, like a stone thrown in a lake that begins to ripple like a tsunami across a placid lake. Bewildered, she put her hands on the small bump of her belly, registering the distress.

As she cried out, she heard multiple steps on the stairs, and the midwife and Daphne flew into the room.

"My little love!" Daphne came to her bedside, the sure weight of her hands upon Althaia's abdomen as she tried to divine what was happening.

"Go, get some clean cloths and warm water," shouted the midwife.

"Breathe, child, breathe, quickly now, in and out, in and out," Eileithyia demonstrated, her hands on Althaia's abdomen, her practiced hands opening Althaia's legs to examine her as Althaia writhed from the ripping pain.

"Come on, all fours now, on your bed. Keep breathing," the midwife intoned.

Daphne hurried back in the room with a pitcher of warm water, a basin, torn cloths, and olive oil. She sat by Althaia, now on all fours, holding her forehead firmly, rubbing her back as the midwife breathed with her, soaking the cloth in the warm water of the basin. Hours passed.

Althaia felt as though her insides were being gutted like a fish, flayed and opened, raked with thorns. She screamed as she felt an involuntary bearing down, a pressure upon her womb. Suddenly, there was a quickening, as though a bird were flying upward out of her body. It disappeared into thin air. Her womb expelled the lifeless tissue of what was a child, a bundle of undifferentiated bloody cells that slipped out of her body onto the sheets. The midwife whisked them away.

Exhausted, Althaia fell onto her side from all fours, weeping.

"Roll over, child," the midwife instructed, gently massaging her belly with olive oil and placing warm cloths there.

Daphne's eyes were moist as she placed a warm cloth on Althaia's forehead, continuing to stroke her hair.

Women were well acquainted with the travail of miscarriage and births lost before their time. It was the women who knew how to minister to one another in these harsh moments.

Tears fell from Althaia's closed eyes. Her golden skin had acquired a white pallor—only intensified by the raven waves of her hair falling in a wreath around her pinched face. She laid completely still as the cramps subsided. She felt the warm flow of her blood continuing, the sheets turning crimson as she lay silent. The midwife busied herself with clearing the sheets and replacing them with fresh ones, as Daphne sat on Althaia's bed, her roughened hands caressing, stroking the skin of this girl woman whom she had known from infancy. She began to hum a lullaby from that long-ago time. Althaia did not move.

The fruit of her womb, the love seed of her union with Adrian, was dead. Her womb was empty. Voided of the life energy that they shared for a time. This baby being had been barred from entering the world, its animating force snuffed out in an instant.

Somewhere far away, she heard an owl. Numb, she wondered if it were Athena.

CHAPTER FIVE

Silencing of Her Song

While in the dark sea,
   I slept,
   And not overwhelmed there,
   dreamt: a star
   blazed in my womb
   I marveled
   At that light
   And grasped it,
   And brought it up to the sun.
   I laid hold upon it,
   And will not let it go.
   (Makeda, Queen of Sheba, ca.1000 BCE)[4]

Days reached into weeks. Althaia moved as a ghost through her life. The midwife left two days after her work was done. The blood flow continued, as though to drain Althaia of her life energy. She felt numb and dead inside.

Althaia begged Mother to let her go see Helena or else allow Helena to come visit.

On both accounts, her mother refused.

---

[4] Makeda, Queen of Sheba, Women in Praise of the Sacred, ed. Jane Hirshfield(New York: HarperCollins, 1994)14

"You are not well, Althaia. You must rest and regain your strength."

Mother had stayed away until the midwife was gone, then she had come to Althaia.

"You are now relieved of your lessons and flute quartet until further notice, daughter. You have become a woman. As you recover from female problems, we must determine what your next step is. You cannot go back to the sheltered life of an underage child. You must now act as a woman. You are no longer an honored daughter under your father's roof, accepting all manner of gifts and special privileges that he affords you. Now we must see how you will make your own way in the world."

Althaia had not the wherewithal to fight her mother's steely hand. The shock of the lost pregnancy on the heels of that fearful and violent afternoon, when she confessed her relationship with Adrian, had overwhelmed Althaia's ability to think clearly. That carefree young girl in the marketplace or on the beach, tossing her hair with confidence, laughing outrageously, and enjoying pretty things, seemed lost to her. Had that girl ever existed? Somedays, Althaia did not know. Her friend, Helena, was unavailable to recognize and affirm the old, high-spirited young woman's existence.

Most days, Althaia could not swim to the surface, escaping the undertow that threatened to suck her under the waves of depression.

One day, as she sat in the garden with Athena on her arm, quietly talking with the owl, sharing her anguish, Father came and knelt next to her.

"My daughter," he began, then stopped.

His voice broke.

Clearing his throat, Lander continued, "Thaia, this has been a difficult season for you. I know you have suffered. My heart is aggrieved."

He did not touch her or gently lay his hand on her shoulder as he often did. His eyes were cast down for a moment. Finally, he looked up, meeting her onyx eyes, which usually flashed with joy to see him. They were dull. Althaia could see the pain in his eyes.

"What is it, Father?" she tried to nudge him to continue.

"Your mother has jurisdiction over your care now, as the woman of the house. She is intent on sending you away." Again she could hear his voice catch. "I will do what I can to preserve your life here. Know that I am doing everything possible."

Finally finished, he stood up and walked away, though not before she saw the tears shining in his eyes.

As the season changed, the air becoming colder, Althaia withdrew even deeper into her own thoughts. Her siblings left her alone now. Even Egan did not come to jar her out of her reverie. There was something unspoken and troubling to the small boy about his elder sister's lack of affect. There was no adult to translate what had happened to her spirit. Instead, he raced around with his twin sisters, peeking at his sister from a distance.

Althaia had no desire to play the flute. It only reminded her of happier times and her meeting with Adrian. Instead, she began to dance. As the shroud of darkness gathered around the city, often when the moon shone into her bedroom, she began to spin. Her hands gracefully flowed out from the center of her body, as though compelled by some music within. Althaia danced—sometimes fiercely, stamping her feet, her head thrown back as her hands tussled and fought an invisible presence, her hands rigid and pulsing, a low growl escaping her lips. Other times, she leaped and soared and twirled around her room. She did not notice the ghost of her mother's presence at the window, stirring the curtains, watching her daughter dance.

As the cover of darkness deepened, she poured down the marble stairs and out into the garden, moving among the thick nectar-scented jasmine bushes and tall cedars. She felt almost herself, and in her body, as she danced. Something frozen was thawing, drip by drip. With the servants gone home for the night, Althaia entered the stables where the warm, pungent smell of the Adamos' fleet of horses engulfed her. As they chewed and snorted and threw their heads about, Althaia laughed. Basil was her favorite, a king-like boy with a cream coat and splotches of chocolate and ginger. He was gentle and always dropped his head when she came to him, his long-lashed eyes looking her over as she stroked his forehead. Soon, she began to bring him dates and almonds as a treat. A bond of kindness held her, and for those moments, Althaia was comforted and felt loved by the creaturely world.

Althaia's blood became a trickle after two months. Her stomach had smoothed out again. The bump was gone. Some days, she would absentmindedly drop her hand on her belly and feel the sharp grief twisting inside of her as she suddenly realized she was barren. Empty. The tears would come, searing her cheeks again.

Her hair fell out in great handfuls. It was rare for her to be out of bed for more than five hours a day. Even Mother seemed worried.

One day, she heard the sound of a strange man downstairs as she listlessly laid in bed, staring at the ceiling.

The voices of Mother and the stranger advanced up the stairs. A sharp rap on the door, and Mother opened it with a flourish.

"Althaia, I have invited Dr. Kriaku to examine you."

"Hello, Althaia."

The doctor had a kindly manner.

"May I approach?" he asked respectfully.

Althaia, now sitting on the edge of her bed, barely nodded.

"Will you please stand, so I might see your full stature?" Sighing deeply, she stood.

"My dear, does this area hurt?" he asked, palpating her lower back. "Is this tender?"

His experienced fingers prodded below her ribs, around her kidneys.

"Yes, it's sore," Althaia spoke in a monotone.

She watched her mother's reaction out of the corner of her eyes, her tight lips, her careful pile of coiffed black and ginger-accented hair, her perfect eye make-up, and the elegant wine-colored silk peplos she wore. This was clearly an inconvenience.

"Please open your mouth and stick out your tongue." The doctor stood before her, his hands on her shoulders to steady her. "Can you stand up tall?"

As he examined her tongue, his eyes made a note of her bald patches and her lifeless hair and dull eyes.

"May I?" He indicated that he would like to listen to her heart.

"It is painful to stand up completely," Althaia intoned, turning her head to the side, allowing the doctor access to her chest.

"No matter. I am going to leave a prescription for you and your mother. Your kidneys are doing poorly. Mrs. Adamos, what herbal emmenagogues was she given?"

Phaedra blinked quickly and stuttered, "We, I… I don't

know. It was left to the midwife."

"Often these strong herbal formulas can damage the kidneys, which are foundational for vitality, energy, and life force. Often young girls are given too strong of a tonic." His tone was clipped.

"But we, I mean, the midwife only gave her one of the three doses. How could that have been damaging?" Phaedra's voice was placating, trying to justify.

Dr. Kriaku ignored her.

"You must give her as many vegetables and fruits as possible each day. I will also leave a recipe for an herbal tonic that includes parsley, ginger, juniper, and nettles."

He turned to Mother and curtly said, "In the future, call me first, not the midwife."

Picking up his cloth bag, he turned on his heels and left without waiting for Mother to accompany him to the door.

Mother took a deep breath and blew it out. For a moment, Phaedra seemed to relent.

"Daughter, we want you to be well. I see you dancing at times in the garden at night. Does that help?"

Phaedra remembered her own years as a young girl, dancing—how free she felt, the joy of spinning and moving in fluid grace, of being admired and seen. She felt a small ache of longing as she watched her eldest daughter in the moonlight, wondering what propelled her forward.

"When I dance, I forget for a moment. It brings me peace." Althaia did not look at her mother.

"I see. Once I danced," Phaedra said softly. "I met your father this way."

Althaia's head snapped up, her eyes flashing for a moment, questioning. But that was all Mother said.

"I will send Daphne with the required things for you." And

she was gone.

One day, Althaia heard the sweet sound of a voice that she had missed for too long.

"Helena!"

She spun out of her bedroom and took the stairs two at a time until she stood in front of her friend, who stood inside the front door. Taking her friend's hands, they spun around, shouting jubilantly until they were breathless.

"Helena, Helena, Helena!" cried Althaia, hugging her friend tightly to her breast.

She could feel their hearts fluttering, pressed against one another.

"Girls, go out in the garden so you aren't underfoot, please," Daphne said in mock indignation.

The girls streamed out the door hand in hand. Althaia took her friend to the furthest corner of the garden, underneath the old olive tree that spread its gnarly arms over them. No one was in earshot; they were safe. The friendly faces of purple and yellow flowers waved gently in the wind.

"Helena, my dearest friend. I have missed you. Please tell me the news. Did you receive my letters? Were you able to deliver Adrian's letter?"

The words tumbled out in a flurry, on top of one another until they were laughing and leaning their foreheads together, hands clutching.

"Thaia, when you disappeared, I was so worried. I sent many messages to your home, but no one ever returned with a reply. Mother said I could not come over to see you until Phaedra allowed it. Finally, your twin sisters came to flute practice one day and gave me a note which said I could come visit. Did you know Calliope and Calista are taking flute?"

"No," Althaia said slowly. "I have mostly remained in my room alone. I have been very ill."

She began to recount the past few months. The scene in Mother's drawing room, where she confessed that she was pregnant. The midwife visit. The strong herbs. The expelling of the contents of her womb. The long bleeding. The season of grief.

Helena's beautiful hazel eyes were wide with disbelief, her brows pulling into a crease. At one point, she sucked in her breathe sharply and clapped her hands against her mouth.

"Oh. Oh. My dearest Thaia. How wretched. When I received your letters, I went to the small temple on our street and offered prayers and lit candles to Athena."

"Where was Athena when Father ripped me from Adrian? How did Athena protect me when Mother told me she wished I'd never been born? Who is Athena now that I am without child and my beloved?" Althaia wept bitterly as Helena put her arm around her quaking shoulders.

"Thaia, I did send your message for Adrian, via my male servant, to the Roman headquarters in downtown Athens. He didn't want to deliver it, but I bribed him with my favorite pearls."

"Helena, thank you! So, you did send it to him!"

The news cheered Althaia.

"But of course! I would do anything for you. I so miss you at our lessons and flute practice."

"Mother said I am finished with the quartet and my lessons." Althaia's face hardened. "She said that she and father will determine what is next now that I am a woman, no longer a child in my father's house. I am afraid I will be given to an ugly old man in marriage. My fate will be sealed. I will kill myself or run away rather than accept this death."

Althaia's tone was low and livid.

Helena's eyes remained on her friend's face. She was silent. There was nothing to say. Both girls knew that their grace period would be over one day, and their parents would have the final say in charting their future. Some girls had the good fortune of kind parents who loved them and attempted to make the best match possible. Other girls, whose parents were intent on climbing the ladder of success, would go to all means possible to ensure their daughters found wealthy suitors.

"Helena." Althaia's breath was shallow.

Her friend could see her torment in her stooped body, her thin hair, her haunted eyes.

"Lena, promise me you will not leave me, even if I am sent to the Orient."

"Oh, Thaia, of course! But it is impossible that you will be sent there. We are friends for life. Forever."

Wrapping their arms around one another for comfort, they sat entwined for a time as Althaia quietly cried. Helena came from a loving family. She was the youngest among many brothers, a beloved only daughter, the last child born. Her life trajectory bode well due to this constellation.

Suddenly, a whoosh, and Althaia felt the claws of Athena through the thin cloth on her shoulder. The girls fell apart with a shriek and the owl fell backwards, rising again to take a perch in the olive tree.

Laughing, they rose from the bench hand in hand, and walked toward the lion gate. The air smelled so pure. Suddenly, Althaia had a sense of wellbeing.

"Helena, I will come visit you soon, I promise," Althaia said.

"I'll believe it when I see you," Helena laughed and rolled

her eyes as they walked through the gate.

Kissing her friend on the cheek, Helena waved and skipped down the path toward her house.

Althaia turned slowly toward her prison. Her eyes fell on a the loose brick where once a young man had secretly stowed a message to her. She went over and ran her hand along the rough surface, where the brick stuck out beyond the others. Something caught her attention.

Her face drawn, she put her fingers around the edges of the brick and wiggled it toward her. A piece of papyrus fell to the ground.

Her breathing stopped. Leaving the brick as though in a trance, she slowly opened the creased and weathered paper. It had been there for weeks, if not months.

My dearest Althaia. I received your message. Our parting was not as I would have wanted it. I regret that I could not speak kindly to you in that moment when you told me of the child, or that I did not hold you in my arms. Your father has made a deal with my centurion, and I am being sent to the far province of Judea. He assured me that you and the child would be cared for.

I am without words, my heart is heavy. I will miss you. Someday, I hope I might come back for you. Adrian

Althaia was stunned. She began to breathe again, this time a shallow, quick breath. He was gone. Something in her broke again. Her joyful reunion with Helena was erased in that moment.

As she walked back toward the mansion, papyrus clutched in her hand, the weight of depression descended again like a dark, suffocating cloth.

The next day, Mother and Father lingered over breakfast. Father did not rush off to the office as usual. The twins were squabbling over who got to sit in front of the chariot on the way to town. Egan raced around the gardens as usual.

In the coolness of the morning, Althaia pulled her shawl closer.

"Althaia, we would like to speak with you after breakfast," Father spoke.

Althaia's eyes darted from Mother to Father. She hung her head.

"I will be in my room."

"No. Come to the drawing room." Mother's voice was clipped.

The drawing room's curtains were closed. Mother pulled them back and nodded to a cushion as Althaia entered. Father stood with his back to her, facing the wide fire pit. He did not turn as Phaedra began to speak.

"Althaia, we have decided to send you to Corinth, the mountain of Acrocorinth, to the temple of Aphrodite. You will apprentice there with the other women to offer your services. Your duty is to serve her, the goddess of love, beauty, and sexuality. We can no longer find a suitable husband for you as you have been used up. Ruined."

Father turned to her. "Daughter, this is our decision. We have no other choice. Sacred temple prostitution is also honorable to our family. There are men who seek out the women of Aphrodite for a fertility rite or a divine marriage. Athena will watch over you and protect you."

Althaia looked in horror from one to another. How could this be? Athena. She cursed the goddess silently. It was as though she was underwater, and the conversation was thick and garbled. Almost unintelligible.

She had no energy left to resist.

"When will this happen?" Althaia asked without emotion.

"It is undecided. I must inquire. It may take months. We must make arrangements with the temple," Father said.

Mother looked out the window, her eyes fixed on the stables.

Althaia felt herself dissociating. It was as though she was sitting in a corner of the high ceiling, looking down at the three of them. She would become isolated and far from her friends and music.

As though in a dream, Althaia turned and walked away.

CHAPTER SIX

The Temple at Acrocorinth

Love of wealth wholly absorbs men, and never for a moment allows them to think of anything but their own private possessions; on this the soul of every citizen hangs suspended.
  – Plato

Lander Adamos debarked from the sea vessel that had carried him from Athens to Corinth. A bustling port city, he knew this place well. He came here often on business and had many clients and colleagues in the city. He walked onto the streets filled with merchants and people selling their wares, jostling one another and vying loudly to be heard above the din.

"Lander! What are you doing here, my old friend?" he heard a voice sing out.

Landers started. He didn't expect to see anyone on this trip. He planned to move undetected due to the serious nature of this trip. But here was Cleomens, a young Athenian from his own city state, who also did business in Corinth.

"Ho! Cleomens! What have you to say for yourself?"

Recovering his demeanor, Lander heard the tone in his voice. It was deceivingly cheerful. It did not bely the heaviness of his heart. He was here on a mission. Phaedra would have it no other way. Lander was aware that wealth and class were a heavy burden for her, as they had become for him. Reputation must be secured at all costs. This situation with his beloved eldest daughter, Althaia, had brought Lander to his knees. He was a man who loved reason. Yet, despite his voracious and enterprising intellect, there was no reasonable way to speak to Phaedra about what had happened. She had become a bundle of emotional outbursts and nerves.

Lander had been raised up as an educated man of excellence who prided himself on virtue in business. He saw himself as the model of a strong, healthy, adventurous man representing the Athenian ideal of *kalokagathos*—a gracious art of living that valued ability, fame, wealth, acquisition, and friends, as well as virtue and humanity.

Sure, when he came to Corinth, he always visited the temple of Aphrodite, but he easily forgave himself for his promiscuity. Landers knew that there was much worse than meeting his passionate appetite in strange cities. He concurred with Demosthenes, who said, *"We have courtesans for the sake of pleasure… concubines for the daily health of our bodies, and wives to bear us lawful offspring and be faithful guardians of our homes"* [5]

What was unforgivable to him was stupidity in the affairs of business and a breach of confidence about his manly adventures at Acrocorinth. He was committed to fairness with his slaves. He offered a denarius to the poor or disabled on the street when he passed them.

It was rare that he became drunk with wine. He was a good husband and provider, offering security to his family and discretion, always, about his philandering. Surely, Phaedra did not suffer from his choices of marital infidelity when he was

---

[5] Will Durant, **The Life of Greece** (New York: Simon & Schuster, 1939) p. 304

away. He had allowed her to keep her firstborn daughter and the twin girls, despite their societal liability. He did not despise her barrenness of sons. Lander saw she was attached to her daughters after birth, though he could have dismissed Phaedra when she did not bring him a son until nine years later.

Cleomens continued, "Man, if you have time, tomorrow I go to the palaestra. There is a wrestling match between the best young men of Sparta and Athens. I will save you a seat for your enjoyment! Might as well have some fun while away from the ball and chain."

He winked and grinned.

His friend was always in pursuit of hedonistic sport. When in town, Lander was easily convinced to join him in the public games, such as wrestling, boxing, or showcasing the physical prowess of young men. Corinth was teeming with landless youth, displaced by debt and families beholden to the wealthy aristocrats. Boys were imported to the city, where they provided endless entertainment for wealthy older men in both sexual and athletic pleasures. Even Plato, in *Phaedrus*, spoke of the love between man and man as nobler and more spiritual than the love between man and woman. Corinth was a seething hothouse of pleasure for the average Greek sensualist enamored with novelty, endlessly curious, and eager to experience all that came with the privileged economic and political freedom of commerce and trade.

But this time, Lander could not bring himself to join his friend.

"I'm sorry, but my time here is short, my friend. I must secure the shipment of silks and inquire about expanding my business to include spices from the Orient. Then I must be off. No time to play, but you go and enjoy, Cleomens."

Cleomens rolled his eyes in an exaggerated manner and laughed. "You go, old man, do what you must. I, my friend, plan to have a good time while here."

After making his business stops, Lander would visit the temple of Aphrodite. Even thinking of it brought a fresh wave of grief to his heart. He could see the hill of Acrocorinth and the temple of Aphrodite rising above Corinth. The goddess lorded her power of sensuality over the city.

Usually, Lander was eager to visit the temple of priestesses and courtesans, all there to deliver him from the troubles and tiresome details of his life for a time. But this time, he felt dread stir in the pit of his stomach. This time was not like the other times.

After a brilliant, blue-skied day, as the sun glowed in the west, Lander hired a chariot to take him under the cover of growing darkness to the hill of Acrocorinth.

The white pillared porticos blazed with torches on all sides of the square building. It was like a beacon atop the city, gazing upon her residents.

As he pulled up before the wide front doors, he was immediately drawn into the beehive of activity. Young men and women came on either side of the chariot to welcome him, taking his bag, and helping him down. There were chariots pulling up on all sides of the square temple. The grounds were a profusion of roses and flowering myrtle bushes, giving off a rich and delicate scent into the night air. Inside, there were tall, graceful statues of swans looking down on the guests. Cages of cooing doves hung from the high ceiling and were scattered on walls within the finely arched vestibule.

Lander's boots thudded on the tiled white and gold floor. The colors represented the goddess well. He knew the smells of myrrh. It calmed him as he entered Aphrodite's temple.

"I'm here to see Tanitha, the Phoenician," he said curtly to the fawning, young, nubile boy and two girls attending him.

"Tanitha is with a patron, my lord. Would you like to wait in here?"

One of the girls, with a simple cream-colored peplos, took his hand and led him into a small room with dim lighted candles, and plush cushions of the finest threads he could import.

"I will bring you some mead to curb your tiredness," she said and quietly transported to another room, soundless as a ghost.

Lander took off his boots and leaned back against the elegantly decorated cushions with a deep sigh, his hand moving into the hollows between his eyes and nose. His thumb and forefinger rubbed the sore spots as he pressed them. He closed his eyes, and his breathing slowed. He always felt safe in this temple of the goddess Aphrodite. It was almost foreign to the hypermasculine world he entered every day. Here, everything was always beautiful and well-heeled, filled with a feminine sensate seductiveness and a maternal comfort alongside an erotic charge.

The young girl returned with a decanter of mead and poured him a long draught. Sitting up, Lander took the cup and drank. The girl quickly sat down behind him, her slippered feet folded under her, and began to massage his forehead.

"Please, no!" Lander barked.

Turning, he pushed her hands away. "My apologies. Please leave me. I will wait in peace for Tanitha."

Seeing the pained hurt in her eyes, he relented.

"I did not mean it, my child. I am tired from a long day," he said more gently.

Wordlessly, she arose and disappeared as quickly as she had come. Lander felt a stab in his heart.

It could have been an hour. A half hour. Or maybe two or three hours. All Lander knew is that he fell into a deep, dreamless slumber until he felt a caressing of his face and heard a husky laugh as he opened his eyes.

"Tanitha!" he exclaimed with a startle, sitting up quickly.

She pulled him back down and continued to massage his temples, her small even teeth shining in the low light.

"How long..." his voice wandered off.

"No matter, Lander. I'm here now. Rest."

Tanitha was his favorite. Sometimes when he came to her bed, they just laid side by side and talked. She was considered a *hetairai*, a companion, not just any temple prostitute or *pornai*—girls or boys imported from the Orient or the far reaches of the Greco-Roman empire. She had clearly come from a well-educated citizenry and could debate with him cleverly with the best of the philosophers. He did not know her story, or why she might have fallen from respectability or fled the seclusion required of good matrons or householders. But she lived independently and entertained only lovers she desired. The oils on her smooth skin always smelled faintly of roses, and her blonde, dyed hair was loose and wavy down the back of her flowery robes.

Yet despite her seeming confidence and strength, Lander knew she was denied civil rights in a culture where women's roles were prescribed. She was forbidden to enter any temple but that of Aphrodite.[6]

Snuggling up next to him, Tanitha continued to comfort

---

[6] Will Durant, The Life of Greece (New York: Simon and Schuster, 1939) 300.

Lander, not knowing what he must ask her.

"What is on your mind, my love?" she inquired.

Lander gazed at this woman who seemed so familiar to him from all his journeys to this temple, yet whom he really didn't know at all. Her life was a mystery to him, as was this temple full of courtesans who were there only to appease weary secular men like himself. They were taught to engage their patrons with the divine mysteries of sensuality and communion. It was something he could not seem to find in his household or with Phaedra. But for a brief moment in time, sometimes an anonymous encounter, sometimes an affectionate affair with Tanitha, could bring him back to balance as he took what he wanted for money.

"Tanitha." His chest heaved. "My heart is heavy. My daughter has made an unforgivable mistake."

His voice was hollow, empty. "She has slept with a Roman soldier and become great with child. It is unacceptable in her station of life, once a promising young virgin. She is ruined now. I have sent the boy away and her mother is refusing to allow my eldest daughter to stay at home."

"Oh, my dear. What is to become of your daughter's child?" Tanitha inquired, holding both of his hands in her smooth, fine-boned ones.

Lander finally allowed himself the grief that had been like an ocean tide, ebbing and flowing for so many moons. First, it came like the sound of a wounded animal, then it became deep-throated sobs that emanated from him.

Tanitha moved closer and put her arms around him, pulling his head to her shoulder, holding him and stroking his hair like a child as he shook violently.

"Her child is no more. Phaedra made certain of that immediately," he moaned.

"Oh," Tanitha said softly.

Pulling his head unto her lap, she stroked his face, wiping the tears with her cloak.

"What will you do now, my dear one?" she asked.

"Tanitha, I have come to ask a favor. Would you please consider taking Althaia under your wing here at the temple? Teach her your ways of independence. Give her a path to respectability here at the temple of the goddess Aphrodite. She needs direction. She is ruined for marriage, but isn't it also respectable to give her a life here at the temple?" he pleaded.

Tanitha looked away, feeling her breath become more shallow, more rapid. Slowing her breath took some doing, as she continued to stroke this man's face, this man of whom she really knew nothing. Breathing from her belly, she felt herself return to the ground of her being.

What could she tell him? That she had little power? That she had her own daughter to consider? That young 'throwaway girls' were a dime a dozen and she had no need to be a part of such a monstrous system?

Aphrodite and her priestesses of love at the temple were indeed considered to bring immortal and divine gifts. The goddess' daughters and sons were trained to conjure up the special powers of love and desire, something a hypermasculine society was hungry to taste. But what was fair about taking a young girl from her family to provide services that even she, as a strong and independent woman, struggled to understand?

"What is it? What? Tanitha!" Lander demanded, taking her chin in his palm and forcing her to look at him.

"Lander. It is customary to select only a few priestesses each year who are young virgins or women beyond their childbearing years. Do you want me to sneak her in the back door? Once it is found out that she is not a virgin, what then?"

"She is beautiful, and her virtue is playing the flute like a muse. We have given her every opportunity since childhood to perform. She is smart and has studied widely of the philosophers, arts, and literature. She is strong at writing and math. Surely you are not worried that it will be found out that she is not a virgin?" He laughed. "She will be a great gift for Aphrodite's temple of priestesses. Is it not we who are indulging you and giving you a great gift?"

Tanitha continued as though she heard nothing that Lander said, "Besides, what can I give her? Hmmm? What kind of a life is it that you and your wife are so ready to give her here at the temple?"

Her voice became less husky, more high-pitched. "She will end her days suiting men's needs. And what of her own hopes and dreams? You have spoken of her as high-spirited. Is this really what you want for her?"

Tanitha felt a painful twinge deep in her heart. A memory rose to the surface—a time long ago, when she as a young woman was forced to give up her own daughter. It was fleeting, as she had become an expert at forcing it into the dungeons of her consciousness.

It was Lander's turn to be surprised at her retort.

"What hopes and dreams does a young girl have anyway? She is recently sixteen years old and quickly becoming a girl with no opportunities." He looked at her quizzically, a frown drawing down his brows.

"All I know is that the mystery religion called *The Way* has been brought here from the land of the Semites to the Greek islands. The messenger is a Hellenist-trained Jew, a man named Paul. Once he was a persecutor of the people of *The Way*. They called him Saul before his conversion. I've heard him speak here in Corinth. Multitudes of women follow him. They are leaders and many have their own trade and wealth. He talks of a society that is not based upon binaries—neither male nor female, Greek nor Jew, slave nor free," Tanitha said, her eyes focused intensely upon Lander's.

"My curiosity is awakened," she continued, "I would want *that* for your daughter."

"Well, we are Athenians. We have no knowledge or interest in this mystery religion or their strange ways. I do know that my daughter is damaged goods, no matter what the culture. I urge you to consider my request to take her under your wing. There will be a large payoff involved for you," Lander said.

Tanitha had withdrawn now to the end of the cushions, troubled by this man's sorrow and cold-hearted willingness to sell his daughter.

"Let me ponder it. I will send word in a fortnight about my decision," Tanitha stated matter-of-factly.

Lander's shoulders sagged. There was resignation on his face. Surely this woman would accept his offer. How could he go back to Phaedra without success? She would be a tempest to live with—more than usual.

At least if Althaia was here, he could visit her from time to time when he came to Corinth on business. Lander felt conflicted. He knew that his visits to the priestesses must end at Aphrodite's temple if his daughter was not to know how he had betrayed her mother all these years. How could he continue to visit for his own selfish pleasure?

"Might there be a place for me to stay here tonight, Tanitha?" Lander's eyes were downcast, ashamed.

He felt her stern stare and disapproval of his request.

"Come with me. I will allow you to stay in my extra chambers. You will be alone, and I will make sure you have a good night's respite and everything you need from our courtesans," Tanitha spoke with authority.

He nodded. It was rare that he was a man without words. He earned his confidence and boldness over decades as a prominent and successful businessman. Lander could order others to come and go at his will. His money spoke volumes.

But with this woman, he was suddenly uncertain. She seemed unmoved by his money or his power. Her authority came from an inner wellspring that he could not put his finger upon.

"Come quickly! I have other commitments."

Tanitha seemed foreign to him with her haughty, distant attitude. He had never experienced this side of her, always counting on her kindness and generous warmth toward him.

Arising, he followed her across the courtyard to a very small room, filled with red textiles—pillows, cushions, towels, and bedcovers. It was decorated with sea shells, a cooing couple of doves in a corner cage, and had the ever-present whiff of roses. All the symbols of the goddess. Tanitha swept into the room, covering the doves with a cloth to bed them down, turning down the red coverlet of the bed, and pouring water into the marble basin for Lander's evening ablutions.

"I shall send a young boy to see if there is anything else you need," she noted.

Lander nodded mutely.

"Thank you." He cleared his throat, catching her hands in his.

"Thank you, Tanitha," he said, looking into her eyes.

She stood a moment looking at him, then nodded and gave a small bow, withdrawing her hands.

"Good night, Lander," she said softly as she closed the door firmly.

CHAPTER SEVEN

Becoming a Woman

Deathless Aphrodite, throned in flowers,
Daughter of Zeus, O terrible enchantress,
With this sorrow, with this anguish, break my spirit
Lady, not longer! (Sappho, 6th BCE)

Althaia had withdrawn even deeper into herself after Father left. Father no longer seemed to be an ally, so it didn't matter if he was here nor there. He said he had business to attend to in Corinth, which usually took three days—two days of travel by ship and one day in the city. But this time, he was gone for more than a week. Mother seemed less angry than usual and even showed small kindnesses to Althaia. She did not yell when Althaia requested to have breakfast brought to her room. Daphne grumbled but not because of lack of affection for Althaia. She was worried about the child.

"When are you coming down to join the others? Are you sick today?" Daphne put her hand across the younger woman's forehead to gauge her temperature. "You seem to be in good health. What is in your heart, child?"

Daphne sat down next to Althaia on the bed. The numb affect and dullness of Althaia's face was even more disconcerting than the endless spigot of tears after the forced abortion.

"Daphne, did Phaedra ever lose a child?" Althaia did not

refer to her mother in a familial way.

"Dear one, is that what is troubling you? You feeling alone inside here?" Daphne tapped Althaia's heart with the palm of her hand.

Althaia's voice rose.

"What troubles me is Phaedra's sacrifice of *my* baby. What troubles me is her compassion-less, self-centered existence. What ***troubles*** me," she said emphatically, "is that Phaedra was willing to sacrifice her own flesh and blood for some kind of reputation that is more important to her than her daughter."

Now she felt the rage rising like bile in her throat.

"What troubles me is her mindless ways of pretending as though nothing ever happened. As though nothing went on to tear me asunder from her and our family. As though she can wipe it away by pretending. Or ignoring. Or denying," Althaia spewed the words out.

Daphne recoiled, pulling her hand back as though she had been burned. Phaedra was still her employer.

"My child, you will need to find it in your heart to forgive your mother someday," Daphne spoke the words slowly, haltingly.

"Oh *really*?" Althaia could no longer stop the rage toward her mother from overflowing.

And as suddenly as her anger had risen, it had spent her energy. Her flashing eyes returned to dullness.

"I... I'm... I'm so sorry, Daphne," she said, her eyes shining with tears. "Please forgive me. It is not for you to take that meanness. My sorrow somedays feels like an endless well. My rage like a monstrous bonfire. It has no place to go."

Daphne patted her hand and then left her large warm hands covering Althaia's for a few moments.

"Don't worry about me. You have suffered as no young woman your age should have to. I'm always here for you."

And with that, she took her leave, afraid that the tears threatening to run down her face would be seen. Her mother's heart ached.

One day, while Lander was gone, Phaedra called Althaia into her drawing room. Bracing herself, Althaia stood rigid in the arched doorway, her feet frozen on the marble floor.

Cheerfully, Phaedra's voice sang out, "Thaia, I have some special silk that your father gave me last year for my birthday."

She walked toward her daughter with the shimmery gold and wine textile, her steps light and bouncy, undeterred by Althaia's lack of response.

"I would like to have it made into a dress for you. It would be so becoming!" She automatically reached out to brush Althaia's hair from her eyes and hold the material next to her face.

She was unprepared for the reaction as Althaia jerked back.

"Thank you, Phaedra. I don't want your silk clothes," she said coldly.

Phaedra stopped short.

"I am your mother, and I ask that you address me as such," she said with mock hurt.

"You stopped being my mother when you forced me to kill my child." Althaia's rage was again pouring, spilling out all over the floor.

Today was the day that the dam broke.

"No," Phaedra said coldly, calculatedly. "You stopped being my daughter when you rejected all that we gave you, including a good life with a good man. You were a self-centered wench, choosing against the very moral basics we taught you."

The standoff had become enflamed. Althaia could feel herself overwhelmed, hopeless. Her mother had always overpowered her energy. She did not see who her daughter really was, and it was no secret that her high-spirited nature threatened Phaedra. She did not protect Althaia before, and she certainly would not now.

In one severe moment, Althaia understood this truth. It settled into her gut. Her longing for a loving, protective, self-giving mother would always be just that. An unrequited longing.

"Mama!" a shrill cry preceded the small boy who raced into the room.

"Yes, my love, my turtle dove!" Phaedra cooed as he stopped short, looking from one face to another.

Increasingly estranged from his eldest sister, he quickly ran to his mother, who picked him up and swung him around before settling him in her lap.

"What is it, my dear?" She held his cheek next to hers.

"Mama, I want to go to the athletic field games this afternoon. May I please, please, PLEEEASE?"

Egan was now seven years old, Mama's little man, but his boy voice still became high-pitched when he became as excited as he had as a tiny boy.

"Yes, of course, my son. I will go with you, and we shall see if your twin sisters want to go also."

She hugged him close before he literally launched from her lap and did another lap around the room, leaping and dancing and jumping up and down as he recounted who would be there and what they would see.

Althaia took a deep breath and turned from the room. She would never know that deep connection with Phaedra. Now even her relationship with Egan seemed to be fading.

Soon, she would be gone from here.

She found herself pulling in the drawbridge to her heart, not wanting to feel the excruciating pain of abandonment and loss any further. There was a hole in her heart that drained away her life energy.

Flashbacks to the moment the life slipped away from her body continued to haunt Althaia. The trauma remained attached to her sense of smell, the olfactory sense being the most basic and wired to the pre-verbal, limbic system of her emotions. Every time she smelled the pungent rue crushed underfoot when walking in the garden, her head spun and she felt nausea rip through her insides.

Or the scab was ripped off her carefully contained emotions when the scent of lavender soap rose as she washed her hands at her basin. She remembered how many times Daphne came to help bathe her as she bled and bled and bled for months.

Then there was the freshly laundered, sunbaked smell of the wool sheets hung out to dry, sheets she had burrowed into for unending weeks. And the overpowering smell of her own hematocrit like a flowing sea tide rising around her.

Althaia found herself attuned to the cycles of the seasons and moon more acutely. The dark moon allowed her to dance without being seen. The full moon was like a bath, healing her with its white glow. The rain filled her with positive ions, the smell washing away the stench of death that she felt wrapped around her very being. The sun burned off the tears and grief that had held her hostage for so long.

She found refuge in the garden with the wild ones. The creaturely world had no judgment, only a neutral, unconditional acceptance. They spoke to her of a more visceral reality that underlaid the refined culture of family, religion, politics—realities that often acted as more real and binding. Althaia pondered how the world of ideas, art, and thought that had entrained her was actually more pretend than all of this living, breathing, planetary drama of creatures, plants, and portents in the sky.

Of course, there was Athena the owl, her familiar. She would often come to gaze at Althaia as she sat on her favorite stone bench. Athena's head swiveled from one side to the other, making Althaia laugh.

There was the lizard with the blue stripe, whose reptilian black eyes blinked at her before rushing away. The dragonfly wore a shimmering, tight-waisted, ruby bodice and sported papyrus-thin wings. She soared and dipped near the fountain, finally coming to light on Althaia's hand, staring at her with large, compound eyes.

She fell in love with the bees, watching them ply their pollinating trade. She could sit for hours and watch them come and go, fascinated by their wings vibrating a million miles a minute, their bodies climbing the stamens like athletes, sometimes buzzing their bodies to shake off the pollen. Once she saw a swarm dangling from a branch in the cedar tree. Drawn as if in a trance, she went up and slowly let her hand drift toward the pulsating ball of bodies, the smell of honey wafting from them. Ignoring her, they continued to hang there in a tight golden orb for hours. It wasn't until late afternoon that she watched, her eyes wide, as the ball suddenly exploded into the air until it was full of bee bodies flying. And in a beautiful arc, in one accord, they flew off like synchronized dancers.

And the snakes. She was not afraid of them. They came to her often in the dreamtime.

It was a reminder that she was on the night sea voyage of her soul. Often debased as dirty, shrewd, and frightening, Althaia found the snake to be a powerful accompaniment of the feminine, of alchemy, the caduceus symbol of wisdom and healing in her dreams. She could only hope that somehow, secretly, she was being initiated into some new birth or resurrection from this time in her life that felt so twisted and tormenting.

And she pondered love and arranged marriage. How had it come to be that she had given a Roman her body and every sensual part of who she was, and it had been ripped from her? *What is love?* she wondered. Was it what Phaedra and Lander had? No, surely not. That felt like an empty husk of obligation. Somewhere inside, Althaia knew she had never wanted that, but yet what *had* she been seeking all along? Was it even possible to find love? What did it feel like? Was it that moment on the beach... or something else?

She continued to walk barefoot through the broken shards of her grief and confusion and rage, day after day.

One day, Father returned.

"Althaia," he spoke her name, but did not come to touch her or hug her.

"Yes, Father? You're back," she said flatly.

He came to sit with by her on the garden bench. They sat, side by side, looking at the brilliant columns of hyacinth, lilies, poppies, and anemones.

Lander inhaled the smell of roses along the perimeter of the fence. It reminded him of his time at Acrocorinth.

"Daughter, I hear you have been disrespectful to your mother."

Althaia's head snapped toward him, and her eyes flashed

with some of the old passion. But this time, they were smoldering."

"I see," she said sarcastically. "Phaedra has already waylaid you."

"Thaia, what has happened with you and your mother? Why do you not call her by the affectionate familial name?"

"Because she has betrayed me for social caste and for climbing the ladder of *your* success," she said accusingly.

"Thaia. Thaia. Thaia." His voice rose in a crescendo. "I am your father. I put a roof over your head! Do not speak with such contempt."

Althaia looked down at her hands, sucking in a deep breath and letting it out as her neck muscles remained rigid and her jaw tense.

"I am tired. I will go rest now. When you are ready to talk in a reasonable manner, I will meet you to hear your heart."

He stood up and walked away.

Althaia watched him go with only a small twinge of her heart in her chest. She was differentiating from these people who were her tribe. It seemed that their approval was of little consequence any more. Her voice was becoming stronger, her sight clearer. The hypocrisy of the systems that held her and her family entrapped seemed apparent to her. Was it not to her parents? She wanted what was real, not what money could buy.

Perhaps this was what it meant to become a woman, she wondered.

That fateful day, when a young boy came to the door with a message, will remain forever engraved on Althaia's memory. She remembered the sun being at its fullest zenith. The midday heat rose from the bricks.

He said he was a courtesan from Acrocorinth, the temple of Aphrodite. His clothing was colorful and exotic. He had the features of one from the Far East, the Orient. His mouth had a strange accent when he spoke.

"Please. This is for Lander Adamos. May I see him?" the boy asked.

"I will take it to him," Althaia said, holding out her hand.

Looking unsure, he asked again to see Lander.

Not knowing that Phaedra was behind her at that moment, Althaia jumped as her mother snatched the message, which was in a fancy beribboned papyrus with a rose flower spray attached.

"I am his wife. I will take it to him," she said curtly.

The boy nodded and bowed, turning back to the chariot that had brought him, climbing onto the colorful, quilted cushions.

Althaia trailed after her mother.

"Who was that?" she queried.

"It is your father and my business. They were from Corinth," she said, continuing to walk ahead of her daughter.

Althaia suddenly felt a clammy feeling in her throat, a queasiness in the pit of her stomach. Was this the dreaded day that she had somehow pushed to the back of her mind? Her father's words many moons ago, so long that it had receded far away, a non-possibility, came back to her. He said that they intended to send her to the temple of Aphrodite on Acrocorinth. Now she distinctly remembered. She felt a shiver of fear up her spine. Her brain became like a reptile; she didn't know whether to flee or freeze.

"Go on, Althaia. This is business that concerns us." Phaedra dismissed her with a wave of the hand.

Althaia stood frozen, her mind and heart racing.

It felt like an eternity, that day did.

She awaited her father and mother's summoning of her to their chambers. She already knew what that message contained. It was now only up to her parents' wishes to dispense the information to her.

She was now in her sixteenth year. The 'event,' as she had taken to calling it, had transpired at the end of her fourteenth year. Her birthday at the end of that summer had transported her through a portal into the misery of her fifteenth year. That year would always remain a blur of pain seared into her tissue, nervous system, and sinew.

Yet, life at home seemed to resume a certain odd normality. The household rolled on as though nothing had rocked its foundation.

Father traveled for business, and as usual, was gone for long periods of time. Mother was deeply involved in administering the servants' work, updating any decorations of the household, and arranging for her youngest children's lessons, athletic events, and parties.

Calista had become a thin, willowy, and graceful classical dancer as she reached her stature at age thirteen. Her demeanor was quiet and coy. Phaedra was delighted to see one of her daughters taking up the art of dancing after her season was cut short by her marriage to Lander. The hope was to send Calista to travel to the islands in the Aegean Sea that summer, bringing her beautiful art to some of the religious sites, and learning for herself the art and culture of the isles. She would be initiated into the ways of Terpsichore, goddess of dance and one of the nine muses. Upon her return, a dowry would be exacted and she would be prepared for marriage.

The other twin, Calliope, though named after the goddess

and muse of poetry, could not be entrained in literature. She had little use for her academic studies and saw them as boring. Her eyes sparkled with her intention to find a husband. She was eager to follow the program laid out for her as a wife, mother, and householder. Unlike her twin sister, Calista, she had no grace whatsoever and developed a strong sense of humor, wicked in her ability to bring down anyone who had any airs about them. As the eldest of the twins, she was down-to-earth and practical. Phaedra leaned on her to take responsibility over her other younger siblings or to manage the household when she visited her sisters on the other side of Athens.

Egan, of course, the apple of his mother's eye, was given the best possible athletic mentors and excelled in the field trainings with his peers. A capable boy, tall for his age but lithe, he enjoyed sport of any kind, but mostly he loved to run.

Althaia seemed to be invisible. No more lessons to resume. She had come of age, somehow, without the proper dowry or even male teacher to entrain her in the ways of the world.

Althaia spent most of her time reading the Greek female poets: Corinna, the lyric poet; Boeo, the Delphic priestess and hymnist; Cleobulina, the riddle maker; Charixene the flautist and poet; Erinna, who wrote prolifically about her dead childhood friend; Melinno, author of *Ode to Rome;* Hedyle, Athenian poet; Praxilla, the lyric poet from Corinth; and Sappho of Lesbos, known for her lyrical poetry accompanied by a lyre.

Her mind was filled with the written word, music, and her imaginings of these women's lives. What were they allowed to accomplish in their families, despite social mores and restrictions? It amazed her.

Since playing and performing the flute had fallen by the wayside, there was no reason to see Helena, her bosom friend.

Once upon a time, they had spent almost every waking moment together. They had giggled over girl jokes and boys who flattered them. They walked hand in hand and spent time exploring their gardens and neighborhoods, creating silly stories or writing five-act plays and then drafting their siblings in for the theatrical presentation. In this lonely time, Althaia's mind often roamed back to those days of freedom, girlish giddiness, and serious musical study.

She contacted Helena once or twice during her year of misery, but Helena seemed to have moved on in her plans of preparing her dowry and this new life of womanhood.

"Althaia!" her father's voice broke through her reverie.

The conversation she had dreaded was upon her.

"Yes, Father?" Althaia sat erect in her simple cream peplos, her wavy, jet-black hair pulled back with a simple bone hair pin.

Phaedra had followed Lander out, and they sat at the table where Althaia was writing on the back portico that extended into the garden. The day seeped with arid heat, and the buzzing of the insects filled the silence between the girl and her parents.

"I have received instructions to take you to Corinth, Thaia. You have been accepted into the community of Aphrodite's priestesses at Acrocorinth."

Althaia did not move. Sweat crept down her stiffened neck. She looked beyond her parents, fixating on a bird high in the tree that was cleaning its feathers vigorously.

Time stopped.

She found herself dissociating from her physical body at the table. These episodes came at times without any control. She was sitting with the bird high in the tree, looking down on this small knot of humans at the white stone table.

"Althaia," her mother's voice, like the scratching sound of

stone cutters' tool on marble, brought her back to the ground.

But she would not look at her parents.

"Thaia, you will see, it will be fine," her father said. "I will come to visit you when I'm in Corinth. You are indeed honored to be accepted to the temple. They only invite four each year. Now that you have come of age, you are prepared to be a woman."

Lander could feel himself vainly attempting to justify and plead for that which had no meaning. He was giving his eldest daughter away. Unlike his wife, he felt the sadness grow and seep through him like an endless river.

Phaedra had always been about herself, more so than her husband. But she did have a fierce instinct for her children. Once upon a time, she had felt a certain bond with her eldest. But through the years of her daughter's stubborn resistance to her way of life, her ideas and discipline, Phaedra had grown cold toward Althaia. It was time for her to go. She had three other children to raise and a household to run. She was tired. Tired of the conflict. Tired of the toll exacted upon her when Lander was gone for extended periods. She sat wordless in her chair for what seemed like eons, her daughter refusing to meet her gaze.

Standing up finally, Phaedra stated, "We will make preparations at once for you to travel. I will send Daphne to assist you. Lander, please let us know the timetable for when you might leave. I cannot leave the children. She must go with you to Corinth."

The buzzing of the insects continued.

Perspiration rolled down Lander's face.

Trying to catch his daughter's eyes, he said, "We will plan to travel after your birthday as the full moon approaches."

But Althaia's chin was tipped upward, and her eyes stared

beyond both of their gazes in stony silence.

Althaia knew that she wanted to contact Helena once more before she left for Corinth. She considered running away. But where would she go? Her cousins on her maternal line were far away on the other side of Athens. She rarely saw them. Her father's lineage she knew even less. They lived in the north of Macedonia. Father had come south to the port cities as a young man, determined to leave the rural agricultural areas, hoping to strike his fortune. He had done well.

She sent a message to Helena via the stable boy:

My friend, please come to me at once. I am being sent to the city of Corinth. I must see you! I will slip out tomorrow in the midafternoon and meet you at the tiled fountain between our houses. I hope you will be free to meet me. Please send word immediately with our servant who delivers this message. Yours, Althaia.

The day crawled by. Althaia made halfhearted attempts to read or occupy her mind. The boy assured her that he had left the message with Helena's servant.

"Really?" Althaia voice grew sarcastic. "You're sure you did? Why haven't I heard from her? Why did you not demand to see her and put my message in her hands?"

He hung his head silently. Althaia relented.

"You may go," she said curtly.

"And thank you," she tossed out to his retreating back.

She could feel her agency slipping away. The ability to come and go as she pleased, to make things happen that she delighted in, to summon friends or objects of desire into her orbit. That reality seemed like another season of her life. A time when she was young and impetuous, confident and strong.

Womanhood appeared to be about the loss of personal freedom and the taking on of the yoke of obligations. Family. Society. Marriage. Children. In her case, the loss of even these things that made sense to her—her social entrance into life as a marriageable woman—were being cast away. All to redeem one decision in her short life—one she didn't regret. She only regretted its harsh ending.

She knew no girl who was dedicated by her family to the priestesses of the Goddess temples. Althaia felt a shiver run up her spine. What was she being asked to do? She must talk with Helena.

In her memory, she heard the gaiety of those times when she played her flute. The frivolity of the girl's beautiful clothing, the music wafting from the amphitheater to the heavens, the appreciative audiences thronging to listen, the expensive food and drink flowing. All of it had once filled her with exhilaration. Now she felt a sadness, a numbness, for that lost girl.

The next day, in midafternoon, Althaia was at the stable talking with the horses and touching their velvety noses. Drawing back their lips, they tried to nip her, requesting a snack. Althaia crooned with them conspiratorially, waiting for the stable boy. She stroked Basil's face, her favorite. She had requested a small horse-drawn cart to take her to the appointed meeting with Helena.

The servant finally slunk through the threshold between the dark intimacy of the stable and the brightness of the day.

"Boy, please prepare this cart quickly! I must go meet my friend," she said lightheartedly.

Without speaking, he fitted the horse and helped her into the cart. Down the cobbled streets they bumped to the aqua-tiled fountain halfway between Helena and Althaia's homes. The water rushed and poured through the mouth of Pan, a god-man creature. There were families bathing in the warm waters.

Helena was nowhere to be seen. Althaia could feel the constriction of anxiety clawing at her throat. She breathed deeply, trying to calm herself.

"Is she coming, miss?" the boy queried.

"I don't know. You're the one who delivered the message." Her voice was unmistakably contemptuous.

She found herself short-tempered with the servants most days now.

"Let me off here. I want to sit on this bench. I will be here for an hour. You can come retrieve me for supper," she instructed.

After he wheeled away, she fell into a reverie, watching the children screaming and laughing, dashing through the water, slapping water at one another. Slaves and mothers sat in clusters, trying to find shade from the oppressive mid-day sun. For a moment, she felt released from her lot in life. She was part of the magnificent drama of human life and creation. Birdsong and the whisper of leaves in the wind calmed Althaia as she leaned back and felt the sun flushing her cheeks, flooding her nervous system with peace. The children's shouts and joyful voices became distant.

The next thing she heard was, "Miss! Miss! I am here to take you home."

The boy barely touching her shoulder as his voice aroused her. Althaia looked up and around, noticing the race of the sun to its slumber in the west. The fountain continued its stream of water from the mouth of Pan, splashing loudly into the pool. It was deserted but for her. There was no Helena that day.

She had become a woman. The ties of childhood were being severed, one by one by one.

CHAPTER EIGHT

Aphrodite's Girls

I am she who cries out,
   And I am cast out upon the face of the earth.
   I prepare the bread and my mind within.
   I am the gnosis of my name.
   I am she who cries out and I am the one who listens. [7]

As Althaia prepared to leave for Acrocorinth, Daphne brought a small bag filled with rose petals and tiny vials of aromatic oils of propolis, oregano, and thyme. There was also a hand-turned wooden chalice, smoothly oiled and nut brown. Althaia grabbed her childhood servant and held her close for comfort, as she could feel the tears begin to burn her eyelids.

   Mother and Father brought her a trunk for her birthday, which Althaia filled mainly with her books, her flute, and a few simple dresses. She left her fine silks and brightly colored peplos behind.

   It was evening, during their final meal together. The wide eyes of her siblings followed Althaia. They were dissuaded from peppering her with questions, but their curiosity got the best of them.

---

[7] 1 (Thunder: Perfect Mind, NagHammadi Library, Tr. J. Robinson, HarperCollins, NY, 1977, 271–4)

"Thaia, where you going?" Egan asked earnestly, pointedly.

"Egan!" Mother fairly shouted, then relented. "Dear one, your sister is moving to Corinth. We have spoken about this. She is starting a new life at the Temple of Acrocorinth."

"I've heard of that temple." Calliope cut her eyes toward her elder sister. "Isn't it for women who don't marry? Are you becoming one of the temple priestesses? One of my friend's had a cousin who went there. They never heard from her again."

Althaia attended to finishing her plate of food, pointedly ignoring her sister's question, as mother gave Calliope a stern look.

Calista was silent.

That night, as the moon rose to its fullness, the time was ripe to leave. She and Father would leave in the early morning. Althaia sat in the garden under the white, milky, luminous moon with the owl Athena, her familiar, sitting in the old cypress tree. Althaia had asked the stable boy to fashion her a crate that could hold the owl for the journey. She would put a thick blanket over the bird as they traveled to keep her quiet.

The owl swooped down from her high branch, the claws engaging Althaia's right shoulder muscles. Athena was small in stature, but still the weight bore down on Althaia as she confided to her familiar:

"Oh, dear Athena, you are my forever friend. Thank you for coming with me to this strange and fearful place. Father has assured me that he will see me when he comes to town for business. He said that I will learn many medicinal arts and religious ceremonies and am blessed to have this opportunity. He knows the main priestess. Her name is Tanitha. What kind of name is that? Anyway, he says she will be wonderful and take good care of me."

The owl swiveled its head and looked into her eyes with its great golden irises and narrowed black pupils.

"Oh, Athena, what would I do without you?" Althaia began to hum a fragment of a hymn to Athena.

The day finally came to make the perilous journey to Acrocorinth. It dawned cloudy. The sun was hidden from view as the chariot was made ready at first light.

Father was shouting to the men and boy slaves, pointing out the trunks of his own wares to take to Corinth, along with his daughter's. Mother and Daphne came with baskets of food and drink to hand up to the driver.

Finally, Althaia emerged down the long marble stairs for the last time.

She went into the back garden where she had put Athena in her covered crate before everyone awoke. The crate had a handle at the top. After peeking at Athena, who blinked at her, she grabbed the handle. The crate was almost as large as she was. Dragging it across the stone courtyard, she finally picked it up as though cradling a child, the weight made her gasp. Althaia carried it inside and out through the front door, down the colonnaded portico, and to the waiting chariot.

"Daughter, what is that?" Lander eyed the burdensome bundle carefully.

Althaia tossed her hair back as she faced Father defiantly. "I am bringing Athena with me."

"I cannot allow this, Althaia," he said gravely. "I know you wish for your familiar to come and bring you a measure of companionship and comfort, but the place you are going is not equipped to take you and an owl," he said sternly. "Hadrian, please take the crate from my daughter and return it to the garden."

Althaia looked at him in shock.

"No. NO," she screamed as she pulled the crate close to her body, the boy trying to wrest it from her grip.

The crate shuddered as it crashed to the ground. Althaia wept as the cloth fell away, revealing the owl on its side, its claws attempting to curl around a wooden slat as it tried to right itself. Athena attempted to unfurl her long wing span, flapping against the crate.

"NO. STOP! You are hurting her," Althaia began to shout at the slave, rushing at him and pummeling him as he tried to shield himself.

"THAIA. Control yourself!"

Now it was Lander's turn to enter the fray, putting his arms around Althaia from the back, restraining her.

"Oh my! Althaia, you really have lost your mind," Mother said vehemently.

And with that, she opened the sliding slat door of the crate, and the owl took to flight.

Althaia cried bitterly, her energy suddenly spent. Somehow the owl's companionship made it seem possible to cross over to this new life. But, alone, her resolve crumbled.

She was inconsolable as they set out on the journey. Her tears flowed. Sobs heaved her thin frame. It was the loss of Athena, Helena, her siblings and father. Childhood itself.

Daphne came close and pressed an object into her hand.

It was a small figurine of a bee. Her hands curled around the soft soapstone.

They reached Corinth after a day's journey across land. This time Lander did not sail the Aegean and make stops along the way for commerce. He was intent on one thing only—delivering his eldest daughter to the temple as had been arranged.

It was early evening when they arrived at the top of Acrocorinth, where the temple's lamps were already trimmed and beginning to punch spots of light in the dusky twilight.

Lander had sent word ahead to Tanitha. She was waiting for them, her elegant flowery dress flowing to the ground.

"Hello, Madame." Lander bowed.

"Please, such formality is not necessary." Tanitha's husky laugh reverberated along the stone corridors in the inner courtyard.

Stepping toward Althaia, she looked kindly at her. "My child, you look exhausted. We must draw a bath with salts and oils for you to restore yourself."

And at that, she clapped her hands, and two young girls immediately appeared.

"What is your name, my child?"

"Oh, I beg your pardon," Lander quickly stepped in. "This is Althaia, daughter of Lander. We just arrived after a day's journey from Athens. Thank you kindly for providing her accommodations."

Althaia's vigilant eyes noticed the kindness of Tanitha and the responsiveness of the girls. She took a deep breath as she moved away from her father. She did not know when she would see him again. Did it matter? She allowed the girls to take her by the hands and lead her into a small room—one of many in this square temple atop a hill—where there was a pool built into the marble floor. The girls gently began to take off her traveling clothes, wrapping her in a soft linen towel. Then they sat her down and began to oil her skin with aromatic herbs, carefully massaging her feet and hands, arms and legs, and shoulders. A soft glow of light cast a circle around the silent girls ministering to Althaia. The tears had been replaced by an emotional paralysis. She breathed deeply of the essential oils and felt the steam rise from the pool. The nimble fingers of the girls began to smooth away all the suffering of the past days, months, and years.

Finally, exchanging glances, they each took a hand again and led her to the edge of the pool and indicated that she could sit on the edge and dangle her feet in the water. The heat crept up her legs. Throwing off the towel, she slid into the pool completely, feeling the healing waters pull her down, down, down into their swirling, shimmering embrace.

The two girls nodded and smiled, one reaching a hand out for her hair clip.

"We will return within the hour to show you to your room," one of them said with an accent Althaia could not name.

After they left, Althaia clung to the side of the pool in the dim light, gently whirling her legs in the waters. Her body and mind became slow as she released her hold and spun in the water, as though in a dream-like trance. The heat and oils were having their effect. She wondered when she would see Father again. They did not say goodbye.

No matter. Now, she was a temple priestess in training. Her new life had begun. Just like that.

Althaia was a quick study. The *Hiereiai*, or priestesses, were comprised of young and old women. The virgins, the young girls like the ones who had cared for her the first night, were fresh-faced and beautiful, often wearing semi-precious jeweled clasps and bracelets, or diadems in their hair. They had kohl outlining their eyes and wore creams or washes to hide any blemishes or freckles. They were usually lightly clad so that prospective clients could examine them before arranging a bargain for any period of time, sometimes taking a girl to live with him for weeks, a month or a year. If a girl was a flute player, they could be hired to assist at stag entertainment, to perform and mingle, often spending the night.

Then there were the women past childbearing age. Their cheeks and lips were often painted with alkanet root, their eyes heavily shaded, eyelashes darkened, and perfumed unguents used to exude a clean smell. Creams and oils softened wrinkles, and these seasoned priestesses were adorned with many fine jewels in brooches, necklaces, or in gold cuffs on their arms and legs. Their garments were distinct from the young girls—brocades and tucks, layers, rich colors, and flowery prints defined them from the thin cream and gold-threaded peplos of the girls.

Then there were the boys, many from far away, the Orient. These nubile boys had no facial or body hair; their skin was smooth and golden. Aging merchants often asked for them.

Althaia began a year of apprenticing with various priestesses, learning the medicines of the natural world. Balms, resins, and herbs that could be ingested to move vital energies and fluids in the body for healing. Aromatic oils and unguents that could be massaged on the skin or applied to the chest to open passageways for breathing. Her favorite was rosemary. There were antiseptics and antimicrobials for infections, such as tea tree oil, thyme, and oregano. There were those medicines used for the subtle calming and balancing power of the spirit, such as mugwort, lavender, and yarrow. Frankincense and wild rue for spiritual protection.

She was steeped in the stories of Aphrodite. The temple was filled with doves, linked to her worship, as were banks of roses and red anemones. The birds did little to appease her sadness over the loss of Athena, her familiar. Althaia learned to tend the sacred fire in the center courtyard as Aphrodite stories, ceremony, ritual, and worship were wrapped like a silk cocoon around everything the priestesses did. Every morning, they came to this fire to begin their day with hymns and prayers to the goddess.

Finally, Thaia was mentored in the ways of soothing and pleasuring the clients who would come to the temple. Aphrodisiacs, water, oils, and things of beauty were always available in the small, well-heeled rooms with overstuffed embroidered cushions. Most importantly, the young girls were under the care of the elder priestesses for the cycles of their menses, making certain that they were not available at certain times of their moon and instructing them in herbal abortifacients as needed.

Althaia was known for her quick mind and her ability to grasp the medicines and healing properties. She could quote poetry and hymns to soothe or enliven any gathering. She had a clear sight and prescience, which made her hyper-vigilant and alert at times.

But overall, she was beginning to settle into the rhythm of the community of temple priestesses and prostitutes, though she had yet to offer her services.

Dionne was a beautiful young girl from the village of northern Greece. She and Althaia became fast friends, as they were assigned to share a room together. She had come about the time of Althaia, and they confided their stories to one another. There was great consolation in finally sharing the sorrow of the past years.

Dionne had large, sad eyes. She was a classic dancer, popular in her village. But her father had lost most of his vineyard and olive harvest the past year due to drought. A dowry would not be possible. The family had four boys, who were sent away to work in neighboring villages or the big cities. Dionne was sent to the temple at Acrocorinth. She grieved for her life in the village, her family, her dreams. She was beautiful in every way, from her slender waistline, ample bosom, tiny hands and feet, and finely chiseled face. Her movements were an honor to the Divine.

They spoke of the newness of everything, about Cressida, Thalia, Galina, Evangeline, Drusilla, Elodie, Hydra, Hyacinth, Iona, Thetis, Artemis, Odea, Persephone, Hestia, Bia, and Astraea. All these young girls had their unique quirks and personalities.

There were the Oriental boys, few though they were, who kept to themselves in their quarters. They spoke little of the language, but knew the work they had been imported to do.

The girls gossiped about Tanitha, the head priestess. She was a force to be reckoned with, but was always just and usually kind. She cared for the girls as though they were her own. There was a rumor that she had a daughter somewhere, lost to her for some unknown reason. Perhaps it was due to financial hardship, or from being a woman of repute in her life at Aphrodite's temple? Tanitha always had an edge of irritation about her, always the sorrow, the loss, eating away at her heart.

The women past childbearing age were fewer. Obelia, Iris, Kosma, Hygea, Lydia, Madalena, Até. Electra, Hera, Pheme, Selene, Urania, and Melissa. They had their own stories of lost children, lost chances for marriage, lost finances and reputations, but all were now seasoned priestesses, mostly celibate and consulted mainly for their wisdom.

Althaia did not share with anyone the darkness that always seemed to hover close by, ready to swallow her up. Depression was like a vise that gripped her brain. It had been changing the patterns of her thoughts for a time now. She did not know what this feeling was, but it frightened her. Some days when she awoke, it was as though an oppressive force was settling around her head and her heart, asking her to hurt herself. The cheerful, extroverted, social butterfly had been buried somewhere along the way. This girl was unrecognizable. A shell of her former self. It was hard to separate out the sorrow. The tidal waves were so frequent, she felt as though she were drowning. Was it from the pain that made her heart hurt when she remembered Adrian, the first flame of love that saw, *really saw* her, and filled her with joy? Or was it the soul that was stolen from her body at the command of her mother and father?

On these dark days, she could hardly gather herself to get out of bed. It was painful to face the tasks and all its external requests and requirements. Althaia felt as though she were slogging through mud in her mind and body. It was hard to think. All she wanted to do was curl up and weep or lay numbly looking up at the sky. During these days of the 'dark spirit,' Althaia could feel her anxiety rising up in her throat, strangling her breath, her heart pounding. She kept a knife that she had taken from the kitchen hidden in her room. Some days, when the pain was too much, she cut herself to feel the pain in her body instead of her heart. Her wrists and ankles had small thin scars that she tried to hide with long shawls, draping her arms now that it was getting colder.

Despite the dark spirit, Althaia learned to be quite functional in her daily tasks. She could tell when the mood was coming upon her, and she would need to guard her sharp tongue. It was so much like Mother—lashing out in her unhappiness. Althaia never wanted to become like her mother. She was disturbed by the growing likeness.

"Althaia! I must speak with you," Tanitha's voice cut across the courtyard.

It was approaching late autumn. Harvest was over and colder days were approaching.

"Yes, Tanitha, I am coming!"

Althaia hurried to Tanitha's quarters.

"It has been over a year now, my daughter," the elder priestess used a term of endearment which startled Althaia. "You have been entrained in the ways of the priestesses and our medicines and worship. Now it is time for you to see those who come seeking our services for comfort and care. You will be under the ongoing tutelage of Kosma, the elder. Are you prepared to begin this week?"

She peered closely at Althaia.

"I, uh, well, I don't know," Althaia stammered.

"What is it, child? We aim to make you ready so you can say 'yes' with confidence," Tanitha replied, noticing her flustered response.

"Tanitha, where is Father? He promised to come see me on business… I had hoped…" Her voice trailed off.

"My dear." Tanitha sighed deeply. "We spoke and agreed that it was best that you focus on your new life here and all that you must learn before you see him or any family members again."

Althaia dropped her gaze, her long lashes beginning to drip with tears.

"Oh my, come here!" Tanitha's husky voice beckoned her, as she pulled the girl into her arms.

"This has been a difficult time for you," she murmured into Althaia's hair, stroking her head like a child. "I do not want to force you, but perhaps we can give it a try, and if it is too much, we will change course."

Tanitha was matter of fact.

"I don't want to disappoint you or the other girls. I am willing to begin." Althaia's voice sounded tiny.

She felt diminished and fearful.

"Yes. We will just give it a try," Tanitha said confidently.

She had no idea of the depth of this girl's trauma or darkness. All she knew was that, at one time, Althaia had been high-spirited and confident, according to her father. She could only hope this part of Althaia would come to life again.

He had no name. He pushed through the curtains where Althaia sat freshly washed, perfumed, and adorned on the cushions, prepared to pleasure and offer consolation to him. He was balding, a bulging stomach beneath his tunic from too much rich fare. His manner was one of entitlement. An air of superiority.

"So, you are my girl tonight?" he said lasciviously. "Please untie my sandals and disrobe me."

Althaia knelt before him and began to undo his leather straps as he began to caress her hair, leaning to kiss her neck. She stiffened.

"What's wrong?" He laughed. "This is my time, I've paid for it, I've earned it."

As she stood up to face him, she suddenly felt that odd sensation of her soul leaving her body. She began to view the unfolding drama from the corner of the ceiling.

He lunged at her, ripping her dress, forcing her down toward the floor.

Althaia heard a low guttural, feral scream begin to emanate from her belly as she whipped her head forward, sinking her teeth into his arm.

It was his turn to scream. The man jumped away as though boiling water had been thrown on him.

Althaia took the moment to gather her dress around her and run. She fled into the night, past the circles of the lamps, past the sacred fire burning beneath Aphrodite's statue in the center of the courtyard, past the square building, and out into the dark land.

It wasn't until she stumbled on a rock, which threw her to the ground, that she began to return to her body. She lay completely still, feeling the pain in her body. The darkness began to engulf her, the pain was in every crevice of her mind, body, and soul. It was a terrifying abyss.

Tanitha heard about the unfortunate incident that night. The man came looking for her in her chambers, rigid with his fury.

"Who is that insolent girl? I've never, ever experienced such humiliation by your priestesses. This will not be the last you hear from me," he raged.

Tanitha tried to calm him. "Sir, I promise it will never happen again. We will refund you tonight and work to please you in the future."

"She should be flogged. Her faculties are not right and must be corrected," he continued to rant.

"Thank you for your patronage, sir. I will make sure it is handled appropriately. She will be disciplined," Tanitha stated firmly. "Now, I will call one of my courtesans and they will arrange for you to come another time, and we will give you additional pleasures to make up for your trouble."

She clapped her hands and a young girl came running.

"Galina! Please come and help this gentleman. He needs some extra time tonight in the warm pools with aromatic oil massage and a rescheduling at no cost."

The man stood up and cleared his throat.

"I will not forget this. But I will give you time to make up for it," he said threateningly.

"We will make it right," Tanitha stated and, with a wave of her hand, admonished Galina to take him from her sight.

Althaia did not see Tanitha for two days. She stayed as far away as she could from the temple, wandering in the hills, coming back only at night to sleep under the cover of darkness in the linen closet at the end of the hall.

One night, as she crept into the kitchen to find something to eat, she suddenly heard a stirring at the door. A lamp illuminated one of the boys in the doorway.

He hurried away, shouting, "Madame Tanitha, Madame! I found her. She is here!"

Before she could gather up her food or run like a wild animal, there was Tanitha in her nightclothes, her hair in a long braid down her back.

"Althaia!" she shouted as she followed the boy into the kitchen. "Stop. What *are* you doing? Where have you *been*?"

She stood in front of Althaia, blocking her exit.

Dismissing the boy, she pulled Althaia to a bench where they sat side by side. There was irritation, but also a strain of concern in Tanitha's voice.

"I know what happened. It is of no matter to me. I am glad you are safe. As I said before, we would give this a try. Clearly it is not time."

"He tried to assault me." Althaia's voice raised an octave.

"I know this man. He is not like your father, a perfect gentleman," Tanitha explained.

Althaia's face snapped toward Tanitha, her eyes like hot coals.

"What? My father? What are you saying?" she shouted.

Tanitha met her eyes with an impenetrable gaze. "Yes, your father. I know him well from many years. I'm sorry to tell you this."

Suddenly, all the scenes of her mother's rage, annoyance, and irritation flooded through Althaia's mind's eye. Years of her father's absence and the loneliness of being discarded.

Now it all made sense to Althaia—what Mother knew in her bones, and why she would always feel like an old garment cast aside. The season of her discontent that would last a lifetime. Perhaps this was why she lived with such anger and irritation always boiling beneath the surface.

"Althaia, I'm sorry." This time Tanitha said it gently, touching her arm lightly.

Althaia shook her head side to side rapidly, then ran her fingers through her scalp, closing her eyes.

"I should've known. All Father's 'business trips' to Corinth. How stupid we all were." Her tone had grown quiet.

"Althaia, I have decided that it would be best for you to learn the art of beekeeping and continue your studies in medicine. I am taking you away from working with the clients. It is not in your best interests—or evidently ours." She chuckled.

"Aphrodite's temple priestesses are well known for our bees and for those who tend the bees. It is time that you learned." Tanitha smiled.

CHAPTER NINE

The Melissaes

"Let us celebrate the hive of Venus, who rose from the sea: that hive of many names: the mighty fountain, from whence all kings are descended; from whence all the winged and immortal Loves were again produced."[8]

Melissa was introduced to Althaia that day by Tanitha. She was the head tender of bees. Her face was weathered by many days in the sun. Her name came from her role as the head keeper of the honeybee hives. The Greek name Melissa meant 'honeybee'. Althaia would come to find out that bees were deeply honored among Aphrodite's priestesses, as well as many other goddess priestess sects, such as Artemis, Persephone, and Demeter. The priestesses were collectively called 'Melissaes'. The hive of Aphrodite was filled with Melissaes. Just as all the workers in the honeybee hive were female, so was Aphrodite's hive of bee priestesses. Alongside the Queen bee, the head priestess, they represented the power of the feminine, fertility, and healing.

Now it made sense why Tanitha's royal seal for all her official documents was in the shape of a bee. Althaia began to remember the small and large bee shapes and statues, and the

---

[8] Wikipedia, Bryant, Jacob (1776). A new system: or, An analysis of ancient mythology. pp. 299–233.

honeycomb symbols embedded everywhere in the temple's architecture. She remembered the tiny bee statue that Daphne had pressed into her hand when she left home. She carried it everywhere.

"Hello, Althaia." The elder priestess' voice was coarse, as though she had inhaled too much smoke in her life. "I hear you are going to join me in the bee yard. There is much to learn, come."

"I will leave you now, my daughter. You are in good hands." Tanitha touched Althaia's shoulder and nodded with a smile, indicating that she follow Melissa.

Tanitha's flowing dress whispered as she turned and walked away, leaving Althaia with Melissa in the courtyard.

"First, you must learn about the craft itself, my child. Along the way, you will hear the stories of the bees and why we hold them sacred," Melissa began.

They were outside the temple, beyond the walls, where the desert lands began. There were craggy rocks and white stone piles. The landscape was interspersed with small, succulent bushes and tiny bright flowers in the arid high lands. It seemed to be a place where life could not be sustained continuously.

"We have created baskets covered in clay and stacked them here," Melissa continued.

Althaia was amazed at the stairs surrounding the temple, carrying one down to a place that had been leveled on the desert floor, cleared in order to set up multiple honeybee skeps stacked upon one another. As they approached big circular pots, there came a sound that was intoxicating. It was the sound of millions of the tiny four winged bees buzzing as they flew in and out of the openings into the pots. Something visceral in Althaia stirred.

She remembered sitting in the garden of her childhood home watching the bees on the flowers, her joy and utter contentment as she felt their energy surrounding her. Then there was that day when the swarm of bees rose like a tornado in the sky. The smells of those warm afternoons, the sounds of the birds in the trees, the water in the fountain were visceral. Tears burned her eyes as her body responded to the memory.

"We use these pots for them to build their honeycomb, which is convenient for us to harvest—though many of the wild bees have built their homes further out in the desert places such as caves, hollow trees, and underground."

Althaia noted a gleam in the elder priestess' eyes as she spoke about the bees.

"See here, behind the pots, we have a way to remove the lid and take the honey!"

Up until this time, the elder beekeeper had not worn any protection against the stinging insects. Now she proceeded to open an old, beat-up wooden trunk, which contained a veil, a few long metal knives, and torches.

"See these tools? They are for when we do come to retrieve the honey. Sometimes we must examine inside the hive if we see there are only a few bees flying in and out. We need to check and see if the queen bee is present and no other pests have invaded. For this, we put on our veils of protection and give them a small signal of smoke so that they know we are coming. We honor them with this warning, so they will refrain from stinging us. For if they sting us, they will die."

Althaia felt the pulsing aliveness surround her, as the orderly whirlwind of bees flew in and out, in and out of the pots. She was one with their energy field. Delight sprang up within her heart. This emotion had become such a rarity, she felt its presence keenly. A smile grew on her face.

"We spend very little time taking from the bees. We do not wish to disturb them for very long at all. They give us the great gift of honey, pollen, and wax from their stores, and we honor these gifts by treating them with utmost respect," Melissa continued. "And for this, they allow us to come here like this, unprotected, and stand among them as a member of the hive for a time!"

Althaia began to giggle, then to laugh, as the bees floated and soared around her. She imagined herself as one of them, no longer bound to the earth by gravity. The younger priestess in training threw back her head and began to slowly twirl and dance among the bees, her feet light and nimble.

"Goodness, girl! You seem to know the bees as your siblings." She coughed and laughed her coarse laugh.

Breathless, Althaia slowed down and smiled, looking at the creased, nut-brown face of her mentor.

"I do. I do know them. I am very eager to learn the way of the bees and the craft of keeping them!"

"Good. Then we shall begin tomorrow. This is only one of many places where our bees live. I shall show you where to find them and we can harvest honey from those hives that are prepared to receive us and offer their gifts to Aphrodite, the blessed one." Melissa nodded.

Althaia's eyes met the elder priestess, a light growing in her own. One that had been hidden for too long.

That night, Althaia slept more soundly than she had for many months. In the dreamtime, an exquisitely beautiful priestess came to her. Her hair was black as onyx, swept up above her head like a beehive. Her breasts were full and exposed, with drops of honey dripping from her nipples. Below her slim waist was the image of a golden bee etched upon her abdomen. One of her hands held a serpent; the other hand was gently placed between the cleavage of her breasts. Flowers grew up around her feet and wings of pure, radiant sunlight curved upwards. She was adorned with a necklace of pure gold. The pendant represented two bees, their abdomens curving toward one another, enjoined at the stinger, their gossamer wings outstretched, legs clasping a honeycomb in which they placed a small drop of honey. The eyes of the priestess were fixed upon Althaia. They were kind and welcoming.

Althaia did not see her lips move, but heard the words over and over, "Return to the mother. Return to the mother."

She awoke from the dream in the dark hours of the morning, as the gray dawn snuffed out the final bright stars of night. Althaia felt something akin to a warm oil creeping over her body and soul. The dark spirit that so often accompanied her in the wee hours of the morning before waking had dissipated. She felt tears of gratitude on her cheeks for this gracious visitation. Who was this woman who came to her under the cover of night? What did her mysterious message mean, 'Return to the mother?' No matter. All she knew was that the depression had been erased for this moment, and that feeling in itself was as sweet as the elixir of honey.

It was the beginning of this apprenticeship with the bees and the elder Melissa that slowly began to melt away Althaia's need to cut herself. Imperceptibly at the beginning, over time Althaia noticed the urge was no longer daily upon her. The dark spirit was still her companion, but not in the way that caused her to want to harm herself. She longed for another dream from the bee priestess to bring her a respite from the depression, but it did not come for a long time.

Before working with the bees, Melissa and Althaia began by building a sacred fire to Aphrodite in the bee yard, saying their prayers before beginning.

"Goddess pure, bees of beauty, we ask for your gracious welcome on this day. With gratitude, we come to harvest your gifts. With honor, we desire always to show you our respect, little ones," Melissa intoned, scattering sacred herbs of lavender and lemon balm on the fire.

When they had completed their prayers, they prepared to go in to the hives.

"See here, this is how we use our smoke," Melissa droned.

They were both suited up with veils over their faces, gloves and thin clothing that covered every inch of their skin. Holding the torch, the elder waved it carefully around the back of the skep as she removed the lid. The bees continued to move in and out of the front of the hive, seemingly oblivious to the two women peering into the recesses of the clay basket pot.

"Please hand me the pot with the lid that we brought for harvest," Melissa instructed.

Her spry adeptness as she reached into the hive and moved about in the bee yard amazed Althaia. She had asked Melissa once about her age. The elder priestess demurred, saying that the gifts from the hive—honey, pollen, the sticky, gummy resin of propolis, as well as the stings—were medicinal and kept her in good health. Her hair tied back in a bun had begun to turn white, revealing the truth of the wisdom of her years.

"I'm going to take my tool and cut out some of the honeycomb," Melissa instructed.

Althaia held the torch while Melissa reached in with her gloved hand and removed some comb, thick with bees.

"Please, give some smoke here so the bees will leave this comb."

Althaia held the torch closer. The bees jostled one another to leave the elixir, as the smoke made their compound, lidless eyes burn. They rose like a cloud swirling around the priestesses, bumping into their veils, some of them angry, clinging to the invader's clothing. It didn't take long to remove some comb from each of the assembled hives. Soon, the clay pot they brought for the honey was heaping and dripping. It was time to return to the temple.

On the way back, Althaia quizzed Melissa about the stories of Aphrodite's Melissaes. Why were they called such?

"There is a long story of women and bees as companions," Melissa stated. "Long ago, on the island of Crete, there was the Minoan King, Melisseus, who named one of his daughters Melissa, which means 'bee'. He was honoring her with the name of the Minoan-Mycenaean goddess, Potnia, also referred to as 'The Pure Mother Bee'. Eventually, Melissa became the first priestess of the Great Mother. All those women who came after her as female priestesses of the great goddesses were named Melissaes. The Melissaes were also the nymphs who fed the god Zeus with goat milk and honey as an infant, sustaining his life. So, you can see how important we are as the Melissaes. We are the priestesses, the Melissaes, the very souls of bees, come to heal and provide sustenance and life for our communities."

Althaia was beginning to piece together the power of the Melissaes as conduits and symbols of life itself. Just as the honeybees offered up their gifts from the hive as medicine for health, so the melissaes represented the honeybees' fertility and healing to those who came to the priestesses.

"Where is the island of Crete, elder sister?" Althaia asked.

"Far away from here. Where the Ionian meets the Aegean Sea. Perhaps someday you will visit. The bee priestesses of Potnia still maintain a temple there and would welcome you!"

Althaia's mind was spinning with the thought of visiting the island where the Minoan bee priestesses had sprung from so long ago. She was curious to meet them, see how they lived, hear their origin stories.

"How did you become the bee tender, Melissa?" Althaia continued to pelt her mentor with questions.

Melissa became quiet. Thoughtful.

"Like many of our sisters at the temple, I was harmed by the events of time. Many, many moons ago, when I was of child-bearing age, I had a child secretly out of wedlock. It was not my fault. I was raped by my brother. My father was enraged. He threatened to kill me. My mother arranged for the child to be given to her sister, who was barren, in another village. She would raise the baby as her own. I was smuggled in the early hours of morning by the horse cart of our neighbor, who sold fruits by day in the city of Corinth. He came and dropped me off here at the temple. At that time, the high priestess was named Melissa. She took me under her wing. She said to me, 'You are a sensitive girl, and you have been through much suffering. You will learn the ways of the bees. There you will find healing.' She gave me her name, Melissa."

The elder fell silent.

Althaia's eyes were downcast as they bumped along in the wagon. She had no words. Somehow, there was a strange consolation in the story of another woman who knew the depth of pain and loss of her womanhood. She wondered how many other women at the temple of Acrocorinth had sustained the same wounds.

"How did you face your pain? How did you heal?" Althaia's voice finally filled the silence.

"My child, the pain never goes away completely. It is only transformed by the work of letting go day by day, month by month, year by year," Melissa said, choosing her words carefully, sensing that there was a similar story with this young woman. "Being of service to a purpose greater than yourself is always healing. That is what I feel through my beekeeping, my harvesting of honey for our temple's economy, and the priestesses' health. But as a young priestess, I was also gifted in the arts of herbal medicine and midwifery. Until I became an old woman, my main work was delivering the babies of the women of Corinth. Now I just tend the bees!"

She laughed. Althaia stared at her mentor. Then she let her head fall backwards, allowing the wind to toss her hair as she breathed in this revelation. They continued on, wordlessly.

Althaia contemplated the commonality of her story with this elder, as she imagined the trajectory of her own life. One thing she was beginning to know for certain, her body was her own, and she was not ever going back to the dominion of men. Fleetingly, she let images of Adrian sift through her mind's eye. What would it have been like to be betrothed to a man with whom she shared mutual respect and purpose?

"Hello, hello!"

The shouts of the courtesans greeted them at the gate, as Melissa stopped the wagon with its beekeeping trunk and the vat of honey. Melissa jumped out and handed the reins to the boy.

"Please bring the vat to the kitchen, my boy," she ordered, not unkindly. "Come, Althaia, let's wash up and prepare for dinner."

She smiled as she extended her hand to help Althaia down.

That evening, Dionne carefully oiled and braided her hair by the lamp as Althaia laid on her mat, her face to the ceiling.

"Dionne, did you know about the story of the Melissaes and why we, as priestesses, are called 'bees'?" Althaia turned her eyes from the ceiling, curling her body toward her roommate.

"I know that bees are important symbols of Aphrodite, the goddess of love, and melissa means 'bee,' but no one has taken the time to tell me the story." She kept her eyes forward as her fingers skillfully braided.

"Well, evidently the stories come from as far away as the island of Crete!" Althaia exclaimed. "I want to travel there someday. Maybe you will go with me, my sister bee."

She laughed, as she watched Dionne.

"If you find the means, the way to get there, I will go with you!" Dionne retorted with a smile.

Althaia did not reveal the story of her mentor to Dionne. It was too close to home for her and would mean she must reveal her own story of sorrow. Her friendship with Dionne was a place of lighthearted playfulness and sharing of gossip around the temple.

"I am in love with the bees," Althaia continued. "Have you ever been to the bee yard?"

"No, and I hope never to go." Dionne smiled.

She tied off her hair and came to lie down next to her friend.

"Tell me, Thaia, what is it like?"

"A million tiny, vibrating bodies filling you up with life!" Althaia put her arm across her friend and pulled her close. "When I am in the bee yard or looking into the hive where the smell of honey fills my nostrils, I am at peace. If I am having a dark day, my attention is only on the bees and I do not remember my sadness at all!"

"They are like an elixir for the soul," she continued.

Dionne fell silent.

Althaia squeezed her arm, saying "What's wrong, my friend?"

"I only wish there were a way I could forget also. I miss my family." She began to cry silent tears. "I hate myself some days. I hate the men who come here."

Althaia pulled her friend closer and stroked her hair.

"I try to attend to my lessons, but the only thing I really care about and long for is my dancing and life in our village, which seems so very long ago and far away." Heaving sobs escaped her now.

"Oh, Dionne. We must find a way for you." Althaia tried to soothe her friend, suddenly realizing that the spirit that often held her in its grip also visited other priestesses there at the temple.

Dionne was like the sister she never had. The twins had each other. She had no one.

They clung to each other for a long time, spooning their bodies until finally sleep mercifully wrapped her arms around them.

CHAPTER TEN

The Pox Pandemic

*Earth, Diviner Goddess, Mother Nature who generates all things
    and brings forth anew the sun, which thou hast given to all
nations...
    hear, I beseech thee, and be favorable to my prayer.
    Whatsoever thy power dost produce, give, I pray
    With goodwill to all nations to save them
    And grant me this medicine.
    Come to me with thy powers
    and howsoever I may use them
    may they have good success
    and to whomsoever I may give them.
    Whatever thou dost grant it may prosper.
    To thee all things return.* [9]

It was early morning, before dawn, and Althaia tended the sacred fire. Every priestess took her turn to make sure the fire was never extinguished. The pungent smell of the cedar and cypress rose up like a familiar friend as she threw a log or a branch on the sparkling fire, its embers ever glowing. It was a reminder of the eternal nature of the bee goddess, Aphrodite, and her presence.

---

[9]Elisabeth Brooke, <u>Medicine Women</u> *Anonymous Twelfth Century Prayer* (Wheaton IL: Quest Books, 1997), 21

She sat down on the wooden bench, huddling close to the fire, her fingers outstretched to the heat in the chill.

Althaia had been at the Acrocorinth temple of Aphrodite for five lunar years. Her childhood in Athens seemed far, far away. On mornings like this, when she was all alone, with the moon melting into the early morning light, the stars going out one by one, she let her mind slip and reel in memories. The smell of Daphne, her girlhood servant, filled her nostrils. It was that pungent smell of olive oil infused with roses. She felt the cool palm smoothing her forehead, the weight of a hand on her heart as she tossed and turned in her bed, bleeding forever, it seemed, after the 'event'. She remembered Athena as a tiny owlet sitting in a large cage in her bedroom until she was large enough to fly on her own. How the shriek would startle Althaia out of a deep sleep. Her best friend, Helena, the brightness of their laughter together and the way they exchanged covert glances at flute practice. The silliness as they walked each other home, arm in arm.

When the pictures of Mother and Father and her sisters and Egan came to mind, she wandered there for only a short time. That last scene as she and Father left for Corinth, Mother's scorn of the crate she had carefully prepared to take her familiar, Athena the owl. As Mother yanked open the door, how Althaia watched her last shred of comfort fly away. Mother's face contorted with rage when she found out about Adrian. Father's matter-of-factness as he told her she was being 'given' to the temple at Acrocorinth.

The waves of grief had become less bitter in the five years she had been with the priestesses. However, if she went too far down those hallways, the tears would often begin, like an artesian well. It was a deep place from which they emanated. How could she ever make sense of, much less make peace, with her stolen girlhood? Even her earliest memories were marred by Mother's contempt and unkindness toward her. Father's silence. She didn't know when the change from beloved first child to rejected daughter transpired, but it felt like a dull knife twisting into her heart. Especially when her siblings came along, and Mother's attention was finally and completely diverted from her eldest daughter. Althaia was invisible to her absent mother. She could do nothing right. The suffering in a child's world was immense and wordless. Only her behavior could demonstrate the pain of rejection. And the ongoing warfare between mother and daughter was locked into place.

"Chaire!"

Althaia was startled out of her reverie. A figure in a dark outer garment with a hood obscuring her face approached. It was Lydia, the priestess who was the head midwife.

"My, it is chilly, may I come join you by the fire?"

"Yes, yes! Of course." Althaia moved on the bench to make room for Lydia.

She was a middle-aged woman, clearly past child-bearing age, with a face that was patrician and distinguished. She had been an attractive woman once, but her face, with its straight nose and high cheekbones, was worn and plain now. Althaia heard she was Roman and had been taken by a Greek husband long ago, but divorced by him when he had come to the end of his attraction to her, seeking a younger Greek girl. She had come to the temple homeless, pledging her loyalty to Aphrodite, also known as Venus among the Romans. Soon, she became known for her skill in midwifery and the medical arts. She was associated with the numinous and sacred, so thorough was her knowledge of the blood mysteries of women and their birthing of children. It was unusual to have an unmarried woman as a midwife, but the temple had a long tradition of offering this service to women. Many of them had trained with Agnodice, the Athenian female doctor who studied under Herophilus, who disguised herself as a man in order to attend medical school in Alexandria, Egypt.

Originally, women were forbidden to practice medicine. Agnodice had to practice secretly, until a jealous colleague brought her into the light and denounced her. She was brought before the high court of Athens with the threat of death upon her. It wasn't until the women whose children she had safely delivered caught wind of this fate that she was saved and elevated to her true dignity. The mothers, many of them relatives and wives of the judges and other powerfully connected men in Athens, marched to the court, and the judge's hand was forced to pardon her. From that time on, she and other women were allowed to practice medicine, but never foreigners or servants. [10]

"Child, it has been a very long night." Lydia pulled her hood back as she sat heavily next to Althaia. "The baby was lying across the woman's opening inside the womb and I needed to turn the baby."

She sighed. "I am afraid there will be an infection for this poor woman. I left instructions for her slave to give her a concoction of mugwort, sage, and pennyroyal to stem the bleeding, garlic and turmeric poultices for insertion, and sage tea to keep the infection away."

Althaia had also been studying the properties of herbs, becoming well-known in the temple and beyond as a budding herbalist. Tanitha had never again required her to work with the male clients, noting her trauma. Althaia bloomed in the bee yard and with the medicines of herbs. She continued to be fascinated

---

[10] Elisabeth Brooke, Medicine Women (Wheaton, IL: Quest Books, 1997) 64

by all the uses of herbs for women and their bodies.

"Lydia, how many years until you learned your skill?" she asked.

"I apprenticed originally for five moon cycles with an elder midwife. She is long gone now. Her name was Hestia, for she loved the hearth and domestic arts." Lydia's eyes focused on a distant diminishing planet in the sky. "Hestia allowed me to begin my own independent practice only after assisting her with one hundred births! She was a tough mentor."

Lydia's laughter pealed in the dawn.

"Lydia, may I ask you if you would consider something?"

Althaia tried to catch her glance. But Lydia continued to fix her eyes on the soon-to-be morning sky in the east.

"Would you consider taking on an apprentice? I, I mean… not for myself, you see… but someone who would be a wonder with women and babies!"

Lydia's eyes suddenly focused on her intently. "Who, my child?"

"Well, I don't… you see… I haven't asked her," Althaia said haltingly. "But I suspect my roommate, Dionne, would be skilled. May I… do you mind if I send her to talk with you?" she finished, her eyebrows raised questioningly.

"Ah yes, Dionne. Such a beautiful young girl. So much sorrow written on her face. Sometimes the medicine we need is to be in service of all that is life giving!" Lydia said.

It was as though she were emphasizing her own story.

"Please. Send her to the dispensary in the Herb Apothecary tomorrow at midafternoon, and we shall talk. Yes, I think this is the right thing." She nodded, her lips parting in a yellow-toothed smile.

"I will tell her." Althaia grinned.

They sat in silence as the sun rose in the east, crowding out the bright jewels of the night sky. Soon, the courtyard would be a bustling beehive of morning activity as the priestesses awoke and hurried to their tasks and duties.

Tanitha, the head priestess, crossed the courtyard and, seeing the two women huddled on the bench, moved toward them in her elegant, quick stride. She clapped for their attention.

"Good women, please join us in the dining area. I must speak to all of us."

Without tarrying, she turned and headed toward the western wing of the temple, where the kitchen and dining area resided.

"Sisters, priestesses, and our young brothers," Tanitha began. "I have received word from some of our clients that there is a disease that is coming to Corinth, yea, is already here."

She continued curtly, "It is a pox that has come upon the Romans in their own country and now is being spread about in Greece through the soldiers and particularly in our fair city because of the port and intersection of trade from all places and peoples."

Althaia looked around the room, trying to find Dionne. There were over thirty women and many young courtesan boys.

"As you know, increasingly many of our visitors are Roman." Tanitha's face was impassive. "They tell me that the disease is raging and will soon be upon us also. I fear what this will mean for our temple and our safety. As much as is possible, let us quarantine. I will appoint two persons to do all the market shopping. Every other request to leave our temple must come to me first. Do you understand?"

Althaia raised her hand, "High Priestess, might we inoculate ourselves with the medicines of herbs to strengthen and protect us?"

"Certainly, Althaia. Please work with Hygea the elder to find the right combination to make our bodies as strong as possible." Tanitha nodded.

"Will we continue to allow the men to come, despite the risk of carrying the pox to us?" Iona's voice was soft, barely audible.

She was a timid girl.

"I do not know, daughter. I will make that decision soon as we see how this unfolds." Tanitha's face suddenly bespoke of exhaustion and worry.

"Shall we set up a checkpoint down the road? Perhaps it's the Romans we must keep out?" Xi, one of the courtesans, piped up in his high voice.

Tanitha sighed heavily. "I cannot do that for now. But if the spread is rapid and quick, we must do this and perhaps even close the temple to the outside."

"Please, High Priestess, tell us about this pox. What is it?"

Electra, an elder, was strong and practical. She ran the kitchen.

"It begins with a high fever, followed by a rash and pustules. Nothing like it has ever been seen before. It disfigures those whom it attacks. I would ask that if you see any visitor with a rash or such pustules on their skin, you move away and immediately inform me. They will be asked to leave. Xi, when we do set up a checkpoint, please be awake and aware of any such symptoms."

Tanitha was becoming impatient.

"That's all, my sisters. Now, please attend to your morning meal and then to your duties for the day."

By that time, Althaia had caught Dionne's eye. They raced across the dining room and hugged one another.

"Come! Sit with me while we eat," Althaia said, taking her

friend's hand.

"I am frightened," Dionne voiced, her eyes darting about. "What if a man demonstrates these symptoms and becomes enraged if I leave him?"

"Dionne!" Althaia snapped. "I want you to be strong. I will make sure you have herbs to encourage your body to be free of this pox. But please, if you see anything, make an excuse and *leave*. Quickly."

Dionne nodded slowly, her brown eyes wide at the foreboding thought of the future.

"Besides, you are going to begin soon with Lydia. It is time for you to apprentice to become a midwife and leave behind this wretched temple service," Althaia stated confidently.

Dionne's smile was wan. Her sorrowful eyes always haunted Althaia.

"What is this you are saying, sister?" she asked.

"Come with me after our meal and I will tell you!" Althaia's eyes twinkled conspiratorially.

One day, unexpectedly, Xi came looking for Althaia in the herbal house. She was straining the antiseptic herbs of goldenseal root, holy basil, and lemon balm into an oil base when he came bursting through the door.

"There's a woman at the front gate; she's asking for you!" he shouted, vibrating his right hand rapidly at her, almost as though he was fanning his face.

Xi's face was always amusing, making her laugh. But this time his eyes were sober and his breath excitable.

Althaia laughed. "I am coming! Give me a minute to set this down!"

She followed him out to the courtyard and to the front arch

that led to the gate.

From a distance, she could see a woman, well-heeled in finery, a veil wrapped around her head covering her face, all but her eyes. Her chariot driver sat still as a statue as Althaia watched them approach. There was something about the woman's countenance and form that seemed familiar to Althaia.

The woman lowered her wrap as Althaia approached.

"Helena?" Althaia cried. "Helena! Helena!"

Helena grinned and gestured to her companion to assist her in stepping down from the chariot.

The women hugged, see-sawing back and forth as they laughed and cried together.

"Please, Helena, can you come inside?" Althaia invited.

"For a moment, just a little visit. I am slated to meet my husband soon as he will be finished with his work." Helena's sweet, tinkly voice warmed Althaia's heart.

They began to chatter excitedly, as though they were again young girls together. Althaia led her friend by the hand through the gate and into the courtyard. Then they walked arm in arm to the pharmacopeia, where just a short time ago Althaia had been mixing potions.

"Tell me. Tell me all about your life, dear friend. I see you have married. I want to know everything!" Althaia exclaimed, sitting across from her friend, holding both her hands.

Helena's head dropped back on her neck, her shining eyes lifted to the ceiling, giggling.

"Yes, it's true! I am married, for five years now. Even as you have been training here at the temple, I have been running a household!" Helena's voice then turned sober. "But I have been unable to have a child. I have lost many souls, sometimes almost full term."

Althaia could see the pain beneath Helena's usual gaiety and joyful spirit. Her eyes were older, seasoned by sorrow.

"My Helena." Althaia came to sit beside her friend, wrapping both arms around her narrow shoulders.

"Yes, three miscarriages now, after five years. But…" she said, leaning her head conspiratorially toward Althaia. "I am again with child," she whispered.

"Helena! Oh, dear one! I am so happy for you! How far along are you?" Althaia hugged her close.

"Three months." Helena smoothed her hand over her belly. "That is why I petitioned Aegeus to bring me along this trip."

Helena pulled away, her eyes searching her old friend's face.

"I know you were given to the temple many years ago, after the loss of your child. My life became a whirlwind soon afterwards, as father set up my dowry and betrothed me to Aegeus," she continued. "He is a good man. I think we are well matched. He allows me much freedom."

Helena rolled her eyes, smiling. "When I told him I wanted to come to see you and receive medicinal herbs from the temple for sustaining the pregnancy, he was eager to allow it."

"Ah, yes, of course, the goddess of love and her powers are respected, even by the men." Althaia smiled cynically.

"My friend, please tell me how you are after all these years and such loss before we parted ways?" Helena's brows furrowed, and her eyes conveyed a kindness.

"I will admit, it has sucked the marrow of life out of my bones at times, but I have found solace here with the priestesses. Early on, the head priestess saw my gifts for the bees and herbs, taking me from the clients to develop these gifts."

Althaia found the tiny bee fetish in her pocket and pulled it out to show Helena, a sign that the bees would come to heal and guide her. She did not recount the dark nights of the soul, the heavy-handed depression that still came unbidden. She was grateful for those days where she felt a lightness of being, which came more frequently.

Helena sighed. "I am glad."

Then she fell silent. So much had passed between them as young girls. And now in their absence from one another, they had passed through rites of passage that brought them through the threshold of womanhood. It felt monumental to try to fill the space and time between their parting with words. Althaia broke the silence.

"Helena, did you ever receive my last message before I was taken away to come here?" Althaia's voice was halting, begging.

She hoped there was a reason Helena had not come that day to meet her.

"Althaia, I did receive your message," Helena's voice broke. "But Mother would not let me leave the house. She intercepted the message before she put it into my hands. She said it was a situation best left alone."

Helena hung her head as she wept.

Althaia took a deep draught of air. Her shoulders slumped. She was silent, remembering the ache of waiting, the unrequited longing to see her friend one more time.

"Thaia, please. Forgive me," Helena whispered, wiping her eyes with her scarf, sniffing loudly.

"It wasn't your fault. I forgive you. I lost everything that day," Althaia continued in a low monotone. "Mother set my Athena, whom I'd had since an owlet, to flight. I did not see Calliope, Calista, or Egan that day. You never came. My childhood was erased. Daphne was there, but I knew I would never see her again. And then it was just Father and me. I cried all the way to Corinth."

Now it was Helena's turn to clutch her friend to her breast, even as Althaia sat motionless. But the presence and contrition of her childhood friend had begun to melt the numbing iceberg of her grief. She sucked in her breath sharply, and Helena drew back.

"It's been many moons since that day, and I lost all hope that I would ever see you again." Althaia's eyes were suddenly shy under Helena's gaze. "But this… this is more than I could ever hope for. Seeing you again has helped me feel more whole."

Helena smiled gently and put her palm on her friend's cheek.

"You will always live right here," she said, putting her other hand on her heart.

Althaia nodded slowly.

The two young women felt the sweetness of Lady Providence shining upon them for a moment in time. The uncertainty of their lives was the only thing that was certain. They knew how quickly the trajectory of their fate could change, steered by the men who dictated their future.

Finally, Althaia stood up.

"Let me find Hygea, the head elder who taught me all about medicinal herbs. I will consult with her about the best herbs for you. Do you have another moment?"

"I must leave within the hour, as Aegeus will be waiting for me. He is a trader, like your father! However, his specialty is fine spices from the Orient. He is longing for a son. I want to give him this gift because he has been so kind to me," Helena stated matter-of-factly.

Althaia did not comment on her friend's sense of obligation. So many women were promised to men of ill temper, who were abusive and violent. To have a husband who showed respect or restraint was a relief. Love, or at least affection, had a possibility to take root and even flourish over time under such circumstances.

"I shall be right back. We shall send you on your way with the very best herbal formula. But you must promise to come and see us again!"

Helena's cheeks were flushed with the secret joy of this seed growing in her womb and her gratitude for her friend.

"Oh, my precious Althaia! Yes!"

It didn't take long for the pox to reach the temple at Acrocorinth. Winter had come upon the city. The chill and rains brought a dreariness to everyday tasks. The epidemic was raging around Corinth, and any visitor to the temple was highly suspect as a spreader of the pox. Men with no symptoms came and Tanitha anxiously kept vigil for any signs or symptoms among her clientele and community. Her elder priestesses, and many of the courtesans, scoured the rooms with antiseptic herbs after each guest left. But they could not scour the girls.

Elder priestess, Hygea, who ran the pharmacopeia and taught the herbal medicinals, worked tirelessly with Althaia and Tanitha to increase the ability of the women's bodies to fend off this disease. They made large quantities of medicine from the root of the carnivorous plant, *Sarracenia purpurea*, commonly known as the purple pitcher plant, or side-saddle flower. They brewed elderberry syrup with dried rosemary, thyme, licorice root, and apple juice, which was doled out daily to guard against the fevers and pustules. They commanded the kitchen to cook all meals with large quantities of fresh garlic for the immune system. And holy basil was instructed to be used daily as a tea or a tincture. Cream of tartar ointment was readied in the pharmacopeia for when the pox would afflict a member.

The night came when a Roman soldier broke out in a fever the morning after his visit. Cressida was the first who complained of the fever days later. It wasn't long after when she broke out in pustules. Tanitha immediately asked the courtesans to close and lock the gate and set up a checkpoint further down the road. All members of the temple were asked to wear a mask, keep their distance, and exercise extreme caution when speaking with one another.

One day, a woman named Phoebe came to the checkpoint, begging to see the head priestess. Tanitha was in the herbal apothecary with Althaia when the word came that she was wanted immediately. Donning her protective clothing and mask, she left wordlessly. Curiously, Althaia followed at a distance. She wanted to see this women from the town of Cenchreae, a village in the municipality of Corinth. Phoebe followed a man named Paul, apostle of the new mystery religion called *The Way*. She was a deaconess in the small house church of Cenchreae. The followers of this strange movement sprang up around a man whose name changed from Saul to Paul after a vision. Jews called it a 'Yeshua cult'. Romans saw them as a nuisance. A new sect of Jews. The Greeks welcomed mystery cults, but there was much competition with the local religions. Tanitha spoke highly of Paul, saying one day she hoped to meet him in person.

Tanitha opened the small window in the locked gate, which had become the fortress between the temple world and the madness of the city beyond. Althaia moved closer to hear the conversation.

"Madame."

Althaia heard the quiet but confident voice of the hooded head on the other side of the window.

"Please advise if you can send some of your priestesses to assist us. Our house churches have been overrun by those pleading for relief from the pox. Your sisters have the medicines that can help ease their suffering. Will you send a few?"

"How can we do this?" Tanitha answered. "We must preserve our own health and safety."

Phoebe continued undeterred, "The Apostle requests this. I come on his behalf to serve the people and the Living God. You will receive many blessings for your aid!"

"Let me take up this matter with my priestesses. I will send word within a day," Tanitha said firmly.

"Yes. Yes. Thank you."

Phoebe turned, and Tanitha shuttered the window.

"Oh! You! What are you doing here?" she exclaimed as she turned and saw Althaia.

"High Priestess, will you send me to help? I can go. My body is strong, and I know the medicines that Hygea the elder has taught me."

Althaia felt a sudden surge of excitement and shivered at the prospect of her skills being of use in the center of this pandemic time.

"I shall let you know." Tanitha turned, her shoes clicking on the stone courtyard, as she went to consult with her elder priestesses.

That evening, Tanitha called all the temple priestesses together after the evening meal. She named five young priestesses—Elodie, Iona, Hestia, Astraea, and Althaia—to accompany three of the elders who were trained in the medicines—Hygea, Kosma, and Lydia. They were to leave at dawn with large ceramic vats of the elderberry tincture and the cream of tartar ointment. That night, Althaia stayed up late into the night, working with Kosma to prepare the herbal remedies.

After the sky had finally cleared of rain, the night was crisp and filled with the luminaries of the sky. Planets and stars and the cascading Milky Way poured around Althaia as she moved silently across the dark courtyard to her room with Dionne.

Upon hearing her roommate arrive, Dionne sat up in the dark.

"Althaia," she whispered. "Aren't you afraid to go?"

Althaia still had her mask on. She sat on the edge of her bed and began to take off her leather boots.

"Dionne, you should be sleeping!" she scolded.

"Thaia, I am worried for you," Dionne continued.

"Don't worry about me. I'm ready. I haven't been away from this temple much since I came here. I'm eager to bring the medicines to those who need it," Althaia said with bravado.

She imagined herself a heroine; the gravity of the risk seemed to elude her. She was ready for an adventure beyond the walls of the temple, to meet other people and see a bit of the world far from this little corner of safety with the women.

Dionne's voice was small. "You are so brave. Well, come home safely."

Althaia sighed deeply and fell back onto her mat, pulling the cover around her face.

"I will, Dionne. You can pray for our safe return."

Both women slept fitfully that night, awaiting the dawn.

The next morning dawned cold and gray. The wagons were loaded, and the horses hitched. The women wore heavy wool garments with hoods over their clothing. Protective masks and head coverings obscured their faces. They worked in silence, gathering their medicines.

Althaia felt the smoothness of the tiny carved marble honeybee that Daphne had given her many moons ago. She kept it in her pocket as a reminder that she was a Melissa, ready to be in the service of healing. It was what the goddesses would want. It was what the bees had taught her.

The journey into town was wordless. They were taken to Phoebe's home, where she greeted them with gratitude, showing them where to set up their pharmacopeia.

"We will make this our central station to dispense medicines, but I will ask you also to come with me to some homes where whole families are ill with the pox," she stated.

"You must keep your protective clothing on at all times, and we will wash them at night with a strong solution."

Phoebe indicated that they could leave their personal bags in a room with a high ceiling and mats neatly stacked in the corner. There were a few basins with soap and pitchers of water to wash.

"I will take two of you with me this afternoon. The rest of you can set up and prepare for the week."

"I'll go with you," Althaia offered.

"I would be grateful." Phoebe smiled tiredly.

"And I will also accompany you," said Kosma, one of the elders.

Protective clothing in place, the threesome began the grueling visits to families and the elderly with the pox. Althaia's heart swelled with sadness and compassion as they came to their first stop, the Ganas family. Living in a simple home, with the bare minimum for furniture and surroundings, the mother was alone with her three small children, two of whom had the pox. The baby lay silent in her crib, her breathing labored, her chest rattling. Her tiny body was ghostly white and covered with ugly pustules.

There were blue smudges under her eyes. The other sick child was a toddler, crying and clinging to his mother's leg as she peered with feverish eyes at the small group of women on her doorstep.

"May we come in, wife of Ganas?" Phoebe asked gently.

Clearly, the woman knew Phoebe well. A small light kindled in her eyes.

"Please, please," she said in an anguished voice.

To Kosma and Althaia, Phoebe stated, "The Ganas family is part of our fellowship. Ganas works in the olive groves for a pittance. He is still working and has not yet come down with the fever. His family has caught it somehow. Let's give them instructions for the herbal tincture and give them the first dose."

She nodded to them to follow her just inside the door, leaving it wide open to decrease any possibility of transmission.

Althaia lifted the heavy ceramic vase filled with the precious tincture, pouring some into a jar for the family. She instructed them to take a cup and continue to do so for the next five days.

"The children should fare well with this, and we want to make sure that you do not become sicker, wife of Ganas. If you have any garlic, begin to use a crushed tablespoon daily in your meal. It is strong, so don't give it to the children. Here, I will pour an amount of side-saddle flower root medicine into your vat for all of you. This is the best for the pox sickness. And here is a paste of cream of tartar to spread on the skin of the tiny ones. As you begin to drink these medicines, you will feel better."

As Phoebe began to speak softly with the woman, listening to her and offering a prayer with her, Althaia stepped closer to the silent baby in the crib. She noticed that the tiny chest was no longer rising and falling with the struggle to breathe. Alarmed, she put her hand over the heart with one hand, and put her index and third finger to the child's throat to discern a pulse.

"Phoebe! Phoebe!" she cried. "The child, come... come quickly!"

Shrieking, the mother responded as quick as lightning. Rushing past Phoebe, she picked up her child from the crib, putting her over her shoulder as she began to rap the tiny back. The baby had become lifeless, her skin bluer by the moment.

"No... NO... NOOOoooooo!" she screamed, as she sank onto the floor, weeping.

Phoebe was upon her in a moment, putting her fingers under the child's nose, her face contorted with anxiety as she put her hand on the chest cavity to discern if there was a heartbeat. But like the child, the heart's motion had been silenced. Moaning like a feral animal, the mother began to rock with her dead child, her voice crescendoing as she wept. Her children added their voices in terror as they surrounded their mother. Taking cues from her face, they screamed loudly. Phoebe sat silently by the mother, her hand making circles on her back as though she were comforting a child. Tears glistened in Althaia, Kosma and Phoebe's eyes as they watched the scene unfold. Their bodies became ground zero, absorbing the sorrow. Kosma sat with the children, pulling them onto her lap and cradling them as they wept with their mother.

"Selene," Phoebe finally said softly, as the mother's moans became a slow chant. "I will send for your husband. We will bring your family food. You may sit with Zoe for as long as you need, and one of us will come and hold vigil with you."

Her voice was soothing for the mother and children. Even Althaia could feel her pulse slow as Phoebe somehow made death seem as natural as life itself.

Althaia had anticipated her own fear of being exposed to the disease or seeing it in its fullest horror as they went from house to house. But all the patients they saw afterwards paled in the face of the specter of this family's misery and heartbreak. There were the elderly in the homes of family members who had lived a good long life and may or may not recover. There were whole extended families sick from the pox. Althaia was confident in her medicines for herself, the priestesses, and most of the young families. For her, the wounds from that first scene became seared into her heart's memory. The inconsolable sight of a sick woman squeezing her dead baby tightly to her body, rocking and surrounded by her children as she moaned and wept, pierced Althaia, taking her breath away. She returned to that image throughout the week of brutally difficult work and the endless, numbing sight of the disease. Though smallpox seemed to be splayed in plain view all over the city of Corinth, for Althaia it really was hidden behind closed doors. The city itself hummed along with business as though there were nothing killing her residents en masse. Althaia's emotions became raw, her compassion fatigued, her body tired at a bone level that she couldn't have imagined.

Every morning, someone, usually a woman and her daughters from the sect of this new religion, would drop off ceramic pots and platters of steaming food for the priestesses and Phoebe's household. Every day, Phoebe's husband would leave quietly in the wee hours of the morning for work, silently coming down the side stairway from the upstairs apartment where the family lived, disappearing into the dawn. Downstairs, the living quarters had become a medical dispensary and a place for the women from Acrocorinth to eat, sleep, and wash. Phoebe kept her children safe and at a distance. But she, herself, was unflagging in offering herself.

The last night of that eventful week, Althaia sat with Phoebe next to the fire in the courtyard. They had finished the final meal together. Elodie and Astraea were cleaning the dishes. The elder priestesses, Hygea, Lydia, and Kosma, were doing their evening ablutions. Tomorrow, all the priestesses would return to the temple.

"Tell me about your work at the temple. How did you come to be there?" Phoebe inquired kindly, curiously.

Althaia took a deep breath. She felt ashamed to tell her story.

"My family rejected me for doing something that dishonored them. My father dedicated me to the temple." She looked down at her hands, her fingers intertwined and fidgeting skittishly.

"And how has that been for you?" Phoebe continued, her voice unabated, no judgment implied.

"I... I... I couldn't do the thing, so I became a master herbalist and a beekeeper, studying with the wise ones who are the elders of our order. Hygea and Melissa taught me everything I know."

Her voice sounded thin and high-pitched. Althaia could feel the rising panic inside her. She almost didn't notice the way her nails cut into her wrists.

Phoebe's eyes met hers unwaveringly. She reached out and covered Thaia's hand with hers.

"You have saved our community this week," she said evenly. "And I have great gratitude and appreciation for the skills of your order and the gifts of your heart. You have much mercy and goodness inside of you, my daughter."

Althaia began to relax. The words of this woman were like an anointing oil of blessing.

Phoebe continued, "Our teacher, Paul, has allowed me to be in charge of one of our small communities in Corinth. It is my honor! He teaches us from the master Iēsous, a Nazarene from the far away land of Judea. He is gone now from this earth, but Paul reminds us that our present sufferings are nothing compared to the glory being revealed to us. And meanwhile, we are all growing in new ways, being redeemed more fully into our highest humanity as we serve the risen Christ, also called Ihidaya—the One. We seek to exemplify his life with a loving spirit."

Phoebe's face had taken on a glow as she spoke.

"The resurrected presence of Iēsous helps us in our weakness, even now in this time of pox. When we don't know how to ask for help, Ihidaya intercedes for us and assists us as we love our neighbor."

"Do you take care of people who are not part of your community?" Althaia questioned.

"Yes, of course. Anyone in need who knows of us and comes to our door, we will serve gladly," Phoebe stated. "We have been taught to love our neighbor as ourself."

It was all very strange to Althaia, this mystery religion. Ihidaya, 'The One'. Her language was Aphrodite, Artemis, Athena, and the many.

"Thank you, Phoebe, for your great hospitality this week. I will share this generosity with our head priestess, Tanitha."

"It is my greatest honor! What can I say? We would not have been able to help others without you and your sisters' assistance. I will continue to visit Tanitha, and we will make a contract for your medicines during this plague and perhaps beyond." Phoebe's worn face brightened.

"Phoebe, where did this scourge come from?" Althaia finally ventured.

"I believe it was transmitted by the Romans who occupy our city." Phoebe's face did not reveal any judgment. "They brought it from their land to our nation state."

"Do you have ill will for the Romans?" Althaia pursued the question.

"No. My husband is Roman," Phoebe offered. "Once upon a time, he was a soldier. But when he came to *The Way*, he laid down his sword and vowed to no more be part of the machinery of violence and war. That is the teaching of our master."

Phoebe's eyes met Althaia's. "In the end, we are all one. A mixed-up and complex humanity who breathe the same air, eat, drink, marry, bleed, and die someday. Until we come to understand this, we will continue to condemn each other and suffer our violence."

Althaia was stunned to learn that Phoebe was married to a 'traitor'. Did not her family understand the Romans who occupied their land? Was not her reputation sullied by marrying such a person? She did not dare to ask any more questions. Instead, she pondered this strange yet compassionate woman's words. Somehow, Phoebe seemed to rise above all those cultural stone walls that Althaia had run headlong into as a young woman. Or perhaps, somehow, her new community allowed her to stand resolute in the face of those petrified norms and say 'no'.

Phoebe stood and stretched, her long face breaking into a smile. "Come, let's retire to bed. Tomorrow you travel, and I will give your sisterhood a blessing before you set out to return home. I hope you will come visit again!"

Althaia nodded. Inside, her heart leapt with joy.

CHAPTER ELEVEN

The Oracle of Delphi

I was sent out from power
I came to those pondering me
And I was found among those seeking me
Look at me, all you who contemplate me
Audience, hear me
Those expecting me, receive me
Don't chase me from your sight
Don't let your voice or your hearing hate me
Don't ignore me any place, any time
Be careful. Do not ignore me.[1]

It was a winter day as gray and chill as the day the priestesses had left. Althaia had been gone a week. It felt like forever. Her world had expanded mightily during her time away. She had seen people from all walks of life. Many of them did not live like her family of origin or her friends from childhood. These families sought to raise their children while living modest, ordinary lives. Often they did not have more than a stick of furniture. The men labored with their hands, not their minds. The great philosophical schools and scholars of Athens were not part of their world. The specter of poverty was always a hungry beast scratching at their

---

[1] (Thunder: Perfect Mind, NagHammadi Library, Tr. J. Robinson, HarperCollins, NY, 1977, 271–4)

door. She remembered the feast of food that appeared at their door every day. The smiling eyes above the veils of the women who delivered their sustenance. There was the practical, even-tempered Phoebe, who never raised her voice with shrill requests, who never shouted abusive things to her children. The quiet form of her Roman husband, his disappearing back in the early morning light. Althaia's inquisitive mind continued to chew on all these places and people she had met in only one week.

Back at the temple, her world suddenly seemed smaller. Tanitha welcomed them back, the lines in her face deeper, the graying strands of hair curling out of her veil.

"My dear ones, I regret to tell you that, in the time that you have been gone, Cressida has passed away and many are gravely ill. The pox has exploded here among us." Her onyx eyes above her mask glistened.

"Xi! Yun Fung!" she called loudly, clapping her hands. "Please unload the wagon, take the medicines to the pharmacopeia. Unhitch the horses so the priestesses can rest."

The courtyard had a deathly silence hanging over it. There were no chatting voices, no laughter or music, no songs as the women worked at their daily chores, preparing for the evening clients. No clicking shoes over the cobbled stones.

The priestesses retrieved their bags wordlessly.

"You will find that many have needed to vacate their rooms and move into a temporary infirmary," Tanitha continued. "This is for your safety. Please do everything you can to stay well. Thank you for your service to the city of Corinth."

She turned and left the bewildered women standing there.

They all had been changed somehow by their time away. The gravity of illness and death had seasoned even the young women, who usually bubbled with giddy laughter. Hestia and Iona peered up from their lowered heads, their eyes dark and turbulent underneath their lashes. They paused, as though for a word of comfort from the elder priestesses, Kosma, Lydia, and Hygea.

"Go, daughters. You heard the head priestess. Stay well and listen for further instructions. You have been of great service. Thank you," Lydia, the midwife, said.

The elder women took their leave, their shoulders weighted down, their steps heavy.

Althaia entered her room to find Dionne's bed empty and neatly made. Althaia dropped her bags and whirled to fly across the courtyard to find Tanitha.

"Where is Dionne?" she demanded. "Where. Is. Dionne?"

Althaia's heart was pounding in her throat.

"My daughter, Dionne has been taken sick. She is in the infirmary."

"I must go see her at once." Althaia's voice was panicked.

"No." Tanitha matched her panic with a measured tone. "You will *not* go to see Dionne now. She is still very contagious. The infirmary has courtesans guarding it. I cannot have you sickened. Your work is with the medicines. I will have Astraea come and work with you to prepare the herbal formulas for the sick priestesses immediately. That is what you can do."

Althaia wanted to retort, "*And what exactly have **you** been doing while I was gone?*"

But she held her tongue. It was the only way to care for her beloved roommate at the moment.

And so, the suffering of the city swept through the temple at Acrocorinth as well.

Dionne was released from the infirmary after weeks. When she finally returned to their shared room, she was wan, and her skin had been severely damaged from the pustules. Her graceful body was a shadow of her former self. She hugged Althaia as Althaia wept tears of gratitude that her friend was alive. They talked long into the night, alternately laughing and sobbing. There was so much to tell. Life seemed as though it would never be the same again.

The toll had been severe on the priestesses. They had lost ten of their community. Tanitha, the High Priestess of the Aphrodite temple at Acrocorinth, had been in this community for over thirty years, the leader for twenty years. Life had always been dynamic in the priestess' temple, not only the clientele of men from all walks of life—longing for some comfort and connection to the sacred goddess, Aphrodite, the goddess of love—but the women coming and going. Some of the priestesses stayed a lifetime, finding their place. Others suffered from the culture of prostitution, even if it was in service of the goddess, Aphrodite. These women moved on from the temple, some carrying a lifetime of trauma unique only to women, emphasized by their service to the clients.

Tanitha was of middle age now. She was restless in her role at the temple, acutely feeling the sorrow of the community's losses. The season of grief also highlighted her own discontent and longing for something that she could not name. She needed discernment and wisdom from another source. Someone beyond her own inquiring heart and mind. Was it time to leave Acrocorinth? Where would she go? What would she do?

Tanitha had risen to power here in Corinth, as the head Melissa of Aphrodite's temple. She had embedded herself in one of the most influential goddess sites in Corinth and the region of Greece. Women rarely had such ability to transcend the cultural norms and restrictions for their gender. She longed to find her daughter and rest after all these years. The thought of mortality had begun to afflict her mind. Her bones were also tired, and Tanitha wondered how long she had left to live. Her health had suffered during the pandemic, the stress of protecting her community left her exhausted most days. She had begun to have heart palpitations. The pox had come and gone through the population of Corinth and Acrocorinth like a wildfire, leaving many dead or disfigured. Many who survived were crippled with anxiety in the aftermath. Though the epidemic had receded to a low ebb, it had not been eradicated after well over a year now. Tanitha continued to worry about putting her priestesses and courtesans in harm's way.

One day, she called Althaia to her personal chambers. "Child, I must go up to the Olympic Games at Delphi. These occur every eight years and we are always invited. We must be represented there. I also would like to consult the Oracle. I am inviting you to come along with me. There will be seven of us, along with two courtesans."

Tanitha's eyebrows were raised in a question to the young priestess. "Would you want to accompany me?"

Althaia eyes widened. She had not been away from the temple since the pox epidemic began. The past year had been spent creating medicines to strengthen the community's immune system and keep them well. The priestesses of Acrocorinth were now known throughout Corinth and the region for wellness and healing. Their trademark had become herbal medicines, which they brewed for a price. Many priestesses now worked with the emerging women physicians in Corinth, as midwives, herbalists, and teachers of the medicines.

"Yes! Yes! Yes!" Althaia responded, jumping up to hug

Tanitha, catching her off guard.

"Well, my dear, that is certainly clear!" She laughed. "We will leave the day before the dark moon. It will be a full day's travel. Prepare your things for that time."

The day dawned warm at Acrocorinth, smelling of spring. The chariots were loaded with gifts for the Pythia, including doves for sacrifice. Althaia was eager for this new adventure. She could taste the opportunity in the breezes stirring the curtains that morning. Hugging Dionne, she promised to bring her something from her trip. Dionne had been recovering her strength and her courage little by little. Now she studied with Lydia, the midwife, and the light had come back into her eyes. Althaia was grateful to see her dear friend begin to flourish and bloom.

Althaia's bag was packed, and she had sewn the small marble bee from Daphne into her undergarments for good luck. For the Melissaes, the bees symbolized healing, fertility, and resurrection. Althaia's apprenticeship with them had taught her all of these things. As she worked with them, learning their bee mysteries, she felt her own healing and resurrection begin to take hold, subtly, almost imperceptibly at first. Among the bees, encompassed by their vibrating bodies that glistened gold and transparent under the orb of the sun, she felt more whole. More alive.

The chariots were ready. Elders Melissa and Hera, a new priestess, Nefeli from Egypt, along with Althaia, Odea, Persephone, and Tanitha, climbed on board. Two courtesans, Xi and Manu, accompanied them. There was an air of celebration as the other gathered priestesses sent them off with a special blessing.

O gracious Goddess, born beautifully of the sea, loving

Aphrodite, hear our **prayer**. *As our sisters go, aid them to navigate the waters ahead, keeping Beauty as their sail and Love as their compass. Give their hearts courage and joy along the path and a safe arrival.*

Soon, the horses were on their way, whinnying with excitement, throwing their heads back and snorting as Manu laid the reins gently to their backs, clicking a command.

The women chattered excitedly, asking questions of Tanitha about the place where they were going. She told them stories of past visits during the Olympic games.

"These began over five hundred years ago. They originally began as a musical competition, with singers accompanying themselves on the *Kithara*, singing a hymn to Apollo, the sacred god whose home is at Delphi. Later, more musical contests and the athletic games were added for prizes. The victor would emerge with a crown of bay or laurel leaves, parading around the stadium. Now it has become a tradition every eight years, with a council representing various nearby city states, with taxes levied to collect offerings and invest in construction programs. The games will continue!"

"How exciting!" Nefeli's eyes glowed with eagerness. "And tell us about the Oracle, High Priestess!"

"The temple is run by many priests who dedicate their lives to the god, Apollo," Tanitha continued.

"But..." She smiled conspiratorially. "The Oracle is a woman, a priestess called the Pythia. She has great powers of vision and wisdom to see into the future. But only the humble, whose hearts are not about individual pursuit and profit, will benefit from her gifts. Many kings, leaders of city states, and even head priestesses like myself come for discernment and actions on behalf of their communities. But those who do not live in the power of their hearts will be led astray or even tricked by her advice. And the Pythia will become silent on the day that only those who seek her for personal gain come to visit. Her role, as is all of ours as priestesses, is to ensure peace and prosperity in our society and communities."

Tanitha then told them the story of Croesus, who was perhaps the most famous consultant of the Delphic oracle.

A fabulously rich King of Lydia was faced with a war against the Persians. Croesus came to ask the oracle's advice. Should he invade? The oracle stated that if Croesus went to war, a great empire would surely fall. Reassured by this, the Lydian king took on the mighty Cyrus. However, the Lydians were routed at Sardis, and it was the Lydian empire which fell, a lesson that the Oracle could easily be misinterpreted by the unwise or over-confident.[12]

The day went quickly, and soon they approached Delphi, the important Greek religious sanctuary of Apollo. Located in the shadow of Mt. Parnassus, a towering limestone hulk near the Gulf of Corinth, it was rumored that the muses lived in the mountain. This was the home of poetry and music. As their entourage approached the mountain, they could see the half-moon shaped stadium of the Olympic Games. The valley was lush and green, filled with olive trees. Althaia's breath caught as they approached the city. She had become accustomed to the rocky acropolis where the priestess' temple was located, looking north toward the Gulf of Corinth.

There was an air of anticipation as Manu steered the procession toward the community of Athena's priestesses, where they would stay for the next few nights. Warmly welcomed by their sister community, the priestesses of Aphrodite settled in for

---

[12] (https://www.ancient.eu/delphi/)

the night. Tomorrow, a few of them would approach the Oracle of Delphi. Tanitha had chosen Althaia and the elders, Hera and Melissa, to accompany her to the temple. The other young women would stay back until the following day, when they could all attend the Olympic Games together.

Tanitha was strategic in choosing which sisters would attend the Pythia, recognizing the leadership gifts of Althaia as a young priestess, and desiring to have the company of her elder priestesses to remember the visit and help her discern the path forward for their community. As Tanitha had predicted, it was a dark moon that night, frightening in its utter blackness. Althaia could hear an owl in the distance. She shivered. Remembering her spirit animal, Athena, she felt an old emotion rise up in her throat. The grip of that last, traumatic memory... a panic clutching her throat as her mother opened the crate and freed her beloved familiar. The image still labored her breath, and tears burned her eyes as once again she relived Athena's wings carrying her far away, disappearing into the distance.

A blue sky awaited the priestesses, who climbed aboard the chariot that would carry them to the Delphian Oracle, temple of Apollo, sun god of many things including archery, music, dance, poetry, truth and prophecy, healing, and diseases. Tanitha had sent word to the female Pythia far ahead of this day, and they were prepared for the high priestess of Acrocorinth. The temple had been rebuilt multiple times after fire and earthquake. The Doric columns, with ornate images carved into the temple itself, paraded around the Olympic stadium. As the horses labored toward the site on the side of Mt. Parnassus, there were great monuments dedicated to military generals' victories. Wealth was represented in magnificent artistry. A great bronze Bull of

Corcyra, the ten statues of the kings of Argos, a gold four-horse chariot offered by Rhodes, and a huge bronze statue of the Trojan Horse by the Argives. [13] The amphitheater seated up to five thousand attendees, and the site around the Oracle's temple was filled with altars to Apollo for dedications and sacrifices. As they went up the winding path to the temple, Althaia felt herself breathless with amazement.

Finally, they arrived. The Delphi had Roman soldiers stationed around the stadium, lounging in the sun. Young priests scurried out to take the horses from Manu and assist the women as they debarked. The women were ushered into the marble-floored narthex. The temple was quiet and dark as a womb. The smell of sweet herbs burning was comforting to Althaia. It felt like coming home.

"The Pythia will see you soon. She is completing her purification," said the priest, who bowed as he left them.

"What does he mean?" Althaia looked to Tanitha, who had visited the Pythia in the past.

"She must wash in the nearby spring, drink the holy water, and burn laurel leaves as part of purifying herself to receive the vision. Then she will take our doves, and they will be sacrificed. Only after all these rituals will she receive us in the innermost sanctum of the temple. We will present her with our offering of a cake, *pelanos* prepared by Electra, who oversees our kitchen."

In the end, it was only Tanitha herself who was able to enter the inner chamber to ask her questions of the Oracle. The other priestesses, Xi, and Manu were invited to walk the gardens, filled with fragrant spring flowers budding.

Tanitha entered the place where the Pythia sat on a tall pedestal with claw feet, the ceramic vase filled with sweet

---

[13] https://www.ancient.eu/delphi/

burning herbs engulfing the dim room with smoke. The Oracle's eyes were closed, and her head nodded as she rocked back and forth. There was a smile of ecstasy playing on her lips as Tanitha came and quietly sat on the cushion before her, leaving her pie on the floor as an offering.

"What is it you would like, Oh high priestess of the great Aphrodite?"

The Pythia's name was Phemonoe. She was a beautiful woman, with porcelain skin and a fine, chiseled nose and ample lips. Her gold-flecked hazel eyes flickered open to gaze upon Tanitha. She had a crimson veil over her hair, and a silk tunic secured over one shoulder. She held a bowl of spring water in one hand and a laurel branch in the other. As the incense smoldered around them, Tanitha began to ask her questions.

"Our priestesses have endured a horrible toll this past year from the pox epidemic. Ten of us have died, out of thirty women. I am tired. I want what is best for the women. I am aggrieved in my heart over our losses. My body is wracked by ill health. I would like to hear your advice, Oh great Oracle. Is it time for a new woman to rise up in leadership? I long to find my daughter and rest from the duties of head priestess for a time."

The Pythia listened carefully with her eyes closed.

"Is that all, my daughter?" she asked.

"One more thing." Tanitha bowed in supplication. "Please tell me about Althaia, a young priestess who has been in our midst for, lo, over seven years now. She came to us with much suffering in her soul as a young girl. Yet she has thrived, learning the art of beekeeping with one of my Melissaes. She is also an expert now in the craft of herbal medicines. What is her future? Will she take the reins from me if I leave? Please tell me, Oh Great Oracle, what is best for the future of our community?"

The Pythia nodded. "Thank you, sister. You may go now. I will discern, and the priest will come to you with my discernments."

Tanitha dropped to her knees, her forehead touching the floor, her arms before her, palms up. "Thank you, my Priestess. Thank you."

And with that, she stood up and turned toward the door. It was the dark moon, and she had planted her seeds. Now she waited for the 'watering' of the Pythia, that the seedlings might begin to sprout a tender shoot from its essence.

The women walked around the campus, marveling at the preparations for the Olympic Games, which started the next day. Slaves were hauling barrels of laurel branches to lay down before the athletes at the final ceremony. A large pedestal for the Olympic flame was being erected at the front of the amphitheater. There were colorful plumes of cloth flying from every colonnade and flags that represented the regions of competitors. The air fairly crackled with the energy of anticipation. The only dampener was the legions of Roman soldiers roaming the grounds with insolent, entitled swaggers.

Tanitha did not disclose what the Pythia had revealed to her. None of the women asked, lest they be cut off in mid-sentence. They had learned plenty about this sacred oracle, even if they were not invited into the inner sanctuary. Even Nefeli held her tongue. If there was one thing they knew about their High Priestess, it was her need for privacy and discretion. It was part of what made her a trustworthy leader and an exemplary model of equanimity.

Soon, as the sun promised to set in the west, the priestesses boarded their chariots and returned to the temple of Athena at

Delphi for a good night's rest before the games the next day.

That night, the beautiful bee woman came to visit Althaia. It seemed so real. She extended her hand with the serpent that she held, reaching toward Althaia. Bees buzzed purposely around her head, and she laughed as she tossed her head, eyes closed as she felt the vibration of the invertebrates. Eventually, the whirlwind of bees came to rest on her whole body, covering her body inch to inch until all that was visible of the bee woman was her exquisite face. Althaia was mesmerized in the dream. She knew that the queen bee had landed on the bee woman with her swarm of workers, resting as one of the bee scouts went to find a new home for the colony. She approached the woman and slowly put her hand out until her palm touched the vibrating mass of honeybee bodies. She scooped the bees into her hands, feeling their pulsating aliveness. This super-organism was a forcefield of power and utter gentleness.

Some bees flew around their sisters, dripping like honey from the bee woman's body. Althaia noticed one of the bees land, waggling her abdomen in a dance that told them where they would go for their new home. Suddenly, they rose up in a spiraling cloud, the air filled with their buzzing momentum. And in one dive, they descended into Althaia's body, disappearing through the very crown of her head. Althaia felt a shimmering as the bees penetrated and filled up her whole being—every sinew, tissue, bone, and cell. Her eyes met the bee priestess, who again nodded and smiled, beckoning her to come and take the proffered snake. As she handed the serpent to Althaia, her eyes were striking in their clarity of vision. They were kind and welcoming, and she heard the words over and over, "Return to the mother. Return to the mother."

She awoke with a start, her face wet with tears. As she sat up in her bed, her racing heart calmed, and she felt again that sense of warm oil bathing her skin and gratitude bursting inside of her. The tears sliding down her face were of gratitude. She felt loved. Who was this bee woman? This priestess? Why did she visit Althaia?

There was a song on Althaia's lips. Even though she was among her sisters, all sleeping side by side in the humble room of the Athenian priestesses, she began to dance in the early morning sun, her arms lifting upwards, her hips lazily gyrating. She began to hum to herself.

Persephone was the first to awaken, yawning and stretching.

"What makes you so happy?"

She rolled her eyes at Althaia, who laughed and came to snuggle next to her sister priestess, whispering, "I have had a visitation by the Queen of Bees! I feel as though I have been initiated!"

Althaia recounted the dream to Persephone. The young priestess yawned again and sat up.

"What does it mean?" she asked, rubbing her eyes.

"I don't know. But I can tell you that she always commands me to 'return to the mother'. I feel so whole, so peaceful, so joyful after her visitation!"

"Maybe she is telling you to go home and visit your mother in Athens?" Persephone posited, drawing Althaia into silence.

"No. No. I'm sure that's not it," she finally said, her words curt and sharp.

She stood up to get dressed, leaving Persephone bewildered.

The women of Aphrodite cut an impressive picture as they arrived at the Olympic Games. The young women were dressed in variegated solid silks of fuchsia, buttercup, periwinkle, and clay, with gold-threaded wraps around their shoulders. Their long hair was braided with gold ribbons and laurel branches encircling their heads. They debarked, as Xi and Manu took the horse-drawn chariots to the stables, instructed by the young men stationed at the gate. Everywhere, there were boys, some with their older male companions. Also present were many young men, their beautiful, bronzed bodies with togas or only loincloths that revealed their oiled, hairless, and muscled chests. The priestesses were led to their special section of stone benches with a birds-eye view of the Olympic field. All eyes were fastened on them as they made their way to the front of the amphitheater. There were musicians playing lyre and flute, and girls with sultry faces dancing next to them on the stage amidst the hubbub.

The Temple at Delphi, and the surrounding stadium, overlooked the green, rolling mountains. It was a stunning and exhilarating sight.

Soon, a loud horn was blown, initiating the beginning of the Games. The crowd became silent as the athletes entered, with one lone boy carrying the torch, the flame of the Olympic Games, to be lit once again. He was then followed ceremonially by many young men, each carefully distanced as they processed into the stadium with the colors of their region on the capes they wore. As the torch caught fire on the front column, a roar went up from those gathered.

"Let the Games begin!" shouted the announcer, his voice reverberating and echoing along the stone amphitheater walls.

Althaia was fascinated by the finely tuned bodies of the young men; yet her eyes were riveted to the field. It had been so long since she had seen so many young men. The temple had its male courtesans, but they were exotic, from far away, foreign places, brought to Corinth for a purpose. These were the young men of Greece, gathered from many families of the city states. It was a novel idea for Althaia, this notion of male athletes gathered in one place to compete. There was the discus and javelin throw, the shot put, running, vaulting, wrestling, boxing, and equestrian events. The announcer noted the various priestess cults present: among them Athena, Aphrodite, and Artemis. And, of course, there was the temple of Apollo and his priests at Delphi. All were invited to stand as the crowd cheered and welcomed them.

The afternoon flew away. At intermission, as Althaia mingled with those around her, a young boy approached.

"Sister!" he called out, catching her attention with the urgency of his voice.

As she turned, there was a familiarity about the young man.

"Sister!" he reiterated. "It is me, Egan. Your brother."

Althaia froze, all the neurons in her brain firing at once, a cacophony in her head. She took in this boy-man. He would be about the same age as she was when her life burned down. Fourteen. Egan was tall and slender, his brown hair closely cropped, his golden face handsome, brown eyes shining and a dimple burrowing into his cheeks as he smiled at her.

"I heard them introduce your temple, and then I saw you!"

His face wore the same exuberant look of that seven-year-old brother she had left behind. It had been well over seven years now.

Reaching out her hands to Egan, she pulled him to her, cheek to cheek, hoping he wouldn't see her eyes filling with tears.

"Come, let's walk, my brother."

Althaia pulled him along the side aisle until they moved past the pressing crowds and came to the grassy hill beyond the stadium. Each sitting on a rock, they faced one another as a torrent of questions tumbled out.

"How are Mother and Father? Calista and Calliope? What brings you here, Egan?"

Egan sucked in his breath and exhaled with a sigh before he began.

"Oh, you know, Father is still busy with his trade, he's gone a lot. Calliope is married and happily so! Mother made sure she had a good dowry before being married off." He laughed. "I have continued with my studies, and Mother made sure I have the best athletic training in Athens. She hopes for me to enter the Olympic Games next year."

"What is your event?" Althaia was curious.

"I do the relays, pole vault, and wrestling!" He smiled again, shyly.

Althaia tweaked his cheek with her fingers, laughing.

"I can hardly recognize you, my beautiful brother! So grown up! How did you arrive here?" Althaia looked at him quizzically. "Are Mother or Father here with you?"

He looked down at his hands. "No, I came with my *Erastes*. Alexander is my tutor."

Althaia knew all too well about this arrangement. A young boy would be paired with an older man, who tutored him in Greek politics, the military, and introduced him to social circles in exchange for sexual favors. Ideally, this arrangement benefitted the young boy's place in Greek society.

"Egan," Althaia said gently. "What is your plan for your life? Does this arrangement suit you?"

Her brother looked away. "I want to participate in the next Olympics. Alexander has many connections."

"Ah! There you are my boy!"

Both brother and sister's heads snapped toward the man's voice. It was Alexander.

"And whom might this be?" he boomed.

"My sister." Egan stood up to greet his tutor. "This is Althaia Adamos. She is an honored priestess in the high temple of Aphrodite."

His face was impassive.

"Chaire. Greetings."

Althaia's face was tight and formal, belying the words. This Alexander was much too loud, seeking immediate intimacy, as though he were intimately part of the family.

Alexander took her hand and bowed deeply.

"My lady. A pleasure." He kissed her hand and she withdrew it sharply.

"Egan, I must get back to my sister priestesses, but you know where I live now. Come with Father someday to visit!"

She embraced her brother tightly.

"One more question, my brother. How is Calista? Please tell me she is doing well," Althaia pleaded.

"Many summers ago, she had the chance to tour the island of Crete and bring her classical dance. She came home changed. She hasn't been the same since." Egan's face was a mixture of pain and perplexity. "Something happened. I don't know what. She mostly keeps to herself now, spending time drawing in her room, except for meals. She doesn't dance at all any more. Mother is determined to make her dowry now that she is almost twenty-one years old. Mother is worried."

Egan shrugged helplessly. "I wish you would come home, Althaia. We need you. Father misses you."

Ignoring Alexander, who had come to put his arm on Egan's shoulder, Althaia took Egan's face in her hands.

"Little fire," she said tenderly. "Egan, my brother, please tell Calista she can also come to see me at the temple. But I cannot return home. Not yet."

Kissing this boy-man, her brother, on each cheek, she stepped back and waved as Alexander guided him back to the stadium for the Games. She felt an overwhelming sadness rise in her. Like the incoming tide, it threatened to drown her in its bitterness.

CHAPTER TWELVE

The Apostle

Love is patient, love is kind. It does not envy, it does not boast, it is not proud. It is not rude, it is not self-seeking, it is not easily angered, it keeps no record of wrongs. Love does not delight in evil but rejoices with the truth. It always protects, always trusts, always hopes, always perseveres. Lover never fails. [14]

After the visit to the Oracle of Delphi and the Olympic Games, a certain heaviness descended upon the priestess community at Acrocorinth. The supreme leader, Head Priestess Tanitha, seemed to be brooding daily about something that was not apparent to the younger priestesses. Her moods were dark and mercurial. She would shout at the inexperienced women, irritated by their lack of knowledge about the tasks at hand. Althaia herself had much to brood about with the unexpected surprise of seeing Egan. After so many years, it had scratched open a wound.

The pox still threatened like a low-hanging cloud, and the word on the street was that the Olympic Games had spread the disease, once again opening the anxiety of public interaction and socializing. The small band of priestesses that had gone to Delphi, however, quarantined for weeks with the growing moon, taking strong herbal medicines to boost their immune systems.

---

[14] The Holy Bible, NIV, The Apostle Paul's letter to the Corinthians 13: 4–8

Thanks to Althaia and her sisters who prepared these formulas, they emerged unscathed from their time away.

It had been over a year since the epidemic first began spreading in Corinth and Helena's visit. One day, a messenger dropped a papyrus note off at the temple. It was addressed to Althaia.

My dear one, I must tell you that after I visited you and received the magnificent herbs to strengthen and fortify my womb, I did not miscarry! Aegeus and I have welcomed a beautiful baby girl whom we have named, Zoe Althaia. She is perfect in every way, just like you, my friend! I hope someday to show her off to you in all her beauty. Perhaps she can be your goddess daughter? Do come visit someday!

Always yours, Helena.

Althaia smiled. So, now she had a namesake. It made her heart sing.

Tanitha continued to be troubled by her visit to the Oracle at Delphi. She took counsel with the elder priestess, Hera, a close friend whom she trusted.

"The Pythia has spoken. I am to leave the community within the year. Where will I go? Who will take me in?" she moaned. "The Oracle said that I must exercise restraint and patience, for the information to find my daughter will appear at the right season. I must trust. But how can I live in this in-between time with no certainty? I am becoming an old woman. I am afraid."

Hera put her hand on Tanitha's and squeezed it with determination.

Tanitha continued, "She said that the future does not bode well for the priestess temples. The mystery religion of Christianity and Gnosticism will spread like a wildfire across

Asia Minor, Macedonia, Thrace, Italy, Spain, and the Near East. Soon we will be a small minority, and our goddess culture and temples will become theirs. She encouraged me to visit the Apostle Paul, who even now is traveling widely to spread what he calls the 'good news'. The Oracle told me to hear him speak, visit with him, if possible, see if the message is sound and of good heart."

Hera continued to listen with sympathy. She knew the greatness of this woman's heart. Her deep love of the women and men who came to the temple. Her desire to always lead with wisdom and compassion. Her suffering over the loss of her daughter so many years ago in Samaria.

Hera was named after the goddess whose marriage to Zeus was troubled and wrought with jealousy and affairs. But Hera was also the one who loved animals. She was known as the one who represented the domestic life. She had her own private suffering, with the loss of her family as a young woman. Because of this, she had great compassion.

"I also asked about the priestess, Althaia, what will she become? She has many gifts and I want her to succeed me. Yet, I see that her attention constantly wanders beyond the temple these days, despite the skills she has learned here. I asked the Oracle if she would take my place." Tanitha looked upward and sighed deeply.

"I was told that she has another life to live. The Pythia told me that I must send her to the Mycenaean state of Pylos, on the island of Crete, where there is a goddess temple devoted to Potnia. Potnia's emblem is the bee, and she is the mistress, the pure mother bee. Althaia will flourish with her skills as a beekeeper and herbalist there. The Isles also need to know the medicines. She will become known near and far for her healing gifts."

Hera nodded. "This is difficult news my friend. I know you had hoped she would succeed your reign. But the Pythia showed you she has another path, and she will only be happy if she is on her own journey, not one superimposed by any of us."

Tanitha looked downcast. "It leaves me completely unknowing of what will happen next and when I must prepare. But I have become more and more unhappy with the temple life and the men who come for services. Is that the best thing we can give our daughters? Is that not also superimposing a whole culture of male hunger, of domination, that we must acquiesce to as women? Is this the only way of sharing Aphrodite's love?"

Her face was flushed as she said this out loud. She cut her eyes away from Hera.

Hera laughed. "It's not that I haven't thought the same! Don't worry, your secret is safe with me!"

Tanitha was beginning to question a whole religious system, goddess culture, and society. It was unthinkable. There were women like herself, the *hetaera*, high-class female companions in the harlot houses of Athens who were independent, outspoken, witty, and confident of speech, not to mention that they had financial security. Then there were the temples, where prostitution was upheld as a sacred honor or duty to the goddess. Other *pornais* were hothouses of lesbian romance, women loved one another more passionately than they loved their patrons. [15]

"And someday, it will all be gone, pushed underground, or changed, as this mystery religion of the Apostle takes hold." Tanitha was measured in her response.

"Some days, I wonder if it is a good idea to see into the future

---

[15] Will Durant, The Life of Greece (New York: Simon and Schuster, 1939), 302

as I did with the Oracle." Her tone was cynical.

"Things are changing. And I must change with it all," she said in a resigned voice.

Phoebe, the leader of the house church in Cenchrea, continued to purchase herbs and consult with the priestesses of Acrocorinth for medicines. She sought to keep her community healthy and well, even as the pox epidemic lurched forward and receded from time to time.

"Tanitha, I would like to invite you to attend our worship this week, if you are amenable?" Phoebe inquired of the head priestess on one of her many visits to the temple. "The Apostle Paul is in town, and so we will have all our house churches gather together. There will be many attending, and perhaps you would feel comfortable coming as part of the crowd?"

Phoebe smiled warmly at Tanitha. She seemed to sense a kindred spirit. Phoebe was not unlike Tanitha, in that she was a woman who was the head of a community—though hers included mixed gender and ages, with many families. She was also a woman of powerful equanimity and good will, with the welfare of her community at the very heart of her service. However, she was more peaceful than Tanitha these days. Tanitha longed for this feeling of calm inside.

And so it was on Sunday, considered the first day of the week for the followers of *The Way*, that Tanitha found herself sitting in a very large home in Corinth, with Althaia by her side. It was owned by Gaius, a wealthy vineyard owner in Corinth. People were filing in from all over the city, dressed in their cleanest clothing. The women wore veils over their heads and covered their faces for protection from the pox. They also heeded the Apostle's instructions on women's modest dress, as they were under the headship of men. Those gathering were clearly, by and large, the laborers of the city. People who worked with their hands and lived modest lives. They did not put on airs or pretensions. Children were laughing boisterously as they played together. Some were crying and clinging to their parents. There were elder women and men in their best tunics or peplos. Young girls huddled in groups together, giggling. Bands of boys chased the children. Many nodded at the new visitors, Tanitha and Althaia, with a twinkle in their eyes, welcoming them. Tanitha felt odd and out of place, uncomfortable in her floral silk peplo and fancy shawl with the gold threads. Did people know where she lived? What she did? Who had invited her? Althaia, in her simple, woven, vanilla-colored peplo, found herself feeling at home.

Suddenly, the two women found themselves next to a woman, who introduced herself as Lydia. The woman was dressed in a beautiful silk of exquisite Phoenician purple dye. She mentioned that she had traveled far to come to this gathering, from the city of Thyatira, due east of Athens, across the Aegean Sea. She was a handsome and gracious woman and invited Tanitha to introduce herself and her 'daughter'.

"I live here in Corinth," Tanitha explained. "Phoebe purchases many herbal medicines from my priestess community. This is one of my priestesses, Althaia. She is highly skilled in the craft. Phoebe invited us here today."

The woman's face lit up. "Oh, if I hadn't inherited this business as an agent of specialty purple and red dyes, I would have studied in Athens with the Asclepius school of medicines!"

She nodded approvingly at Althaia.

"But this man, this simple tentmaker, his words have changed my life. I am glad you could join us today!"

"Shhh, shh, shhhhh…"

A hush began to descend on the crowd. The doors were thrown open, and many sat in the colonnaded courtyards, pouring out into the well-manicured gardens of the owner, Gaius. Those in the main marble-floored room continued to call on those gathered to silence themselves. Children were sent outside. The young girls and boys came to sit with their families.

"Friends and neighbors, sisters and brothers in the faith, I am delighted to host our worship today! We will have food and drink to share after our teacher, the great Apostle Paul, brings the message of Iēsous. Thank you for coming!"

And with that introduction, a man stood up to speak. He had on a simple purple tunic with a cream woolen cloak thrown over his shoulder. His dusty feet were bound by leather-strapped sandals. His Jewish features were swarthy and dark. He sported a coarse beard and curly, unkempt hair. As he began to speak, Tanitha was mesmerized by his speech. His oratory skills were persuasive, and he spoke with an intellect that appealed to the mind, but the passionate flame glowing in his eyes awakened the heart. He was clearly a learned man, trained in rhetoric and literature, with a fluency in Greek philosophy.

"I have visited Athens, the Aeropagus, and the philosophers of that city were very eager to speak with me!" he began. "You know how I love a good debate."

The Apostle garnered laughter from the crowd.

"They called me a babbler, those Epicureans and Stoic men of rational thinking. Well, yes, I do babble. But I am also a scrappy fighter!"

Again, laughter from the crowd.

"But, my friends, here's what happened. When they said I am a 'proclaimer of foreign divinities', I used some of their language to help these wise men of reason and logic understand that I am not so far and distant from their own hearts and minds!" The people at Gauis' home that day were mostly unlearned in the ways of the Athenian philosophers' reason, law and order, and logic. They felt the contempt of those who were intellectual and well-trained in oratorical skills. So Paul's message fell on eager ears. But the Apostle's message was for all people.

"I said to them, 'I see you are a very religious people by all your objects of worship to the gods and goddess. There is even the altar with the name '*to an unknown god*' in your city.'"

The Apostle's voice became louder, to emphasize his next point.

"I told them, 'You can *know* this god. Look about you and see all that has been created. This is the God who does not live in shrines made by human hands but is infused everywhere, all around you, and through you! I am here to tell you that in *this* Creator we live and move and have our being.' Thus, I quoted the words of their very own, Plato's student, Posidonius!" the Apostle shouted. "And I ended with their very own Stoic poet, Aratus, 'For we too are his offspring.'"

"Yes indeed, we are this God's offspring! Not gold, silver, stone, or an image formed by the imagination of mortals, but the flesh and blood of the One God and good Earth herself!"[16]

And with that, the Apostle Paul wiped his sweating brow and fell silent for a moment.

"Did you challenge them to a sparring match in the public square?" shouted a man from the back of the room.

Raucous cheers and shouts erupted.

"No, no! My friends, it is not in matching with the same competitive spirit that you will have a stage to share your

---

[16]The Book of Acts, chapter 17, NRSV

message!" the Apostle boomed. "No, my friends. I look to teach a secret wisdom that comes only from the heavens. For only God is wise! Don't deceive yourselves. If any of you thinks he is wise by the standards of this age, you should become foolish. For the foolishness of God is wiser than your foolishness!"[17]

"How can this be?" people murmured amongst themselves, trying to understand a deity as foolish.

"Good people! The weakness of this God I speak of is stronger than your human strength. Look to the innermost chambers of your heart, as our Master taught us. Examine your hearts! Pray for humility, wisdom, and a kindness that is much larger than your little ego. Do not live with contempt and superiority inside your heart. It will eat you alive and be your downfall."

The Apostle then went on to speak a personal word to the gathered: "Look, my dear family, I have heard about the divisions among you. Do you think only of yourselves? Are you ignorant to the needs of others? Do you hoard the holy bread of the Last Supper, grumble, and complain, withhold your resources from one another? I have heard you bring lawsuits against your brothers. And what of you men whose sexual thirst causes you to harm your wife and family?"

The crowd became so quiet, one could hear a child's toy drop.

Paul sensed the change in tenor of the meeting. He had struck a nerve.

"For those who love and follow Iēsous and his teachings, remember, you are now One Body. All of our communities together make up this Body. Each of you has a special function to make this Body healthy. Even the unpresentable, private parts

---

[17] I Corinthians 3:18–19 NRSV

of this Body have a special honor.[18] Those who are different than you, whom you want to shun. Those who work behind the scenes to cook or care for children, the sick, the elderly, the widow. Like Phoebe, my dear sister! She singlehandedly cared for our communities, quietly and with great compassion, during the peak of the pandemic. She was not a boasting or loud mouthpiece like myself."

The crowd snickered at the Apostle ingratiating himself.

"Not one of the parts of the body is dispensable, not even the weaker parts."

They quieted. His voice rose and flowed in a cadence that held the audience.

"There should be no division in the Body, but its parts should have equal concern for each other. If one part of the Body suffers, every part suffers."[19]

Then he began to eloquently speak of what he called the 'most excellent way': "Love is patient, love is kind. It does not envy, does not boast, it is not proud or rude, self-seeking, or easily angered. It does not hold grudges, delight with evil, but rather rejoices with the truth. This love always protects. Always trusts. Always hopes and perseveres. This love never fails!" [20]

Finally, the Apostle ended his message, "Be of one mind, live in peace. And the God of love and peace will be with you!"[21]

Althaia was entranced. She knew that most of the people of Corinth in this room were a practical people, the working class. But sprinkled among them was also the class of the well-off, the owners, those who held powerful roles in the city. The city itself

---

[18] I Corinthians 12 NRSV
[19] Ibid
[20] I Corinthians 13:4–6 NRSV
[21] II Corinthians 13:11 NRSV

was a competitive and thriving economic environment, and those who participated in it were trained to succeed. Drachmas, the silver currency, flowed in the street. Amidst the shadow of the Roman occupation, it was known as a pleasure capital, whose aim was to please through flamboyant shows, food, sex, amusements, and pastimes—anything to distract through excess and acquisition.

The Apostle was appealing to their hearts, waking them up to a God who cared for them. To how they cared for one another. There was more to life than vanity and self-serving pleasure. These charitable people did something that the city of Corinth shrank from during the pandemic. They visited the sick and contagious, bringing relief and kindness. Suddenly, she understood Phoebe's great compassionate service for her community.

Her heart had been awakened to this love.

The gathering brought much lively conversation as Tanitha and Althaia bumped along toward home in their chariot.

"The Apostle's reach and influence continues to grow here in the city and around Macedonia and Asia Minor," Tanitha noted. "Even the Romans are setting up house churches!"

"Do you believe what he preaches?" Althaia questioned.

"Well, of course he is persuasive. He is trained in rhetorical debate and the Greek philosophies, after all. I can appreciate that." Tanitha laughed. "But what I find most compelling is his followers."

She grew more serious.

"They do not practice infanticide, which we know are usually baby girls in our society. Also, they do not shout their beliefs on the street. They illustrate *caritas*, a love for others.

They have cared for Corinth during the worst of the pox pandemic. Who else did you see going outside of their own tribe and home to do this?" she wondered out loud.

"Yes, I have grown very fond of Phoebe. I like that the Apostle has many women who are leaders," Althaia emphasized. "We met Lydia, a woman of means and power in her own right. And during the agape meal, I met a couple named Prisca and Aquila. Prisca has the best humor. We laughed and laughed as we shared stories!"

Tanitha smiled at her priestess. "They certainly do seem to enjoy one another's company. People from all walks of life—not so different from our community at the temple. We have all learned how to live together in some semblance of peacefulness. It's not something you see readily, all organized around this One God idea."

"I would miss the female deities," Althaia countered. "But one thing the Apostle speaks of in common with our goddess religions is the wisdom of the created world. According to him, this 'unknown god' can be found in all that has been created! I believe this. I have found peace and wisdom in the bees, the birds, the animals, flowers, and trees. I have found healing in the medicines from the herbs. Surely the Divine is alive in all of these things. At the temple, I have learned from all our sisters about the holy, healing powers of the created world."

She tilted her head quizzically. "Perhaps we do not know this One that the Apostle speaks of, but we do know love of one another and see the unknown god in the bees and herbs and moon, sun, stars and skies and all the animals."

Tanitha took Althaia's hand in hers. In the silence, they felt a warm, shared glow between them as the horses turned toward home.

Tanitha continued to attend the house meetings of Phoebe. Sometimes she went to Prisca and Aquilla's home when invited. She had developed an affinity for the warmth of the communities. They practiced a simple method of worship, which involved a message, a collective prayer called 'The Lord's Prayer,' and an agape meal with a common cup and bread to remember the master, Iēsous. They were humble people who would give you the clothing off their back. They shared their money. Everyone giving generously as able, and those receiving if in need. This was not odd to Tanitha. The temple also practiced such a common purse and assistance.

They claimed their teacher had resurrected after a bloody and torturous crucifixion by the Romans. Their shining faith and kindness, their fierce fidelity to caring for one another in community, enveloped this soul-weary High Priestess as she grappled with her next step.

She had come to question almost everything about her role and the temple prostitution as a sacred vocation. Tanitha had seen its harm to many of her young initiates. She thought of her own suffering and sacrifices. She wondered if this system was truly what the goddess had in mind, or if it had been instituted by men as a way to secretly address their appetites.

Most of all, Tanitha grieved the loss of her only child, a daughter. As a Phoenician, her people were seafaring people from Northern Israel. Her family was poor, with ten children. Her father could not put enough food on the table, so, one day, he sold his eldest daughter into slavery in Sidon. It rescued her family's sagging coffers for a short time. In servitude, she bore a child, who was taken from her and given to the temple of Astarte, the goddess of fertility and sexuality, the productive power of nature and war in Samaria.

Eventually, Tanitha was able to purchase her own freedom. She fled to Egypt, to the temple of Astarte, since she had nowhere else to go. Before leaving, she inquired after her daughter in Sidon, who would've been only five years old. She turned up nothing. No one would speak to her of her daughter. In Egypt, she studied the philosophers and poets. Literature was her passion. She became a learned *hetairai*, a companion at the temple, but also a woman of independence and means. She was never able to find a trace of her daughter. She had named her daughter Diana.

Tanitha soon rose in the ranks of the priestesses, known for her intelligence, wisdom and equanimity. It didn't take long for her to be sent to the temple of Acrocorinth as the Head Priestess. She remembered the early, giddy days of the flourishing temple. Her charisma that drew the circle of the community wider and larger. Because of her witticism, intellect, and ability to recite poetry and debate the philosophers, her services were sought after by men from all over the Aegean coastline. The high reputation of the temple increased in visibility. The priestesses grew in numbers. Many cottage industries were added for profit, including herbal medicines, beekeeping, honey bottling and candle making, sewing, and offering of special rites of passage for young girls in the local families. Priestesses aged and stayed on until the end of their lives, so content were they with the community. Soon, they were known as more than Aphrodite's girls for their services.

But all that was, lo, over thirty years ago. Now, Tanitha found herself seeking a community where she could worship and serve as one among many equals. She desired a quiet life. And so, one day, when she awoke, she knew it was time to go.

That day, she called together the priestesses, and as they gathered, she felt the tears well up.

After a long season of discernment, the finality of it all had finally hit her. Her heart felt sore.

CHAPTER THIRTEEN

The Bee Priestesses of Crete

Do what you are most naturally suited to do and do it to the best of your ability through your life.
— Plato

Springtime arrived after a long winter of discontent, sorrow, and uncertainty. Tanitha had announced her leave-taking. She would soon move into the spare room in Phoebe's home in Cenchrea. She had decided to join the community, and her friendship with Phoebe was strong. The new movement needed more women workers and leaders, and Tanitha was eager to participate after a long rest.

Hera, her best friend, would take over the leadership of the temple at Acrocorinth. Unlike her friend's flamboyant and charismatic style, Hera was hearth, womb, and earth mother. The women could sit at her feet and pour out their hearts, and she would listen carefully, with deep concern, offering her shoulder to cry upon. It was not so much that she had great wisdom to offer but that her merciful, listening ear would elicit each woman's deeper intuitive understanding of their situation and what was being called forth in them.

Before Tanitha left, she called Althaia into her presence.

"My daughter, I have two things on my mind. Since you arrived over eight years ago, I have felt your sadness and have seen the dark night of your soul, which visits you from time to time. I realize that there has been tragedy and trauma in your life before you came here. I thought it best that your father or family not come to see you so that you might make a life for yourself here. But now that you have matured, I have sent a message to Lander Adamos, your father, to tell him about you and invite him to visit."

Althaia kept her eyes fixed on a beetle crawling across the floor toward her. She did not respond to the Head Priestess.

Tanitha took her hand, as she often would when she wanted to connect with Althaia.

"You are like a daughter to me, my dear. The one I never had the privilege of raising."

Althaia brought her head level with her mentor and leader, her eyes unwavering and clear, her face impassive, even as she saw the shining tears in Tanitha's eyes. Now she was losing a spiritual mother. What would her home here be without Tanitha?

"I am petitioning the priestess community on the isle of Crete that you might come there to live. I believe it will be a place for your dreams to flourish. I see your time here has also come to an end, according to the Oracle. You are longing, even hungry, for a larger world than the temple at Acrocorinth."

Tanitha suddenly looked tired and old, her face worn. Gently, she put her right palm against Althaia's face. Then, the Head Priestess placed her left hand on Althaia's heart.

"Home is here, wherever you go. Know that I will be with you here in your heart, as will Dionne, Melissa, Kosma, Hera, and all the others who love and know you here."

Something inside Althaia broke. As the tears slid down her face, Tanitha soothingly reminded her of her name.

"You are a child of Love. You come from Love and to Love

you shall always return! Remember your name's meaning, my sweetness, Ἀλθαία. She is one who heals, one who takes care. You are *She Who Knows*. The keeper of the medicine of herbs. You are Honesty."

Tanitha took the young woman in her arms, and their tears mingled.

A year after Tanitha left, Father never did arrive for a visit in response to the message the Head Priestess had sent to him. But the priestess community of Potnia on the Isle of Crete sent word that they would welcome Althaia warmly.

Althaia began to pack her trunk with the simple things that comprised her life there. Her three simple, woven peplos, her one silk dress for fine occasions, the veil, gloves, and protective clothing she made for herself in the bee yard. Her worn copy of the *Papyrus Ebers*, which contained hundreds of herbal recipes for women's diseases, and the *Kahun Papyrus*, with classifications of diseases for women and children. She was proud that she had a copy of prescriptions from clay tablets, written over six hundred centuries before in the ancient civilization of Sumeria.[22] She took a small apothecary of herbs to begin anew on the island.

And so, on her twenty-fifth birthday, in the August month, when the Mediterranean sun was bright hot in the arid, periwinkle sky, a chariot came to take her to the sea, where she would take a ship to Crete, accompanied by Xi, her longtime friend and courtesan.

Dionne stood weeping in the long line of gathered priestesses. She had now become a skilled midwife after many years of training. She had taken Lydia's place as the head

---

[22] Medicine Women, Elisabeth Brooke (Wheaton, IL Quest Books, 1997)

midwife. After the long, dark years of the pox pandemic and ten dead and gone from their midst, new priestesses had come. Althaia felt a surge of anticipation, alongside the heavy weight of grief, as she hugged each one of her sisters. Coming to her longtime roommate, they threw their arms around one another, wailing loudly.

Finally, Althaia pulled away, and she pressed a small marble bee carving into her friend's palm, whispering into her ear, "I will come and dance with you. When you need me, watch for the honeybee! She will come and whisper my words and sing my love to you!"

Dionne nodded through her tears.

Althaia climbed into the chariot beside Xi, and they lurched forward. Althaia remembered another day, so many years ago, as a young sixteen-year-old girl, shattered into a million pieces as the chariot rolled away from her childhood home. How she wept all the way to the sea, with Father looking straight ahead. This time, a smile tugged at the fullness of her lips. This time it was not like a bitter drink, only sweet sorrow, tempered by the exhilaration of this new adventure before her. She waved to her sister priestesses and turned to look forward to a new day.

The ship was waiting in harbor for Xi and Althaia. Though they had known one another for many years, Althaia had never spoken to Xi about his life. But this time, they had hours in a day to hear one another's stories.

"Where did you come from, Xi?" Althaia asked, after they had settled their bags and sat at the hull of the ship, imbibing the moist air of the Aegean Sea.

"My home is far away, in a land of dynasties, many rivers, silks, and spices, and also many philosophies and deities, like your country. Confucius was our teacher and the Tao taught us balance in all things."

"Where did your people come from?" Althaia continued.

"From the countryside, in a region near the Silk Road at Nanyang. My people were farmers, and they also kept silkworms. I learned to spin, with brothers, many silk textiles to sell to the city for dying and trade. As a young boy, my mother grew very ill and died. My father's sorrow knew no bounds. He sent me to the city to trade our silks. One day, I was in the marketplace and a man came to purchase. He lured me to his chariot and took me to the boat, binding my hands and ankles so I could not escape. He brought me, with many other young boys, to your country where I was quickly sold to a man who called me slave, dmōs (δμώς). One day, your Tanitha came to market where I worked for this man. She made a trade of wares with him, bringing me back to live at the Acrocorinth temple."

Althaia's brow was furrowed. She had never known a slave's story so intimately.

"I'm so sorry, Xi. It should've never happened to you. How do you deal with the sadness of your loss?"

Xi hung his head. His good humor had always been a mainstay for Althaia at the temple. They had joked and laughed and played tricks on each other as young teens. He was like a brother to her.

"I carry it here." He tapped his head. "And here."

He laid his hand on his heart.

"It will never let go of me, but I can carry on because I have met many good and kind people. Not everyone is cruel and driven by profit."

He brightened. "Besides, I am too handsome to resist! Everyone, of course, loves me!"

Althaia stroked his smooth, chestnut-colored forearm and then held his hand as they laughed together.

The boat docked after three days on the Aegean Sea. Xi and Althaia looked toward the great Mediterranean Sea before them, its endless, unruffled cobalt and emerald waters. They drank in the pure sea air as they debarked onto the Island of Crete, gateway to continents untold. The island was a gem set in the waters between worlds.

"I will attend to you until we reach your community to ensure your safety, then I will return to Corinth," Xi stated matter-of-factly.

The port city of Heraklion was abustle with ships. The marketplace seemed to lazily wander through the downtown, with buyers and sellers. It was much less busy than any port cities Althaia had ever visited.

Xi hired a chariot driver, and they set off through the winding, narrow cobbled streets, with whitewashed mud-brick buildings with ornate wooden doors. They turned south and east toward the ancient Minoan settlement of Knossos, now a Roman colony named *Colonia Iulia Nobilis*. Five kilometers from Heraklion, they entered a valley and rode up the hill of Kephala along the Kairatos River, where they entered the walled city, rolling into the center of a beehive flurry of activity.

It was high noon. The city was a vast network of over a thousand rooms, five stories high, represented by doors facing into the large commons, with colonnaded open-air walkways connecting the stairwells to the center of the city. It was clearly an administrative and commercial center, with storage buildings scattered around the interior. Roman soldiers lounged against the ceramic stone walls.

Althaia could see giant ceramic *pithoi* or five-foot-high

storage jars lining the interior of the walled city, filled with the goods of oil, wine, grain, and water. There were artisans wrapping large bales of wool for sale. It was a remarkable scene.

Xi directed the driver of their chariot to take them to the quarters of the small collection of Potnia's bee priestesses that remained there, remnants of the Minoan kings and queens of bygone days. A lone woman came scurrying out as they pulled up to the door. She was dressed elegantly, her gown—with puffy sleeves and a wide flouncy skirt—flaring from her bodice. Her hair was swept up and pinned above her head. Bowing, she welcomed the travelers.

"Come! Come in. We have been expecting you! My name is Selene, and I will take you to our beautiful queen!" She smiled warmly. "Please, wait here. I will have one of our sisters bring you refreshment of pomegranate juice."

Selene disappeared into a side door.

The interior of the main hallway was dim, even in midday. Their quarters were decorated with frescoes from the Minoan Age. As Althaia stood in the main room with Xi, her eyes began to follow the carvings and colorful, tiled pictures that decorated the room, telling an ancient story. There were legendary marine creatures, rocks, vegetation, ornate frames of the elements of sun, moon and stars, mountains and sea. Suddenly, she saw something that gave her a start. It was a statue of the bee woman who had come to her in her dreamtime. A winged woman with a skirt overlaid by golden leaves that resembled a beehive, breasts with honey dripping from her nipples, crocuses around her feet, a serpent in one hand, a large pure gold bee necklace, whose pendant showed two winged bees gently bowing forward, their large compound eyes touching as together they embraced a pollen granule with their front legs. Althaia went toward it as if in a trance, her fingers lightly tracing each detail. She turned with widened eyes toward Xi.

"Xi! Look! It's the bee lady! She has come to me in the dreamtime," Althaia whispered excitedly.

"Very, very nice. Lovely bee lady without her proper clothes." He giggled.

Althaia remembered the words of the bee woman in her dreams. 'Return to the mother. Return to the mother.' Had she finally come home?

The priestesses of Knossos were kind and hospitable. But the weary visitors could only stay one night, as Althaia was still on her journey to a community in the high altitudes of the island.

As morning dawned, Althaia's original bravado began to wane. She realized that soon the only familiar being to her in this strange and unknown place would leave her. She began to feel trepidation. It was a breathlessness and anxiety that clutched at her throat. A gnawing in her stomach. A burning sensation of fear in the back of her head.

Xi would leave her now and return to Acrocorinth.

After a breakfast of lavender tea, fish with olive oil and bread, Xi, in his usual inimitable cheerful manner, tugged at Althaia's hair and waved.

Swallowing hard, Althaia grabbed the unsuspecting boy-man and held him tightly to her, warming her body, which suddenly felt cold and rigid.

"My, my!" he intoned in his sing song voice.

"You are taking my air away, Thaia. I can't breathe!" he playfully whined.

"Go then," Althaia said with mock indignation, watching him for any sign of sadness.

All she could see was a shadow cross his eyes like a cloud across the sun for a moment.

Kissing him on each cheek, she grabbed his hand and squeezed, then released him to be on his way. Perhaps surprised by her emotion, he took one last long gaze and waved as he hoisted himself into the chariot.

"Goodbye, my friend. Until we meet again!"

And he was gone in a whirl of dust rising from the wheels and the horses' hooves.

Two priestesses watched his leave-taking. One was Selene and the other, Penelope. As Althaia turned to them, they nodded knowingly.

"It is not easy, sister. But come. You must be on your way to Limnakaro, our sister community. You will love it there. Your heart will be filled to overflowing once your homesickness has been cured."

This time, the small chariot Althaia rode was quick as lightning. Her things were not many, and the horse was young and strong. They headed even further eastward, crossing valleys, toward the Lassithi Plateau ringed by the Dikti mountains. Through gorges and along pulsating, rushing rivers and green rock fields, the horse toiled along. The sun was low in the horizon when they finally arrived at the Limnakaro plateau. Soon, they could see a couplet of stone walls in the distance where the Minoan bee priestess community nestled on the fertile soil of this plateau. Alluvial runoff from melting snow on the Dikti mountains made the soil rich.

As they rolled up to the buildings, young men surged out of the main building and surrounded the chariot.

"Chaire! Chaire!" Their voices echoed in the early evening.

Despite the summer day, the evening was cool at one thousand one hundred and twenty meters above sea level.

The fires and lamps were being trimmed and lit as Althaia was ushered into the spacious main courtyard. There was a feeling of lightness of being and warmth despite the darkening evening. Greetings sang out to the visitor as the smells of a meal rose up from the commons. She was immediately taken to the Head Priestess with the namesake of the great bee goddess, Potnia.

Like the women of Knossos, her ample figure was elegantly dressed, even in this isolated place.

"My name is Potnia, High Priestess of the Melissaes. Welcome!"

She extended her hand to Althaia, who bowed and kissed her gold signet ring with a bee inscribed.

"How was your trip, my daughter?" she inquired kindly.

"It was a magnificent view!" Althaia exclaimed.

"And how are you?" Potnia peered closely at her face in the twilight.

Tears welled up in Althaia's eyes. This sense of homesickness was unlike anything she had ever known. It was not tinged with anger, helplessness, and fear. Instead, it was like a tide, ebbing and flowing, carrying her along on its waves of sadness and gratitude. All of it was mixed up together.

"I am sad, but happy to have reached my destination."

"Tanitha spoke highly of you. She said you would bring many gifts to our communities on the island here. We are eager for you to settle in. I will have one of the priestesses show you to your room. Please wash and change your clothing, prepare to come to dinner within the hour." Her voice was strong and gracious. "Please allow yourself to feel your sadness; know your tears. Only then, when the rains have passed, can the well-watered earth of your soul come to fruition!"

She smiled, her front tooth overlapping slightly in a mouth of small, white teeth. She was beautiful.

Althaia could feel a small flame of warmth curl up from the embers of her heart as she took in the good will and compassion extended toward her by Potnia.

"I will," she said resolutely.

Potnia was right. As the months passed, fall into winter into spring, soon Althaia's homesickness began to recede. She threw her energy into setting up her herbal house that winter. The lush fields became crackly and barren. All the harvests of grain and beans, fruits and vegetables were in the storage house.

During that first winter, Althaia was taught many new skills by her sister priestesses. Sophia taught her to spin wool and spool it, ready to be dyed in the large vats come spring.

Ophelia taught her clay works. She learned to make the Minoan *pithois*, with colorful waves and spirals, adorned with winged horses, radiant suns, and sea creatures. She added her own signature images of herbs to the large storage pots or delicate decorative vases of azul, cinnamon, burnt orange, and earth tones.

Iris taught her how to care for their menagerie of animals, from sheep to chickens, donkeys and doves and corvids.

In return, Althaia taught them herbs and took over the care of the honeybee hives in the skeps stacked three high, built into the stone walls. That winter, she bottled the honey preserved in vats and made bottles of mead for purchase in the spring. It was a time of unparalleled wonder for Althaia, as she experienced the industrious and joyful energy of Potnia and her Melissaes. The priests of Zeus lived close by, and they traded food, wares, skills, and assistance to one another.

Winters were times of rest, reflection, creativity, and healing. The time of harvest and storing away had been completed. The cold time was for community. Many days, the women soaked in the steaming baths that had been constructed at the perimeter of the commons. Sacred herbs were steeped in the waters, and Althaia settled into them with a sigh of pleasure and relief. Afterwards, the woman smoothed on warm olive oils infused with flowers and myrrh and thyme essences, massaging one another's feet and hands and limbs.

At night, the women shared stories around the bonfire, lit once every seventh day in the commons of the courtyard. There were recitations of poetry, speaking heart messages, and visions from the dreamtime to one another. There was sharing of delicious food, fresh from the cooking hearths. It was here that Althaia first heard the myth of Aristaeus, the god of beekeeping.

After causing the death of Eurydice, who stepped upon a snake while fleeing from him, her nymph sisters killed all of his bees to punish Aristaeus. Witnessing the empty hives, he wept. It was then that the wise Porteus advised him to sacrifice four bulls and four cows to honor Eurydice. He complied, leaving their fat lifeless bodies to rot. As their corpses decomposed, bees rose up from the putrid stink, returning to fill his empty hives.

"You see," said Evangeline. "This is a story of repentance when one has gone astray. Amends must be made in order for healing to happen, and the resurrection of bees and their fertility of new life will spring up again!" she said triumphantly.

As the night wore on and the honey wine flowed like an underground cistern, the women brought out their instruments of flutes and harps and drums. The moon rose cold and bright. Their dark figures danced around the fires, singing and whirling under her white eye.

The music was what pried open the lid of Althaia's heart, opening up her wellspring of joy again. She remembered the sheer grace of playing the flute as a young girl, and all the tunes and melodies came cascading back. She associated this time with her dear Helena, with unbounded laughter, silly play, a young girl's freedom. Then there came the memory of Adrian. The sweet warmth of his breath. The touch of his skin, bringing all her senses alive. If music was the food of love, it swelled within her like a banquet.

Years ago, she had stopped the cutting of her wrists, but now the despair of that long night of her heart began to lift bit by bit. She began to understand the bee woman dream more intimately. The serpent represented an offer of healing to her heart. The bees that swarmed into her head as messengers of wisdom. They came to inhabit her with the sacred knowledge and intelligence of creation's gifts through her healing herbs and the bees. The Great Mother, Potnia, the bee queen, offered her, finally, belonging. She was a part of community.

In so many ways, it resonated with her heartstrings, who she truly knew herself to be. An equal among equals.

The bloody wound of why she landed in Corinth began to form a smooth scar in this place. The temple business at Acrocorinth was stern and austere. It stood as a fortress in the midst of an economic system of social, political, and intellectual pursuit driven by endless profit and competition. The temple was a place to assuage the hunger that grew out of a hyper masculine world. To sooth it by the feminine soul of love, sensuality, beauty, and fleeting connection. The temples of the priestesses provided ample generosity for the body and soul. Even if a man could not find these in the domestic spheres of his home, he could come there for a time to forget his troubles. Yet, for the priestesses, this temple was still set within a patriarchal system.

Potnia's temple, however, was filled with color. Her fertile grounds were awash in art, literature, domestic peace, the wisdom of the animals and earth, collaboration, healing, and health. It was a place of peace, creativity and joy, music and love, minus the services of pleasuring male hungers.

Here, Althaia could pour out her gifts like libations, and grow in new ways she could not have imagined. There was a reciprocity and joy in sharing life together. It was on a level she had not heretofore known.

Yes, she had returned home, true to the Bee Woman's clarion call.

CHAPTER FOURTEEN

Mary the Tower

Then Mary arose, embraced them all, and began to speak to her brothers:
"Do not remain in sorrow and doubt,
For his Grace will guide you and comfort you"[23]

Spring came late that year. The earth was moisture-laden, creating mudslides everywhere. But as the sap rose, the energy began to rise in the women of Potnia. Soon, it would be time to plant as the equinox approached and the dark moon beckoned. The queen bee had already begun to lay her eggs in the beehives. As the sun drew closer to the earth, soon the bees' transparent bodies would shine and soar in the sun-drenched mornings. They would begin their long forage for nectar and pollen through the peak of the harvest season. Much like the Melissaes, their lives were dictated by the sun and the cycles of the seasons.

As warmth crept across the dormant land, drying up its excess, the crocuses pushed through the soil. The women of this sister community of Knossos dedicated their annual celebration of spring and thanksgiving to the fertility goddess, Cyprian, also known as Aphrodite, daughter of Zeus and Dione. The men's

---

[23] Jean Yves-Leloup, The Gospel of Mary Magdalene (Rochester, VT: Inner Traditions International, 2002), 99.

community of Zeus would join them for this big celebration. There would be worship, music, and dancing, with tables laden with rich food, honey wine, and pomegranate juice.

A new woman had joined the community that spring. Her name was Diana, and she had come from afar, from the northern Israelite and Samarian lands of the goddess Astarte, Aphrodite's twin. She was very small in stature, standing neck to neck with the goats. Her countenance was childlike and full of mischievous fun and playfulness. She was the same age as Althaia, give or take a year or two. Diana was filled with stories of the land from which she arrived. A free spirit, she seemed unattached, footloose, and fancy-free. She became one of Althaia's fervent bee apprentices, so enamored with the bee's vitality, communal thriving, mysterious habits and ways. But, of course, she was most delighted by the gifts of honey and wax from the beehive, choosing to spend long days in the honey house shaping small images from the wax—creatures of her imagination and those around her on the farm and in the forest and sea.

"Diana, what was your community like in Sidon?" Althaia queried, as they rattled along in the mule drawn wagon to check the hives in the grasslands around the community. The spring flowers were popping, and the food was a most excellent habitat for the honeybee pollinators.

"My goodness, it was very large compared to here. There were many more women dedicated to the temple of Astarte!" Diana exclaimed. "I was an artist there, making fine jewelry out of gold and silver and semi-precious stones. I hear I had been there since a tiny babe, but I don't remember a thing!"

Her face grew serious.

"I have no memory of my real mother. Instead, I had many, many mothers! They all fawned and fought over my attentions. I was as well-loved as a little piglet. My feet rarely hit the ground as a babe!"

Her laughter erupted from somewhere deep within, a cross between a giggle and a snort.

Althaia smiled.

"May I ask why you were sent here?" Althaia continued.

"I think I had become a nuisance." Diana grew sober again. "I sold my wares in the market at Jerusalem once a month. There, I met a woman whom I loved. She was like a big sister to me, visiting my stall of jewelry often. Her name was Mary. She hailed from the town of Magdala, which means, 'The Tower'. It fit her well because she was such a giant in soul stature. Her beauty was legendary. But her chosen taste was simple. She dressed in plain clothing and pulled her mahogany hair pulled back in a tie. No jewelry, except for a dove necklace I had configured for her as a gift. I heard rumors that she was an Egyptian princess once, with much wealth. But she never confirmed this for me. She shared her wealth with those who followed the master. His name was Y'shua, the Hebrew and Nazarite teacher who eventually became the figurehead of *The Way*, a Messianic Judaic reform movement."

Now she had captured Althaia's attention. Her ears perked up. *The Way* was the name of the bold movement catching fire throughout Asia Minor, Greece, and Macedonia. All the names associated with this movement rose up in Althaia's mind. The Apostle Paul, Phoebe of Cenchrea, Prisca and Aquilla of Corinth, Lydia of Thyatira, and now Tanitha.

This young woman had been exposed to the same movement at its origin point, Judea. It was known as a hotbed of Jewish zealots, who clashed with their Roman occupiers.

"What did this Mary, the Tower, say?" Althaia's curiosity

grew.

"She shared so much with me about the teachings of this master rabbi. I learned that she was his beloved. She was at the foot of the Roman's torture tool, the cross, where they killed him. She never left him until he took his last breath and they brought him down for the grave." Diana's usually cheerful lips became grim.

"After he died, she was the first eyewitness to his empty grave, along with her sisters in the faith. Those who followed him believe he was resurrected, according to Mary's testimony."

Diana's eyes grew distant as though she were reliving the story.

"In Sidon, we heard of this man, Y'shua's great suffering. Once, he had visited our land and met one of our own, at our ancestors, Jacob and Rachel's, water well. Her life was changed forever from the oppression of her life as a woman at the hands of many men. You see, rabbis never speak to Samarian men, much less their women. Though we are half siblings, we are hated as 'less than' orthodox Jews."

"So what does all this have to do with your coming here?" Althaia held the reins of the horse and stilled its motion as the wagon came to a stop at the first bee yard.

"I began to question too many things at the temple. I wondered about the message of this rabbi and his beloved, Mary. It was a simple message of loving one's neighbor as they loved their one god and themselves. Even loving one's enemy!" Diana smile was wry. "It seemed so simple. Yet so hard. A message of peace for all the strife in our society. Don't we live with such divisions in our politics, religion, class, and sex in society?"

Her question was rhetorical. Althaia nodded in agreement.

"Such loving kindness is not readily given among all the

sects of gods and goddesses, between men and women, among leaders, occupiers, nation states, and common people. Mary believed that's why her dear one was tortured and killed. He had also become a nuisance." Diana's eyes were fiery.

Althaia saw the heart of a rebel shining in her new beekeeper and sister priestess' eyes. For one so young, her words were clear, her heart courageous and strong. She could see why her queries and passion would be a threat to the temple.

"I was barred from leaving the temple to go down to Jerusalem to sell my jewelry. There was little I could contribute any more, either financial resources or ideas. Everything I said seemed so dangerous to my sisters. I tried to help them understand that we could absorb and practice his teachings to make ourselves and our community better. But they wouldn't hear of it. Even after our Syrophoenician sister confronted him about a comment that showed the racism of his culture toward ours, he was willing to listen and change his heart. Truly a master. His maleness unthreatened by a woman," Diana said quietly.

The conversation had been plenty for one day. Althaia swung herself down from the wagon and began to unload the equipment for smoking and prying the honeycombs apart in the ceramic skeps. She gave the protective clothing to Diana and they suited up side by side. She handed the smoking jar to Diana to light.

"You are a brave heart, my sister. I am glad you think for yourself. Now I see why you have come here to our community. We need strong sisters! Aphrodite… Astarte, as you know her, is no shrinking violet." Althaia smiled at her through their veils and reached out to draw Diana close in an embrace. "Welcome!"

They laughed together as the bees danced around them, soaring toward the sun. They returned in an eternal circle, to dive into the hives that held their precious treasure, pollen, and honey.

Food and nutrition for the future generations of the whole hive.

As summer came to an end, Potnia called Althaia to her quarters for a visit.

"You have been here for over twelve full moons. Our harvest is stored. I would like you to consider a long journey to Athens to study at the Temple of Hygiea. There resides one of the great clans of Asclepiads, in the tradition of Asclepius, the god of healing. Many women physicians have studied there. I believe it is time for you to gain more knowledge to bring back to our Knossos sisterhood."

Althaia's eyes widened.

"You... I..." she stammered, with a small nervous laugh. "How do I deserve this, Head Priestess?"

Through her head cascaded a cacophony of voices. What if I encounter my family members? Will they find out I am there? How will it feel to return to this place of so many memories?

"Do you know that was my childhood home?" Althaia said in a low voice.

"So Tanitha told me," Potnia said kindly. "I think it is time to return there and make peace in your heart with those family members lost to you."

Althaia's eyes were fixed on the small circle of light to the sky beyond that room. She blinked back tears.

"My dear daughter, I would not send you alone. You will have the company of a few of our sisters, including Diana. Also, some of the priests of Zeus will come along to study." Potnia implored her priestess to look at her by laying her plump hand firmly to quiet Althaia's fingers, which mindlessly twisted the shawl draped over her lap.

Finally, Althaia looked at her. She felt the chill of a

premonition. This would be an adventure unlike any other. The excitement of traveling again, the enticement of studying the medicines even more deeply—these things riveted her attention. The old family sorrows, however, brought her again to the edge of that vast canyon of despair. That place where she felt she was falling, falling, endlessly. She felt the clench in the pit of her stomach, the cold fear gripping her heart, strangling her breath.

"I will go." Althaia grasped Potnia's hand as a lifeline.

"I will go." She sighed heavily.

Potnia drew her close to kiss the top of her head.

"You will leave by the end of this month, traveling by sea to Corinth, and then a chariot to Athens. I will make all the necessary arrangements for you, including lodging. I promise, it will be fine. You are strong in body and spirit. This will only make you more whole. You'll see."

Potnia's face was radiant, as always. A light beamed outward from an inner landscape that Althaia imagined with the eye of her own heart. She longed for that radiance.

Athens came into view as the chariot caravan of assorted priests and priestesses from the Minoans rolled along together. Athens sprawled before them in her white, limestone buildings. The Acropolis and four hills of Lykavitos, Hill of the Nymphs, Pnyx, and Aeropagus stood above the city. The Parthenon, housing Athena, the goddess of the city, rose in majestic, marbled splendor. A feeling of restlessness settled on Althaia. Eager to be settled and begin her studies. Anxious to face the demons that lived here, and longing to reclaim the joyful memories, she would send a note to Helena as soon as they arrived.

Diana was bubbly and funnier than usual. The travelers often dissolved in laughter at her antics, her elastic face mimicking the people, first of Corinth and now of Athens, with the Stoic in earnest debate. She imitated haughty women dragging children behind them. The fat merchant at the docks screaming at the ship's captain. The dog following the huckster as he tried to sell his wares.

Finally, they came to a stop outside the temple at Hygeia. The ornate facade of the double-carved wooden doors were inscribed with the Rod of Asclepius. The stone walls were impassive. Other than the doors, there was no indication of the greatness of this community.

The group was warmly welcomed by the Hygeia herself, the Head Priestess. They were settled in their separate quarters, men and women. They would live in simple rooms, with only a table for their books and personal items, a single bed with a worn woolen blanket, a basin with a pitcher of water, and one shared lamp.

Althaia quickly dropped her bag in her room, took her ink writing utensil, and scratched a note to her Helena:

My dear friend, who would believe it! I am in the great town of Athens again. I have come to my old home, this time as an accomplished woman of herbal medicine. I live on the island of Crete now, and the Head Mistress of Potnia has sent myself, two other sisters, and three brothers to study here with the Asclepians! I must see you at once! I cannot wait to visit my darling Zoe Althaia. Please do call on me here at the temple of Hygeia.

Always yours, Althaia

She also wrote one more note, this time to Daphne, her servant from long ago, beginning with the affectionate salutation from her childhood μητέρα.

Mama Daphne, I have longed to see you for so many years

now. I wish I had written sooner. But as you know, my heart was heavy when I left so long ago. I could not be weighed down further by seeing Mother or Father. But I always remembered you and longed to see you again. Perhaps you know I spent eight years at the temple at Acrocorinth. Now I live on the Island of Crete with the Melissae priestesses of the Knossans. I am very, very happy there! I will be studying here in Athens, at the Asclepian community, for three full moons. My heart longs to see you and also my sisters and Egan. May I come to visit?

All my love, Althaia

Folding the notes carefully, Althaia put her seal of the honeybee on each one, along with the address, and went to find a servant to take the messages to their intended recipients.

The studies were satisfying and deepening. Every morning, as the students gathered, there would be an altar draped in white cloth, vervain burning, the smoke rising above the anemone flower-bedecked altar. There would be songs and prayers, interspersed with silence. It was a time of centering and peace before the onslaught of the new day.

In the classroom, Althaia learned maps of the body and the web of energy that connect the physical tissue, bone, and breath. She learned about the subtle energy fields, which could also become blocked, keeping one from feeling vital and balanced in emotion and spirit. The seven vortices of energy extended from the crown of the head down to the forehead to the third eye, the throat, the heart, the abdomen, and finally, to the base of the spine. These seven energy fields extended through the dense physical body, and any disturbance in the physical structure, through trauma or unresolved suffering, could dull the vital energy, creating listlessness, disease, and eventually death.

As Diana said, "The Creator has put all this into place, and we are called to bring this wisdom through our compassionate touch and understanding."

Althaia brought her knowledge of herbs to the table, and the gathered students discussed the properties and essences of plants, mapping them with the body's physical and energy fields. Herbs were well known to carry healing through their high vibration, attuned to the soil, waters, sun, moon, and the earth's fields of rotating energy. All the elementals of the earth worked in a synergistic way to bring healing for all creatures—human and non-human.

Althaia also taught about the gifts from the honeybee hives as tools of health and healing. Flowing from the queen herself, honey was a magical and sacred substance that could be used for healing wounds. Turning nectar into honey was a task completed by thousands of worker bees. The libations of honey wine and a dollop of honey each day could strengthen the immune system. Honey was the food of the muses and poets! This sweet elixir, with endless preservative qualities, was also used to embalm at the end of life. A pot of honey was placed next to the deceased loved one to guide them to their eternal home, since bees were seen as resurrection and the fertility of life itself.

Diana was becoming Althaia's shadow, absorbing everything possible from her sister's apothecary of wisdom. At night, the two women, sharing a bedroom, talked endlessly about the days' studies.

Again, Diana brought Mary the Tower to bear on the conversation.

"Mary showed me the path of self-emptying love. What an awakened heart looks and feels like! She said Ihidaya, the single-hearted One, the Rabbi Y'Shua, showed her the way and she became his equal."

There was that word again that Althaia had heard years ago from Phoebe. Ihidaya.

Diana continued, "As he was facing his very own death, Mary sensed his heart. Acting as his priestess one day, she poured a year's worth of the unguent, nard, onto his feet, wiping them with her hair. This prepared him for his end. Her heart was broken, but she loved with so much purity, integrity, and intentionality. My sister, Mariam, showed me that this path of The Way only requires a fidelity of heart. Not a perfect life, but a purity of love that is self-giving, over and over."

Diana continued undaunted, "She taught me that learning to love in relationship with others is the only way we can truly be transformed. It is about reciprocity and mutuality. We cannot live in a high-minded tower by ourself."

"She sounds like a very wise and advanced woman," Althaia responded absentmindedly.

"It was her passionate relationship with Ihidaya, the single-hearted, single-minded one that healed her completely. It was their trusting love that transfigured her. The marriage of their bodies and souls changed her life!" Diana said excitedly. "Don't you see? She is a living example of what we are studying! She was healed in *all seven* of her energy vortices through her love of Y'Shua. She wrote it down in her very own book, called The Gospel of Mary Magdalene."

"Did you read this book?" Althaia stopped what she was doing to listen to Diana, who never seemed to tire of talking about Mary the Tower.

"No, but she told me everything she was writing," Diana continued. "She was the most fully human and enlightened woman I have ever met. Humble and loving at the same time. She was not afraid. She looked into the jaws of death and became free of all it threatened."

Althaia laughed. "You have become quite the orator, Diana! Maybe you should join this movement, *The Way*?"

Diana jumped up on the chair, catching her balance as it shook under her force. Taking a mock stance of the Apostle Paul, she began to stroke her imaginary beard. Throwing back her head, she mimicked his booming voice. Althaia laughed at her antics. Inside, she sighed. If only she could be freed in the same way as she faced the demons of her own family.

Diana's voice continued as the Apostle, in her best bellowing voice, "*Yes!* She *was* delivered from seven demons or cravings. This woman, Mary of Magdala, haunted and clinging to the past, finally released all the baggage when she met Y'Shua."

Diana flung her imaginary baggage across the room with a flourish, lost her balance, and dissolved on the floor.

Quickly picking herself up, and brushing herself off as though offended, she moved closer to Althaia, whispering with emphasis.

"Mary taught us to let go of *False* pride. *Endless* desire for things. Judgment. A craving to die. *Enslavement* to her body's needs. The *false* peace of pleasure. *Rage*." Her voice rose and fell with emphasis as she held up her index finger, shaking it at Althaia.

"That, my dear, is quite a list!" Althaia rolled her eyes.

But inside, she was calculating her own list. She could identify with the craving to die from endless grief and sorrow. The bouts of despair that drove her to the brink for so many years. The rage toward her father. The judgment of her mother. The clinging to comforts to distract herself from her depression. Althaia could feel the congestion of her emotions as Diana spoke.

"Come, Diana. Please, stop talking!" Althaia threw her soft

slipper at her friend, hitting her in the head as Diana, pretending to be stricken, fell across her bed. "Let's go to the baths here on the grounds. I am done with your words, words, words for this day."

"I am going to go with my birthday suit this time." Diana's giggling snort made them both laugh as they took their towels and headed to the warm spas, the moist air filled with the scent of sweet herbs.

It was a place of deep relaxation for their minds and bodies.

Both notes arrived the same day, one from Helena and one from Father.

Althaia should have known. Daphne was not literate. Of course she had handed it over to Father.

Helena was falling all over herself in eagerness. She asked Althaia to come to her and Aegeus' home at the end of her time of study. They wanted to have a special rite to dedicate Zoe Althaia to the goddess Athena.

The note from Father was more ominous. He was sending a chariot for her on the next day after her studies, in the midafternoon, as the sun began to sink from its zenith in the sky.

Althaia began to feel her heart beat in her mouth. She was frightened.

Father's chariot was exactly on time. Althaia stood in front of the temple with a small bag of herbs and personal items. She was determined not to stay overnight.

"Daughter of Lander Adamos?" queried the driver, who hopped down and bowed, offering his hand to assist her up into the chariot.

It did not take them long to drive from one side of the city to the other. Memories tumbled over Althaia as they drove past the park where she and Adrian had parted ways. The side street where she had often raced from her home to Helena's in the next neighborhood. The wide boulevard of flowering bushes and towering cedar trees that led to her childhood home.

Finally, they arrived. The sun was slipping in the western sky. Surely it was time for dinner.

Althaia took a deep breath and walked up the stairs to the portico that protected the front door. She tried the handle. It was open. As she entered, the cold marble floor rose up to meet her. The latch clicked behind her. It was silent. The darkening halls were gloomy and shadowy. No sounds of children laughing or chasing one another, the twins' laughter reverberating. Yet these sounds still rang in Althaia's head. Suddenly, she heard steps, a sound of shuffling in her direction.

"Father?" Althaia made out a bent figure toiling to approach her.

Lander's neck bent his face toward the floor. He had a difficult time lifting his head, his hair now completely white. His eyes rolled up to meet hers as he moved toward her. He did not pick up his feet. His arms were stiff as they stretched out to meet her. She could see tears shining on his cheeks even in the dim light.

"Father," Althaia said, almost as an exclamation of anguish.

Without her consent, he moved toward her, putting his stiff arms around her, and pulling her to him as he wept inconsolably.

Diana's words rang in her ears, *"Only in learning to love, in relationship with others, can we be transformed. It is about reciprocity, mutuality—not in a high-minded tower by ourself."*

Father pulled away and shouted, "Daphne! Daphne! Come quick. Daphne!"

Althaia saw a woman scurrying toward them as she wiped

her hands on an apron. Daphne also was looking old. The lines of her face etched deeply. Her gray bun sagged onto her neck. But her love shone and sparkled as she saw Althaia.

"Dear Althaia!" she shouted. "Althaia is home! Praise be to the goddess above!"

And she fell on her knees and bowed her forehead to the floor before Althaia.

Althaia, embarrassed, touched Daphne gently on her shoulder, then knelt down and took her beloved servant's hands in her own.

"How I have longed to see you, dear Daphne."

The women wept as they embraced, their arms wrapping around one another, their tears spilling down their clothes to wet the cold marble floor. They sat shoulder to shoulder, breast to breast, cheek to cheek, and rocked gently back and forth, back and forth.

As the chill of autumn surrounded them, Daphne lit the fires so they could continue to sit out in the garden with the pungent smells of the fallen leaves wafting to their nostrils. She called to Calista to join them, the only one left in the large mansion of what was once 'home'. Egan had gone off to the Peloponnese Peninsula to learn the skills of war and prepare for the athletic games with his companion. Calliope had her own household to run with six children.

"Calista sits in her room all day long," Daphne said, her brows deeply furrowed. "I don't know why she is so troubled since her dancing tour of the islands many moons ago. She came back almost mute. Refused to talk to anyone. Shut herself away and mostly draws, reads, and sometimes takes a walk in the neighborhoods or takes a horse down to the Mediterranean to ride for hours."

Althaia noticed immediately that Mother was nowhere. She felt a deep sense of relief but also concern. Where was she? When would be the right time to ask? She walked among the garden, spent from its summer's finery. The evening flew away, and soon the stars were lit above. Finally, she came to the table with Father, where he sat reading papyrus documents for work. They both waited for Calista to join them, waited for Daphne to serve the meal.

"Father, why is Mother not here?" Althaia finally got up the courage to ask.

Lander looked up at her, his gaze resting upon his eldest daughter after nine years. His heart had ached for so long to see her. The sorrow of what he had done aged him way beyond his fifty years.

Finally, he sighed heavily. "Althaia, after you left, I wanted to come and see you. So much. But Tanitha would not allow it."

He hung his head in shame. "I know the temple at Acrocorinth well. I visited there often. Tanitha was a favorite of mine, intelligent, witty, and kind."

"I know this already, Father," Althaia said coldly.

Looking up again at her, his eyes darted about as he contemplated whether to tell her the whole truth.

Althaia softened. "Go ahead, Father. I'm listening. I do not hold it against you after all these years."

Nodding, he continued, "Your mother was a very unhappy woman. She caught a whiff of my infidelity. She began to have an affair with a man I know. A colleague of mine. This is punishable by death, my daughter, you do know this?"

Althaia sucked in her breath and nodded.

"I try to be a reasonable man. I believe the law is there to restrain. To rebuke. And to punish. Truth must eventually come out, and morality be restored and elevated. Wisdom is learning from one's mistakes. I failed your mother. She could've divorced me on grounds of cruelty or excess, but instead she chose the love of another man."

He became silent for a moment.

"Or perhaps it wasn't love but the feeling of being lusted after, seen, desired, welcomed. Either way, I was absent and she longed for my presence. And she betrayed me. So, I chose to divorce her instead. Through mutual consent, we parted ways. The man with whom she had an affair did leave his wife and family. They live together in Corfu, a most beautiful island. I hear she is dancing again and very, very happy. Me? I am an old man, destroyed by my lies, my overwork, and my poor decision to send you away."

Lander leaned toward Althaia.

"Can you forgive me?"

Again, the tears glinted in his eyes. Althaia had always known her father to be gentler, more kind, and of good heart than her mother. But rarely had he shown such tenderness through his tears.

"Father," she whispered. "I forgive you."

As he put a large hand on top of hers, they both were startled by the ghost of a presence that had silently appeared to stand behind Althaia.

"Calista!" Althaia leaped up, sending the chair careening backwards.

Calista recoiled. "I'm, I'm sorry, I'm sorry. I… I… I… Is that you, Althaia?"

Calista began to weep, her face wrenched by pain.

"Oh, yes! Yes, my dear, it's me!" Althaia approached her

sister to hug her, only to have Calista step back into the shadows, beyond the circle of the firelight.

"Calista," she said more gently. "Please come and sit with us. Daphne will bring the dinner out momentarily."

Calista put her head down, a strange, anxious tic causing her head to pull to one side. Althaia patted the chair next to her.

"Come, my beloved Calista. Sit near me."

Calista was breathing heavy and fast. But she came to sit as Daphne bustled onto the fire-lit portico with the rich feast she had prepared—roasted chicken rubbed with garlic, fresh flat bread with olive oil, and a leafy green salad of arugula, cress, asparagus, celery, and fennel.

And the small family of three sat together, mostly in silence, and ate.

The last week of her studies came to an end. Althaia was ready to return to the island of Crete. But she had one last, joyful obligation. She was invited to Zoe Althaia's blessing ceremony. It was at the high temple of the Parthenon, with the priestess of Athena presiding.

O Sacred Mother. You will never leave this little one. We give gratitude for your life energy that has animated Zoe Althaia. Sustain her in body, soul and mind. May she offer back her whole self and being one day, just as her parents now dedicate her to you in this, your temple. You are love. You are fertility. You are life itself. Now guard this child to her dying day. Blessed be.

And the child received the sacred incense, as her parents Helena and Aegeus placed a myrtle wreath on her tiny head, sprinkling holy waters upon her soft baby skin. Then they sat her down next to the bowl of water as she splashed and laughed heartily, her pink dress becoming soaked.

"Come, Althaia, namesake of our baby girl. Please give her a blessing also!" Helena cried as Aegeus nodded approvingly.

Althaia stepped toward the child and picked her up. The baby turned and looked at her intently, not taking her eyes off this woman who suddenly held her in her arms.

Sweet Zoe Althaia, may the dove of peace fly with you all the days of your life!

May the bee touch your lips and bring you health and sweetness and beauty.

And may no hair on your head ever be harmed as the red, red rose of Athena guards and protects you.

Althaia then turned to hand baby Zoe to her mother, as she dug in her bag to pull out a small pot with honey in it. It was a beautiful pot, made in the Minoan style, with turquoise and dolphins swimming through the waves zigzagging around the clay circumference.

"Here, my dear friend. Put this among Zoe's things to remember her auntie Althaia. Tell her who I am. Tell her I will come again to see her and, some day, perhaps she will visit me!"

The two women hugged, with Zoe squeezed between them until she began to squirm and cry out. They laughed and pulled apart, each putting up a hand toward the other, interlacing their fingers, and holding them together for a moment in midair.

"Please do join us for some food and drink as we make merry in our garden!" Helena begged.

"Yes! Althaia, come to our home and celebrate with other family members!" Aegeus enjoined.

Althaia shook her head. "I must go, dear friends. Even now, the chariots to return are being readied."

She kissed Helena on the lips, and Aegeus kissed her cheeks as they stood in a circle of friendship and care, savoring these last moments. What she knew she still needed to do was spend some time with Calista. She would go pack and ready her bags this afternoon and evening so she could spend the whole day tomorrow with her sister.

As her time in Athens had come to an end, there was a bitter sweetness, which was the way of life itself. Some small triumphs and other unfinished things.

That night, as she drifted to sleep, Althaia heard an owl.

"Hoo hoooo. Hoo hooo."

Its haunting voice rang through the darkness.

CHAPTER FIFTEEN

Loss of a Soul

O hearth, O heartbeat of the whole, your dark light dance began the times, the days and seasons, seconds, years, the ages' rhythms and the rhymes. O Fire, O firmament and sea, your center did conceive and bear its male and female, waltz of life each plant, creature and its seed. (O God, Great Womb)[24]

The day dawned bright and cold as they entered the last of the calendar year. Winter was afoot. The travelers would leave the day after tomorrow to return to Crete via way of Corinth overnight. Althaia was eager to spend the day with her sister, Calista. Perhaps they could take the horses down to the sea to ride on the beach and talk. But before she could hire a chariot to take her to the home of Lander, a somber messenger came and pressed a summons into her hand.

"Come quickly, daughter. I must see you immediately."

The messenger hoisted her up into the chariot after she told Diana she must go.

"I will return soon, Diana."

"Enjoy some windblown sea air for me!" Diana teased.

The round, fading orb of the full, bone-white moon was still

---

[24] text, Harris J. Loewen, Assembly Songs 1983, Music, James W. Bixel, Assembly songs 1983, (Newton Ks: Faith and Life Press) 155

high in the sky as the sun began to lift the blanket of darkness in the east. Althaia entered her father's house, as she had done so many times. Father shuffled toward her.

"She's gone. Calista is gone. By her own hand. We found her this morning, Daphne and I." He began to cry.

Althaia saw a broken man standing before her. She stared at him, her gaze unwavering. She could not take it in. Beautiful Calista. Tall, slender, willowy, graceful, quiet Calista. Althaia felt the same old dissociation begin, her awareness, her consciousness rising out of her body and moving to the corner of the room to look down on the tragic scene. Only she and her father, alone in Mother's old parlor room. There was something sinister and eerie about the house. Althaia no longer wanted to remain there. Her soul was not safe. Perhaps Calista had known the same feeling.

Lander began to retell the story in a halting way.

"Thaia, Daphne came to prepare breakfast in the early hours of the morning. When she went to call Calista to come for breakfast, she was not in her room. She asked me to attend to finding her so the first meal of the day could be served."

His voice broke, "I found her… hang… hanging from the old Cypress tree."

Lander was unable to finish as he breathed heavily.

"Where is Daphne?" Althaia demanded.

"She was so overwrought that I sent her home to be with her family." Lander's voice was almost inaudible.

"Calista left a letter addressed to you." Father handed her a papyrus page, rolled and tied. In her neat handwriting, she had written Althaia's name.

As Althaia began to read, she understood that her sister had always been the most vulnerable, the least resilient and equipped in their family for the cruelties of life. The invisible demons of the family had haunted her, but the very real abuses of her own experience had eventually destroyed her sister.

My dear sister. Seeing you again after so many moons has been a small joy in my sea of endless pain. I never knew why you left our family when you did. I was fourteen. You were the same age as I when, two years later, I went on my tour of the islands, bringing the art of classical dance to many. It was an exhilarating tour. Many were grateful. I haven't told anyone what happened one night. So, now I will tell you. There was much frivolity and gaiety at one home where I was to stay that night. The rich food and wine flowed. After the guests left, my travel companion went to bed. The man of the house invited me to continue to perform my dance for only he and his sons. I resisted. I did not feel that this would come to a good end. It was true. But I also felt obligated to my host. Each of them had their way with me that night. I was a virgin, and they were eager. I awoke the next morning with shame and a body pain so overpowering, it seared my mind. From that I never recovered. I could not tell anyone. So, now I have told you. I so longed for you to come and rescue me for many years. One by one, everyone left. You, Mother, Calliope, Egan. I fantasized and imagined how you would look as you rode to our house. But you never came. Then, I realized, when I finally met you this week again, after so many years, that I could never put such a burden upon your shoulders, to care for me. You are so happy and content. Your life is rich with possibilities and your service to the community. Your herbal medicines and bee mastery is a beautiful thing. Please don't be angry. I can no longer carry on in the prison of my mind. Every day, it is as though I am drowning in the sea, struggling to keep my head above water. Pray for me. Perhaps the underworld will be a better hell than this. Your sister, Calista.

Lander watched her face as she read. But her features were impassive, rendering no information. Finally, she rolled the paper back up and carefully replaced the tie. Looking at Father, she began.

"Calista was raped by a family of men on her dance tour. She never told anyone. She suffered for many years."

Stopping, Althaia let her hands drop into her lap. She felt herself watching from the far ceiling of the room.

Lander began to remember, his voice dull, how important it was for Mother that Calista continue her classical dance and go on this trip. How Phaedra was so eager for her daughter to pick up where she had left off after her marriage and children. In a monotone, Lander finally revealed a family secret that made Althaia's numbing complete.

"Your mother, Phaedra, knew suicide intimately. She was damaged by your grandmother's death, also by her own hand. Grandmother, wife of Demopoulos, who left her abandoned after he died at sea. It was devastating for your mother. She never recovered."

Althaia began to understand that the soul sickness in their family ran deep. Her mother's desperate attempts to keep her own head above water as the sea closed in around her so many times. She imagined the meanness that comes from a lifetime of trying to outpace the demon of dark despair. She began to understand how her mother's trauma had been inflicted upon her own daughter, Althaia. Unconsciously and unknowingly, Mother lashed out in a desperate attempt at self-preservation from a world of judgment. Now, the despair from her own trauma, that had afflicted Althaia for a lifetime, had taken her sister in a moment, without warning.

Though Athenians normally cremated their dead, Father and his two daughters, Althaia and Calliope, determined that Calista's perfect, porcelain beauty would not be destroyed in the fires. On the second day, though her neck and jaw showed ugly black and blue bruises and swelling, the sisters set about with Daphne to wash Calista's body with myrrh and aloes in her bedroom. Surrounded by all their sister's things—pictures of dancers, her harp, the chartreuse silk bedspread, her small dainty shoes—the sisters chatted casually about Calliope's life and children. They rubbed the sweet rose oil into her now cold, lifeless skin, dressing her in one of her flowing periwinkle dance peplos, and crowning Calista's head with a laurel wreath. Except for the bruising, she looked queenly.

Suddenly, nothing was normal. There was a gash in the air, sucking the breath out of the room.

"Althaia, how could I have missed the signs?" Calliope sobbed as she rubbed, her tears mingling with the oil they smoothed on their sister. "I knew she was unhappy, but I ceased my regular visits to Father and Calista after our third child."

Althaia's usually matter-of-fact and wickedly humorous sister was now kneeling, face downward, forehead on the cold stones beside the soft cloth that nestled Calista. She rocked to and fro, moaning with grief. It were as though the pain were physically assaulting her.

Daphne's jaw was set and her lips were tight, tears glistening in her eyes as she continued to apply the rose oil. Althaia stopped her work. Rocking back on her heels, her eyes rolled up toward the sun in the winter sky as she sighed heavily. Then, hanging her head, her arms reached out for her sister, and as their hands found each other, they embraced. Heaving sobs shook Calliope.

Althaia stroked her hair, murmuring as to a child, "I am here with you. Hush. Hush."

Finally, as her tears parted for a moment, Calliope pulled back and blew her nose. Althaia put both her hands on her living sister's shoulders and looked her straight in the eye.

"Dear sister, it's not your fault or anyone's. Calista never trusted to tell any of us. You couldn't have known the depth of her sorrow and self-contempt. Now, it is time to honor her as we lay her to rest."

Daphne nodded silently.

"What of Mother? Or Egan? How can we let her go without them here?" Calliope's breathing was labored from her sobs.

"Father has sent word, but it may be weeks before they hear or can make arrangements. We must go forth and prepare Calista for burial. They will visit her grave when they can come," Althaia said quietly.

"Our family has been torn apart these past years. First, you left suddenly. I never understood it. Years later, Mother went. Calista went silent after returning from her dance tour. Then Egan left for good." Calliope searched Althaia's face for answers. "Only Father has remained constant, but I see how he is aged, and the suffering of loss has ravaged him."

Althaia nodded slowly. "Calliope, do you know about Grandmother Demopoulous' death by her own hand? Did you know that Mother carried this inside of her heart?"

Calliope slowly sat up, wiping her eyes, now wide with shock. "No, I never knew Grandmother, and Mother never told us that story. She must have protected us from this."

Daphne suddenly joined the two sisters, fully present, her face sad.

"I knew this," she said simply.

Her sorrowful eyes were fixed on Althaia and Calliope.

"She was an unhappy woman for it," she continued. "I'm sorry for the pain it has caused your family… pushing Calista to take this dance tour unaccompanied at such a young age. Your mother's rage, always at the ready."

Finally, she cast her eyes down.

A silence settled over the circle of women, bound together by ageless trauma and shared experiences.

Finally, Althaia spoke. "Yes, this generation of our family is a body with many wounds. We must heal these through our own forgiveness. Of ourselves and of each other. This is the medicine for our hearts that we all must take, if we are to carry on."

Gripping Calliope's hand in one and Daphne's with her other, Althaia continued, "Calliope, we must make certain not to pass along this suffering to your children, by forgiving yourself, Mother, Father, and Calista."

"The weight of this burden is much too harsh of a yoke for my children to bear for even a moment. I will do what I can to forgive," Calliope said in a small voice.

Althaia knew her sister had great powers of denial, as she had protected herself and her growing family these past years, even as the sea of sorrows rose around Lander and Phaedra's family. But she knew her sister also possessed great gifts of resilience and healing due to her practical nature and fun-loving spirit. She would be okay.

Daphne nodded quietly, returning to the preparation of Calista's lifeless body with oil.

Althaia did not know and couldn't imagine how this might impact her mother and brother, but she would not be able to stay for much longer. Later, Daphne and the outside servants would wash Calista's room with hyssop and seawater to purify it from the sorrow. The burial would be on the third day, tomorrow, with only immediate family, including Daphne and her children. They would leave at dawn to follow the funeral bier carrying Calista. It would take them to the family plot of land near their home, where Father would have the grave ready. The stele, or tall headstone, would be engraved with a likeness of Calista, lithe and fluid, and a small prayer for the goddess Athena. The stele would be ready to place when Mother and Egan could return home for a second funeral in the future.

Althaia planned to place a libation of honey next to her dead sister in the grave. The bees would wing her to her new life. They would resurrect her to a place where never again would she suffer, only be fleet of foot as she danced in the meadows of a more beautiful and just world.

CHAPTER SIXTEEN

Soul Retrieval and Healing

The caravan was eager to leave Athens after these months. It was time to return to their communities in the high plains. The temperatures continued to dip, increasing the urgency. They had stayed for an extra week, beyond their welcome at the Temple of Hygeia. It had given Althaia time to mourn the shock of her sister's suicide with her family.

The tone was hushed that morning as the loaded chariots came to the gate. One by one, the Hygeia priests and the priestesses solemnly embraced Althaia, offering their condolences. Suddenly, there was a rustling high in the trees above them. It appeared to be a scuffle between birds, until a blood-curdling scream pierced the airwaves of the otherwise silent street. Startled, Althaia stared up into the treetops. It was a pair of nesting owls. One of them looked down at her sternly with blinking, round yellow eyes peering over a beak, framed by a round, furred face. A chill went down Althaia's spine. Athena? A fleeting thought captured her. Could it be? Was this the owl she heard the night of Calista's death?

The goodbyes continued, drawing Althaia's attention back to the trip before her. They would sail to Corinth and stay overnight at her old Aphrodite temple, at the request of High Priestess Hera. The next day, they would travel overland to Knossos to stay with the sisters there for a night before returning to the high Lassithi

Plateau.

It was a quiet trip. Althaia was in her own world of thought. Diana tried to draw her out, but it was fruitless. Her friend was in mourning. Althaia only wished to be left alone. Eventually, her travel mates allowed her to be as they murmured and laughed among themselves, recalling the past months and all they had learned.

The sun was slipping down behind the hills as the chariots rolled to the gates of Aphrodite's temple above Corinth. The footman scurried out to unload their bags and take the horses for the night. Soon the group of travelers was surrounded by laughing, chattering women priestesses, old and young, welcoming them with great delight. The High Priestess, Hera, came running out, clutching her skirt with her hand to lengthen her stride.

"Althaia! Althaia! You are here!"

She swept the young woman into a tight hug. Pulling away, she turned to the small knot of women.

"And here is your dear friend!" she exclaimed as she turned aside to clasp the hand of a shy but radiant and smiling Dionne and pull her forward.

Althaia threw herself on Dionne, her laughter and tears mingling with her friend's hair. Somewhat taken aback, Dionne put her arms around her old roommate, and they stood there for a long time in an embrace until Althaia's tears subsided.

"But where is Xi, my old friend?" Althaia looked around.

"My dear, he has moved on," Hera said soberly.

"It was for the best. He found a stable place to live in the north and went to serve a family there. We miss him terribly," she ended.

Althaia looked at her closely. There was a further story there.

"Here are my sister Melissas from Potnia's community and Zeus' brothers from down the way!" Althaia turned to her companions and introduced each one.

"Well, come on, come on!" Hera exclaimed. "We must settle you all in your quarters for the night. Althaia, you get to stay with Dionne."

She smiled affectionately at both of them.

The small, merry band began to move inside the walls of the temple, the eternal fire sending a sweet and pungent cedar smoke to welcome them all to this hearth of love.

After a night of giddy reconnection, Althaia and Dionne crossed the courtyard for the morning prayers and then the first meal of the day. The chill air engulfed them as they hurried to the warm kitchen commons, where a fire was roaring. As they entered, a tall woman in a dark cape turned.

"Tanitha!" Althaia found herself laughing and weeping again as she threw herself into the familiar warm embrace of her former, beloved leader.

"Ah, my daughter!" Tanitha rocked her back and forth as they held onto one another.

Finally, Tanitha cupped Althaia's face in her hands as she gazed into her eyes. "How is your soul?"

Though Tanitha had grown a few years older, she was still beautiful, and the weariness had left her aura. Her eyes were soft, shining stars.

"I... I am blessed by my new community. You made the right decision, my mother. But I have just come through the flames of purification, as I finally met my father after all these years and attended the death of my sister by her own hand." She hung her head as the tears flowed afresh.

Tanitha drew in a sharp breath, for she knew this family. She knew Lander Adamos. She was the one to whom he had dedicated his daughter at the temple all those years ago, almost seventeen now.

"Oh, my dear. Oh, my dear. Oh, my dear."

Again, she took Althaia into her arms as the young woman wept.

The other women began to gather. Soon, Diana was there, her hand quietly and gently resting on the small of Althaia's back.

Finally, Althaia drew away, her hand still clasping her beloved former high priestess'. "Tanitha, this is Diana, a new priestess with Potnia's Melissas. She came to us from Northern Israel. Diana, Tanitha was the Head Priestess here during my time and, lo, almost thirty years all told!"

Diana bowed to her elder, missing the alarmed look that crossed Tanitha's face as she set her eyes on the young woman.

"Daughter, may we sit alone together at this meal?" she requested urgently.

"Yes. Yes. Of course!" Diana said clearly, her eyes roaming from Althaia to Tanitha, trying to ferret out some information for this request.

But there was none forthcoming.

The time was all too short as the community shared the simple meal of eggs, flatbread, olives, dried figs and apricots, and pomegranate juice. Soon, the band of pilgrims would need to move along their way from this warm reception in order to be at Knossos by nightfall.

Althaia noted that Tanitha and Diana had been in riveting conversation, barely touching their food throughout the meal.

"Come, Diana! Don't take Tanitha away from me one moment longer!" she teased as she sat down by her friend, putting her arm around her.

Tanitha voice was resonant and clear as she put her hand on Althaia's arm and leaned toward her.

"Althaia, I must tell you something." She paused with the emotion of the moment. "I have found my daughter. The one I have longed for my whole life, since she was taken from me. This. This is my daughter, Diana."

Her eyes fixed on Diana until a smile lit up both mother and daughter's faces and a giggle escaped from Diana's lips, as she reached to pull her mother's hand to her lips and kiss it.

Althaia shook her head as though to clear out the cobwebs.

"What? What?" Her eyes were burning with questions.

"Yes. When I laid eyes upon her, I saw the likeness of my child. In my heart, my mother's instinct, in my heart of hearts, I knew immediately that this was her. The one taken from me and given to Astarte's temple at Sidon."

Althaia continued to shake her head.

"Mother, please don't be offended by my questions, but how can you know for sure?"

Tanitha smiled widely, and Diana began to laugh.

"It's this, Althaia. See this birthmark?" Diana pulled back her cape and pulled aside her woolen peplo to reveal a cherry red birthmark below her right breast.

"Mama Tanitha remembers carefully examining me, every inch, before they took me away that next morning. She asked immediately to see my birthmark," Diana said breathlessly.

"And I showed it to her! I have a mother!" she shouted in delight, drawing the attention of tables next to her as they smiled at her ebullience.

"What will you do?" Althaia asked, almost incredulously.

"Diana will stay here with me for a season, my dear. You must pass along this information to Potnia. I will send a message soon about our plans."

"Potnia will be so happy for you, Diana!" Althaia smiled.

"We have much in common, including my daughter's passion for *The Way*! We will explore that together." Tanitha grasped her daughter's hand and nodded her head vigorously.

Althaia's heart felt an inner fire of warmth, despite her mourning season. It was so good to be here among beloved old friends. To meet the goodness of this moment with a fullness of being. Bitter sadness could reside next to joy, she realized. The heart's tent was large enough. Family came in all sizes and shapes—biological and spiritual. Althaia's heart capacity to love was expanding moment by moment, day by day.

The final leg of the journey would be an overnight at Knossos, the walled city where the Melissas lived together. The priests of Zeus would sleep with their brothers' community, while the women would find haven with their sisters.

Penelope was the one who greeted them this time, as the dusk settled. She wore her veil tightly across her face, so it was difficult to discern who was attached to the voice.

"Friends! Welcome! I must tell you the news that we are experiencing a resurgence of the pox. It is not such a good time to come to the city." Penelope's hazel eyes blinked above her veil. "But we have scrubbed and cleaned two rooms in quarantine, and you can stay there as long as you need. We will leave your food at the door each morning."

Althaia was hesitant from her seat on the chariot. "Shall we just continue on, Penelope? We don't want to cause you trouble."

"Bee sticks! No! Of course not. We knew you were coming and will keep you safe. We are prepared. Come. Come!" she said insistently, her hand rapidly waving, beckoning them to debark and follow her.

As the torches in the city were lit, the weary women pulled their veils over their faces and hurried through the wooden door that swung open. The Head Priestess had been alerted, and she came toward them and pulled her palms together to bow to the small band of priestesses. Her gaily colored scarf was pulled tightly across her face.

"Welcome! I am the Head Priestess here. My name is Nefeli. I regret that you have come at such a time as this, when the pox is ravaging the city a second time. But have no fear. We will make sure to keep you safe in all ways. How was your trip?" she inquired.

"Nefeli?" Althaia stared at her Egyptian sister, remembering when she was a young priestess at Acrocorinth, after the loss of so many sisters to the pox. "I am so glad to see you after these years! You have also come home!"

Nefeli beamed.

"Thaia, it is an honor to meet again and have you stay here with us. How was your trip?" she inquired again.

"It was... dynamic," Althaia spoke for all of them. "We left one of our priestesses back in Corinth, as she unexpectedly met her mother after a lifetime of separation!"

Nefeli's eyes widened, and then the lines around her eyes crinkled with a large smile.

"A delightful reason to lose a sister!" She laughed.

Zoe, one of Althaia's companions, stated, "We had a wonderful time in Athens at the Hygeian community. We learned so much about medicine!"

Her eyes shone. Nefeli nodded.

"Sadly, I buried a sister." Althaia could feel the rawness of her heart even as she spoke this truth out loud again.

"Oh, dear. My heart aches with you." Nefeli's forehead knit tightly together.

"Returning to Limnakaro will do my soul good," Althaia finished with a ragged, sharp breath.

Nefeli nodded. She did not step forward to touch Althaia, given the raging pandemic, but her eyes conveyed an endless pool of compassion.

"I will have you all shown to your rooms so you can rest. Althaia, may I spend just a moment with you in our common room?"

"Yes. Yes, of course." Althaia nodded.

Leaving her bag in the entryway, she followed the Head Priestess.

They walked past the bee woman statue and entered a very large room, the fire spirits brightening one corner, infusing the room with cedar, heating their bodies as they relaxed on colorful cushions in the dimming light. For Althaia, fire was always comforting. It was a place where she felt accompanied by the elemental world in a kindred and loving way.

Nefeli began, "Althaia, I know your gifts as a medicine woman from Corinth days. Your reputation proceeds you. Potnia and I have been in touch these past months, and she suggested you and your sisters stay a few days extra to assist us with setting up an apothecary of herbals to treat the pox in our city. The Romans are willing to pay for anything we need. They are desperate. We can stay separate in our quarters; our community will be safe. We realize that, without treating the whole city, we all continue to be at risk, and this savage disease will not go away."

Her eyes were watchful of any reaction as Althaia heard her request.

"I spoke with the Roman commander yesterday, and he will prepare a building where they will stock the things we direct them toward."

Althaia's eyes held Nefeli's in a steady gaze.

"That is fine," she said calmly. "Zoe, Kynthia, and I will prepare a list of the herbs needed for oral use to strengthen the body and reduce spread. It will include propolis from the beehives to make salves for application on the pustules. Also, you will need to teach them how to make poultices of herbs for external use, to reduce the disease replication. We will leave instructions."

Head Priestess Nefeli nodded. "They will need to find and purchase their own herbs and medicinal properties from the hives. The Romans will need to find their own distributors of the medicines. We do not wish to be forced to play doctor."

For a moment, there was a flash of anger that crossed Nefeli's eyes, a reminder of the ongoing discontent and even contempt between occupier and occupied.

After two weeks in Knossos, finally Althaia and her companions were on the last leg of the journey back to the high plain of the Lassithi Plateau. Their trip was undertaken in midday, as the sun was high. It would only be a few hours. They would be home in time for dinner. Soon, the city was far away. The silence began to deepen. The humming sounds of the planetary community became louder than human noise. The wind whirled around the moving vehicle, and its pilgrims huddled together for warmth. The chill of the winter season cut through even the women's layered woolen garments.

Althaia's heart began to sing as she could see Limnakaro in the distance, late in the day. She began to hum as she imagined the community of Potnia and the Melissas nestled among the wintering fields, the dormant bee skeps with the pulsing orb of bees staying warm inside, the sacred fire always glowing, and the sweet smell of earth. She felt a deep gratitude in leaving behind the hustle and bustle of the cities to return to the countryside. Here, there was more sky visible, and the sun in his glory moved across the firmament. Here, the land was not so full of humans. Instead, it was filled with the rock and creaturely communities, the tribes of plant life, and the tumbling crystal water that their chariot followed.

After many, many years, Althaia felt that she had finally found her soul's calling. A place that was safe and peaceful and creative. That night, in her own room and her own bed, Althaia had a dream again. This time it was not the bee queen who came to visit her.

It was a boy-child. His laughter tinkled as he ran toward her, taking her hand in his warm grip, pulling her along with him.

"Who are you?" Althaia asked.

"I am Iēsous," he giggled.

"Iēsous?" Althaia looked at him, startled.

How could this be?

"The one whose followers call themselves *The Way?*" she queried. "But you are only a child!"

"Yes, yes, yes! Now, will you come and dance with me? Let us go and play!" he insisted, tugging at her hand. "Love rejoices when we play!"

Althaia awakened with a start as the dream evaporated. She realized that her cheeks were wet with tears. Perhaps it was the delightful presence of a child after a lifetime of her own childlessness. Perhaps it was the season of sorrow that had clamped down so tightly on her soul.

She laid completely still in her bed for what seemed like hours, watching her life story rerun in her head. All the losses, the trauma, all the changes, the transitions. Her exhaustion from the past months weighed upon her chest like a stone. Winter was a good time to sleep. She wanted to stay wrapped in this liminal state for as long as it took to welcome spring back to her soul.

Days and weeks passed. It was as though Althaia moved in a fog. Winter began to release its grip. Spring solstice was around the corner.

One day, Potnia summoned Althaia to visit with her.

"My sweet girl, you have been troubled for a long season. Sorrow has become your food day and night. I know your heart is heavy from your sister's death. I would like to call upon your Melissaes to kindle the sacred fire and sit in circle ceremony with you. We will midwife you from this season of grief so you can release your sorrow with our loving witness and birth the next season of your life. I want you to know you are not alone, my beloved daughter." Potnia was tender in her carefully chosen words. "I want you to live from the center of your fullest self, of whom you truly are."

Althaia kept her eyes fixed on her hands resting in her lap, even as salty tears began to splash on her fingers and then rain down like a spring thunderstorm. The kindness of Mother Potnia was beyond anything she had ever experienced as a young child. Her compassion preceded her everywhere she went, like a beacon of light.

Althaia's words began to tumble out. A whole lifetime of pain, it seemed. Phaedra's contempt of her as a young daughter—the strange meanness, bordering on jealousy. A father who would not, could not protect her, as the words and sometimes blows from her mother rained down on her. Falling in love for the first time with the Roman soldier. The forced abortion. That long journey of silence with her father to Corinth as he 'gifted' her in servitude to Acrocorinth's temple prostitutes and the goddess Aphrodite. The loss of her childhood and siblings. Her sister's suicide and the revelation of her maternal grandmother's death by her own hand. Her mother and father's divorce.

As the story poured out, eventually the crescendo of her emotion began to abate, her sweating and shaking body quieted as Potnia came and sat close to her. Potnia's plump body seemed to absorb all the sadness and sorrow and trauma that flowed out of Althaia like a river.

"Potnia, for years I would leave my body when I found myself in a distressed situation. Part of me would flee to the ceiling of the room where I could look down from a distance and feel safe. It would reduce my suffering and pain. Then, at Acrocorinth, I began to slice my wrists. That is when Tanitha mandated that I would learn the bees and the healing arts, no longer serving the men who came. It got a little better. But still, there are times a darkness covers me. I feel as though I will suffocate. That is how I feel now."

Potnia nodded, listening carefully.

"Through all those years, I had a dream of the bee woman who always would say, 'Return to the mother.' I saw her statue in Knossos. Now, I know she is you. You are the Great Mother. The bee priestess in my dream knew I had gone far from home— perhaps I was homeless... until now." Althaia's eyes met Potnia's.

Potnia smiled and took Althaia's hands into her lap.

"You are a woman full of wisdom. Perhaps the bee woman was myself, or perhaps it was the Great Mother who has initiated you into all the forms of the Universe of Love. Your suffering has manifested the pure alchemy of gold in your soul. Yes, you are home, my dear. You have returned."

Althaia continued, "And then I had another visitation. Just a few weeks ago. It was the boy, Iēsous. The Nazirite who would teach his people in *The Way*. Yet in this dream he was a child, playful as a puppy, calling me to come dance with him! What does it all mean?" she murmured.

Potnia took a deep breath and replied, "Althaia, all of us are wounded as children. But some, like yourself, experience more tragedy as a child than most will know in a whole lifetime. These are carried as scars inside your soul. They erase your ability to play. To see life with a lightness of being. To carry out your tasks with joy and ease. I believe this boy-child, Iēsous, has come alongside the Great Mother, perhaps it is his very own mother, to heal your sorrow. To remind you to leap and dance and play again. I hear he has been imbued with great gifts of healing through his resurrection!"

She smiled kindly at Althaia and took her face in the palms of her hand. "My love, invite Iēsous to come again and teach you to play. He will be a good brother for you."

In that moment, Althaia felt the whirlwind leave. It was as though she had been relieved of many demons that had lived inside the house of her body, mind, and soul for too long. She had expelled them merely by sharing with this wise and loving Mother Bee, who sat with her, before her, beside her. She felt calm. Clear-headed. A warm glow had been kindled in her heart chamber. A tiny light was at the end of the tunnel she had been traversing alone for so long.

Spring equinox came, and the Melissaes were planning a special ceremony for Althaia. It was a new moon, the best time to plant seeds and intentions.

Preparation included preparing herb bundles and a special ceramic pot of the honeybees' elixir and medicine of honey wine.

There would be drumming and music. Althaia's body had been decorated with indigo paint by her sisters. Ornate designs and tiny pictures of insects, the sun, moon and stars, and sea creatures swirled from her soft belly, around her back, down her arms and legs, up her neck to her face, where a tiny bee was etched on her cheek.

Potnia had determined that they would have this soul retrieval and blessing circle for Althaia, to call her to resurrection from a lifetime of the 'dark spirit'.

As the fire was laid with stacked cedar wood, in between the stacks were laid the herb bundles, prepared with prayerful intentions. As Potnia taught, prayer is a force of consciousness, focused attention, or loving intent that can seed change around and within oneself.

Night came, and the bonfire was set as the Melissaes flooded to its warmth, chattering and laughing. Each woman brought an element to contribute to the goodwill 'cake' that would be offered back to the earth in gratitude for her many sustaining gifts of life.

First, a bed of leaves was laid, then an herb sprinkled for each one of the powerful ancestors—mountains, sun, moon, river, and spirit animals. Salt was sprinkled for the bitter. Fava beans represented the fetus, the unborn ones. White corn for energy of the sun and health. Seeds for flowers in this new moon, sprinkled with sage for protection. Finally, a dollop of honey in the center, representing the sweetness of life, fertility, and resurrection into new life.

As Potnia approached with Althaia, dressed in her finest

woolen peplo and heavy warm shawl, the women moved as though they were a shining swarm of bees in the firelight, surrounding the two women, singing as they pulsed and moved in one unified body.

Althaia found herself laughing as the sea of celebration rose like a tide around her, carrying her along. She felt light-hearted, ready to be initiated into this new time of life.

Potnia stepped toward the fire as the sea of women parted. Her tall hat was regal, and her comportment dignified as she offered an invocation:

Great Mother, earth of all being, we your daughters are awake tonight to your goodness. We offer gratitude for your constancy and infinite blessings, your sustaining mercies of every element and abundance of the earth. We call upon you, at this special time of equinox, the beginning of spring planting season, to bless our efforts with your intelligence, wisdom and power. Let us be in daily communion with you and all our ancestors, spiritual and biological, human and nonhuman. We offer our breath, our heart, our whole self and being to this path of purity and fidelity of heart and conscious love. Protect and guide us. We invite the animals and all the plant beings, heavenly realms and earthly beings to assist us on our path, revealing their wisdom also.

The women's voices rose in sweet accord, their melodious hymn to the earth and the Great Mother.

The honey wine was passed around the circle multiple times, as the group swayed to the drums. Time passed. The night grew pregnant with their songs and dances. Finally, it was time to bless this one Melissa, Althaia. To call forth her song and honor the season of sorrow that could now come to a close.

The women gathered close together, surrounding Althaia. It was a tightly woven web of safety like none other Althaia had ever experienced. With their gentle coaxing, she leaned into them, allowing her body to go limp as many hands lifted her up. As her body was carried around the fire, she felt her sisters' support on a visceral level. It was something she would never forget. A lightness of being in that rarified air.

Circling a few times, they slowly brought her down, but her feet still did not touch the ground. As her sisters cradled her, Potnia began to speak. Her voice sounded far away, and yet echoed inside of Althaia in that intimate moment.

"Althaia, the bees and plant world have taught you of their gift economy from their spacious lives. All that they offer is from the great gift apothecary of food, of medicine for health and well-being, and the endless cycle of fertility. Their work is for the commonwealth of the community. Always. The plants and bees teach us of an everlasting and reciprocal economy of good, poured out for all who learn to live in right relationships. That is why we revere them and understand them as the winged ones of the heavenly realms, the next life. They are our little resurrection messengers. The bees sweep the dead from the depths of the underworld and fly them to their joyful reunion with the Great Mother. You have already been initiated into the bee realms as a priestess. You are a Melissa, keeper of the beautiful secrets of the world of honeybee, as well as a doctor of the plant medicines world." Potnia was eloquent.

"This ceremony is not an initiation into the Melissaes. Instead, it is a coming of age, an initiation into the profound mysteries of being a fully alive and awakened wise woman. Through all your travails, you have been courageous of heart and have learned, to the best of your capacity, how to walk through the fires of loss, rage, grief, and confusion. You have allowed our sisters to accompany you as you picked your way through the ashes. Even as you stand here before me, you have come of age as a full human being, called to serve. We call back all parts of your soul, that you may live in strong, unified vitality of body, mind, and spirit. May all that is unhealed be utterly transformed and made new!"

And with that, Potnia, the High Priestess, offered Althaia a half moon of a pomegranate, spilling forth her ruby seeds. Althaia raised it to the moon, then to her lips, feeling the crimson red juice streak her chin and drip onto her breast as she bit deeply into the succulent pockets of bitter sweetness. She threw her head back and began to laugh with her sisters, the whiteness of her teeth glistening against the juice in the fiery light.

Althaia remembered how her heart had been awakened so many years ago by the natural world. As she learned to tend the bees and the plants, she fell in love—awakening to the mysteries of the universe, after a childhood so famished from soul-nourishing love.

She understood now how her plunge into the discipline of apprenticing with bees and the plant elders had also taught her about the interior landscape of her own heart in the process. Throughout those years of living in the shadowlands of trauma, there were moments and glimmers of communion with Divine joy. But this time with her sisters was the pinnacle of ecstasy. Of belonging. Becoming a part of something greater than herself. A purpose calling her to serve with compassion for all beings.

Under the cold field of stars that night, she finally felt forgiveness flow through her like a molten river, burning away shame and blame. It was a moment of surrender to something much, much bigger than herself. A marriage with her own soul, of sorts.

She smiled as she saw the vision of the Bee Woman standing before her. She heard the words as in a dream…

"I am Sophia. I am the Great Mother. I danced with the Creator at time's beginning. I am Ihidaya. Iēsous. The Great love. I am all in all. We are one. You are home."

The sparks flew upwards. Althaia was laid gently on a woven blanket. Many hands wrapped her, tucking the cloth around her. They offered her soothing valerian, and she began to feel sleepy and lightheaded. The women continued to speak softly among themselves as the fire turned to glowing embers.

The sweet, pungent smell of the soil coming to life enhanced the night air. The fecund moisture mixed with the burning cedar. Althaia would not forget this night.

It was early in the morning, when the stars flickered, and galaxies poured like a waterfall of cold milky light into the moonless night. The women roused themselves and moved off to their beds. Potnia had long ago left them. This circle had shown Althaia what truly was at the heart of the beehive. Community. Caring for one another. Always, the sisterhood.

It would be some days later that Althaia would leave for solitary time in a cave, the womb of mother earth. She would become silent, listening for this new voice that had replaced the old tyrannical voices. It would be a time of prayer and fasting, with increasing and intense levels of Love as the Great Mother took her into the fire of the depths of her being. She would come to know her body as a sacred temple, her sex and spirit, body and soul unified. In this time of communion, she would experience a deeper rebirth. She was no long a woman bound by time and space and the culture around her. She was a non-binary human being. Equal merits of left-hand masculine and right-hand feminine. Balanced in one accord.

It was much as the Apostle had said, "In Christ, there is no male or female, slave nor free, Jew nor Gentile."

Now she was free to serve truth, unhindered and unfettered by the systems that oppressed herself and her sisters at Acrocorinth. Her timeless, deathless self now guided her.

POSTSCRIPT

Adrian

Give heed then, you hearers
And you also, angels and those who have been sent,
And your spirits risen now from the dead.
I am the one who alone exists,
There is no one to judge me.
For though there is much sweetness
In passionate life, in transient pleasure,
Finally soberness comes
And people flee to their place of rest.
There they will find me,
And live, and not die again.[25]

After Althaia's sacred soul retrieval ceremony, she found herself light-hearted, even playful, as the spring sun warmed the countryside. There was a new resolve in her to live in the light of Love, more and more. To release, release, release the shadows of cruelty, narcissism, stupidity, ignorance, addiction to power, and control which a whole society had wounded her with. To heal and forgive the fear, depression, starvation for love, generational trauma, and need to 'be seen' in her family of origin. To allow

---

[25] "The Thunder: Perfect Mind", Women in Praise of the Sacred, ed. Jane Hirshfield, from the Gnostic Gospel: Nag Hammadi Library, 2–4th c.(NY: HarperPerennial, 1994) 33.249

the transformation of the sorrows that had fueled a whole lifetime of violence in the Lander Adamos' family lineage.

The bees were her companions during this tender season of naming and reclaiming her truest soul. She spent much time not only with her hands in the hive but sitting next to the dizzying busyness and buzzy aliveness of the ceramic hives, daydreaming or resting. She gave thanks daily for the resurrection of her heart from a very dark place to this joyful communion.

One day, she heard a chariot rumbling in the distance as she was in the bee yard. Its wheels kicked up dust as it toiled along the rocky road. It was a very fancy and ornate chariot, with white horses. From a distance, Althaia could see that the men riding were also well-heeled. They appeared to have tunics that were bright and colorful. Perhaps they were on their way to Zeus' community of priests.

She turned back to her task of scooping honey from the hives. The girls were expanding rapidly with vast new broods of baby bees, their honey stores swelling with the nectar foraged from the spring blooms.

Soon, she heard the bell clanging out across the land, calling the community to midday meal. Althaia quickly packed up her tools and carefully sealed off the honey pots, bowing to the honeybees in gratitude and breathing a prayer for their health and prosperity. She began to walk across the field, even as a tall male figure moved toward her, his features blurred at a distance. His tunic was bright orange—the man seen riding atop the chariot. His hair scattered from his face in the spring winds.

As they approached one another, her eyes were quizzical, as the lines between her eyes deepened in disbelief.

She noted the skin, crinkled like crows' feet around his sea-green eyes, as he flashed his gap-toothed smile. His flowing black hair was sprinkled with gray, framing his bronze skin.

"Chaire, Althaia. What a sunny day!" he greeted her with the traditional Greek greeting, *Rejoice! Be glad!*

Althaia froze. That voice. This face. That tall, lithe body. Those kind eyes. All carried her back in time and place to over seventeen years ago. The smells and sounds of the marketplace, the tugging of Egan's small hand in hers as she chatted with a Roman soldier.

Forgetting even basic amenities, such as returning a greeting, Althaia stammered, "Wh... what?"

She could feel her face flushing in the bright sunshine, her hair, caught in a leather tie under her bee veil, unraveling to frame her face like a wild woman.

She stopped and her hive toolkit clanked to the ground as she stared at this man. Older, but still boyish and playful.

Adrian picked up her tools in the respectful manner she remembered of him.

"I will carry these for you, lady priestess!" he said kindly, with a hint of teasing.

"Adrian, *what* are you doing here?" She finally found her voice. "How did you know...?"

"It was easy. I merely followed your scent from Knossos!" He laughed. "I know all about you from Penelope at the temple. She raves about your magical knowledge and powers with the medicines. Perhaps you saved our fair city. Certainly, the Romans are deeply indebted to you!"

Trying not to stare at Adrian, suddenly self-conscious of her honey and propolis-stained peplo, and the increasing beehive of activity as her hair whirled out of the leather holder, she finally gasped. "And so you came to find me?"

"Yes," he said gently, almost tenderly. "Yes."

"I've been stationed at Knossos, on the island of Crete, for over seven years," he continued, "When I heard of the wise Melissa, Althaia Adamos, doctor of medicine at Limnakaro, I resolved to come and find her to see if she was one in the same as the young girl who stole my heart."

At this, he looked closely at her, gauging her reaction behind the veil.

"Indeed, she is," whispered Althaia.

"There are not many Althaia Adamos' this side of Greece." He laughed, lightening the moment.

Gathering herself after the shock of seeing this man again after so many years, still fresh as a newborn in her own spirit, Althaia found herself breathing shallowly.

Flashing her smile, small white teeth shining through the veil, she said, "Well, come on then, let us get reacquainted. Will you join us for the midday meal?"

Adrian nodded eagerly, his eyes glowing like embers.

"I'll introduce you to our Mother High Priestess, Potnia. We will find you a place to stay, and you can follow me around here. I'll put you to work!" She laughed.

"Come here, you." Adrian stepped toward her, encircling her in his arms.

Her arms went around his waist as he pulled her to his chest. She smelled frankincense on his tunic. She could feel eros begin to rise up like sap, something that had been dead and wasted within her for too long.

Drawing back, he pulled the veil from her head, gazing into her eyes, his arms still holding her.

"Oh, how I have missed you and longed for you. You cannot imagine." His voice was thick with emotion.

Althaia remembered that moment before she was ripped

from him by her father. His last papyrus message laid under the loose brick in the wall around her family home. His understanding that she and their child would be cared for, even as he was sent to the far reaches of Judea. As distant from her as Mother and Father could manage.

"Adrian, there is no child," she said dully, pulling away, fixing her unwavering gaze on him.

Adrian's shoulders sagged. He dropped his head. The weight of the moment ripped open a scar for Althaia.

Putting her hand on his shoulder, she said softly, "I'll tell you about it. But I want to hear also about your journey and years in Judea. Time has passed like a river. It has carried us here. All is well. We can begin from this place."

Adrian's breath released jaggedly.

The seductive spell of the moment was broken, as Adrian and Althaia dropped into a more spacious place where grief and longing could sit side by side.

"I will tell you about my life, Adrian. I simply hold the light and work within the frequencies of love." Her eyes were golden and shining orbs. "And you must tell me who you are after all these years."

Shouldering up Althaia's toolkit, Adrian took her hand, and they walked toward the commons of the bee priestesses of Minoa, side by side.

BIBLIOGRAPHY

Brooke, Elisabeth. Medicine Women (Wheaton, IL: Quest Books, 1997).
Durant, Will. The Story of Civilization: Life of Greece (New York; Simon and Schuster, 1939)
Slough, Rebecca, ed. Hymnal: A Worship Book (Newton, KS: Faith and Life Press. 1992)
The Holy Bible, NRSV
Hirschfield, Jane, ed. Women in Praise of the Sacred (New York: Harper Perennial, 1994)
Robinson, J, translator. Thunder: Perfect Mind, Nag Hammadi Library (New York: HarperCollins, 1977)
Yves-LeLoup, Jean. The Gospel of Mary Magdalene (Rochester, VT: Inner Traditions International, 2002)

Digital References:
https://www.ancient.eu/delphi/
https://itsallgreeklondon.wordpress.com/2014/10/22/the-minoan-honeybees/
https://sharedveracity.net/2019/01/17/was-pauls-philosophical-speech-at-mars-hill-in-athens-a-failure/
https://www.biblestudytools.com/classics/barnes-scenes-in-life/paul-at-corinth/
Wikipedia